Louise

Louise

CAROLINE ASHTON

Published by

The Paris Press

Cover design based on a A Woman of the Empire by Walter MacEwen, used under a Wikimedia commons licence

For translation rights and permission queries please contact the author's agent Lisa.eveleigh@richfordbecklow.co.uk

About the Author

Caroline was born in Durham City but has lived in many different parts of the country before finally settling in Norfolk. Aged eleven, she began writing stories for the school magazine and has continued whenever work, marriage and raising three children have allowed. She started writing (almost) full time during a creative writing degree with the Open University. Caroline's favourite activity, other than writing, is walking with her husband and two cocker spaniels.

Acknowledgements

My thanks as usual for the continuing support of that group known as The Snug, and in particular to Janet and Judy. My best wishes to Judy for every success with her proof-reading business: judymanvilleproofreader.wordpress.com.

For DEC

Chapter One

Miss Louise Devreaux was sitting on a chair drawn into the window embrasure of an elegant drawing room rendered gloomy by the miserable weather outside. She was occupied in skimming the final six pages of a novel to see if the idiotic heroine would find enough common sense to extract herself from her predicament. Deciding there was no hope for the creature, she closed it and set it on the small table beside her. A far more inviting novel, sent down that week from Hatchards in London, lay beside a vase of early daffodils she had rescued from the blustery March wind. The bookshop was almost the only thing she missed about her former life in the *ton*. That, and the availability of an accomplished *modiste,* of course, something that was easily overcome by an occasional visit to town to replenish her wardrobe. A life in the country was no excuse for looking dowdy.

Her hand rested on the book; her gaze lingered on the daffodils. They had been her sister Amelia's favourite flower. 'Twinkly trumpets' she had called them in their childhood. Louise's throat constricted. Five years. Five long years since Amelia had run off with her beloved Gerard, the man their father would not countenance her marrying. Even after all this time, the longing to see her still had the power to hurt, so much so that she had rather abjure society than endure the arch comments of 'Have you seen your sister yet?' or 'How is Amelia?' from those *haut ton* ladies of catty disposition.

She swallowed, blinking eyes that had suddenly grown hot, and opened the book, hoping to dispel the sorrow that always sat in her heart. She had barely read the first page when the door opened and the family's ancient butler creaked across the floor towards her.

'A visitor, miss,' he said, holding out a silver salver.

Louise lifted the visiting card. The name *Sir Ranulph Trent* was inscribed in flowing copperplate across the middle.

'I don't know of him, Dorkins. Is he a friend of Papa's, do you think?'

The elderly butler wagged his head. 'I can't rightly say, miss. He did ask for the master afore you, though he don't look old enough to be a friend of his. Have to say as I've never seen him afore.'

She considered this. Her gaze fell upon the novel. With a sigh, she laid it down.

'You had best show him in.'

The butler bowed and shuffled out of the door.

When it had closed behind him, she rose and cast a quick glance across the room to the glass above the mantle. Owning to some five-and-twenty years, she was generally held to be attractive and even-tempered, with an oval face and eyes of so mysterious a blue they frequently looked violet. A dusky curl had tumbled onto her forehead. Her fingers twisted it back into place. Straightening the cuffs of her blue print gown, she waited by the chair she had vacated.

The man shown into her was certainly not of her father's generation. His hair, as dark as hers, showed not the least strand of grey and his figure was that of an athlete. If he were many more years older than thirty she would be surprised. Aware of a pair of cool grey eyes examining her she was prompted into speech.

'Sir Ranulph? You wished to see my father?'

'Indeed, ma'am.' The athletic figure inclined in a shallow bow of considerable grace, but no civility of expression covered his face.

'I much regret to find him absent from home; it is inconvenient, to say the least.'

Both his chilly tone and his words annoyed her, and she was betrayed into saying, 'Had he been expecting your visit, sir, I'm sure he would have remained at home.'

The fleeting expression that crossed his face could have been one of impatience. A gaze of the most dispassionate kind replaced it. 'Might I enquire when he *is* expected?'

Her fine brows rose. 'I am not at all certain. Possibly not for some hours. Is there some way in which I might assist you?' Her voice betrayed a noticeable lack of willingness.

'I have some tidings to report to Mr Devreaux. I would much prefer to pass them to him personally but as he is not here – and I have little time – I regret I must relate them to you.'

'Indeed? I must own to some surprise, sir, that a person quite unknown to us should have news that affects us. However, pray tell me what it is.'

Sir Ranulph inclined his head briefly, and told her.

These few short words turned her face ashen and plunged her into a nightmare world. She swayed and grasped at the back of the chair for support. Her breath dried in her throat.

'Dead?' she managed at last. 'What do you mean, dead?'

'Dead, ma'am. As in no longer alive.'

'But it cannot be true. She was barely two-and-twenty.' Louise's knees weakened. She sank onto the seat.

The wish that he had kept to his original plan of sending the news by post overcame Sir Ranulph. He deeply regretted that Dernstone Grange stood such a little way off the journey from his home to London that he had decided to call instead. 'I regret, ma'am, that she and her husband drowned. Christopher has survived – although by pure chance.'

'Christopher?' Louise was quite bewildered.

The feeling that he had entered some sort of madhouse supplanted Sir Ranulph's emotion. 'Christopher is your nephew, ma'am.'

'Oh.' Louise pressed her fingers to her cheeks. '*Oh*. I didn't know about him.'

Her anguished eyes rose to the elegant figure before her. His expression gave her no comfort. Colour flooded her face. She snatched her hands into her lap and stiffened her spine. 'You must know, sir, that my parents turned against Amelia upon her marriage.'

'So I was given to understand.'

'We have heard nothing of her since then.' Her lips trembled. She folded them tightly.

'Gerard said your sister had always hoped to have word from you.'

'Hoped?' The violet eyes opened wide. 'But I wrote to her as soon as I discovered her address from my grandmother, Lady Melthorpe.' Her head shook briefly. The dark curls on it trembled. 'She never answered.'

Sir Ranulph studied her. His expression grew harder. 'I know that she wrote to you.' He glanced at the nearest chair in the dismal room, unwilling to sit unless invited but fearing this interview would take longer than he wished. Abandoning the dictates of politeness, he sat, placing his hat and gloves on one knee.

'I must conclude you never had sight of Mrs Aveley's letters.'

'But how...?' Puzzlement was printed on her delicate features for several moments. Then her face hardened. A wave of fury such as she had never known gripped her. She bounced from her chair, glaring beyond him.

'Oh, how could he?' She trod a quick pace forward. 'It must have been him.' The urge to throw something engulfed her. She pulled herself up short. Her hands gipped together so fiercely the nails dug into her skin. 'How *could* he?'

The aristocratic eyebrows rose. 'Your father, ma'am? I fear in seeking this interview I have gone against his wishes.'

'His wishes? *His* wishes, sir?' Her hands transformed into fists. She took a hasty step towards him, her face flushing. 'Never mind his wishes. I insist you tell me all you know of my beloved sister.'

Sir Ranulph regarded her with amazement. Unused to feminine hysterics, his hand lifted his hat. He had no desire to see the creature before him lapse into a frenzy, magnificent as she looked with her sparkling eyes and chest heaving with quickened breaths.

She fixed her gaze on him, striving for control. 'You must understand I have learned nothing of her since she ran away with her … with her … her what?' She paused briefly.

'You called her Mrs Aveley – she was married then? And, forgive me, but how do you come to you to know her?'

Sir Ranulph's hand released his hat. 'She *was* married, ma'am. And to my cousin Gerard.'

'Married? Oh, how wonderful.' Eagerness replaced the tension in her face and figure. 'In Scotland, I collect? We assumed they had fled to Gretna.'

'No, ma'am, nothing so improper. He lodged her with a university friend and his wife in Derby until the banns were read. No-one in that parish knew them so, naturally, there could be no questioning of their entitlement to wed. It was all perfectly legal.'

'Legal? In a church?' A hand raised to her forehead. 'Then Papa had no need to cut her off?'

Sir Ranulph's eyes narrowed. 'It is hardly for me to say.'

The hand fell. 'So it's all been to no purpose.' The extraordinary rise and plummet of her emotions overwhelmed her. Disorientation replaced her anger. She strayed back to her chair and sank unsteadily onto it.

'It could have been passed off.' Her shoulders drooped. A cry broke from her. She stifled it with a hand. 'We could still have been sisters,' she all but sobbed.

Sir Ranulph eyed her with caution.

A dejected laugh replaced the cry. 'I need never have retired from society.'

'That must have been for your parents to decide, ma'am.'

'No.' Her fingers stirred her dark curls. 'It was my decision. I had only some twenty years when she left. The opprobrium ... the gossip that abounded...' Her head shook. 'Old-maidhood seemed preferable at the time.'

Sir Ranulph, whose affection for his own − older − sister was tepid at best, was conscious of a degree of pity for the pretty woman drooping so disconsolately opposite him. The deep eyes that had shot fire at her parents' infamy had softened into sorrow. The glossy ringlets drooped as her head lowered. For a moment her hands twisted in the lap of her muslin gown. Saddened she might be, and surprisingly moved was he, but he had business to conduct.

'I must inform you, ma'am, that you and I are named as guardians to Christopher.'

Louise's head jerked up. 'Guardians? Both of us?'

'Indeed. It is my intention to take him to live at Crestings. My house in Gloucestershire.'

'Your house? But that will remove him from the only world he knows − wherever that may be. It will cause him even more distress than he must already feel.'

'He will soon become accustomed.' he said indifferently.

'Soon? How old is he?'

'I believe him to be in his third year.'

'Believe? Don't you *know*?'

Sir Ranulph's features hardened into the look his friends decried. The one that greeted what he deemed an impertinence. Before he could depress Miss Devreaux's pretention he was favoured with a steadily freezing shaft from her eyes.

'Who will have care of him? Your wife? A stranger to him too, no doubt.'

'I am unwed, ma'am.' He leant back in the chair, confidently at ease. 'It will be my mother who oversees him.'

'Oversees? *Oversees*?' Louise's weakened grasp on her serenity vanished. She erupted from her chair for a second time and glared down at him.

'He is not some farm animal, sir, or a household account to be *overseen*.' Her hands could not rest. They swept the air, they grasped at her arms, they struck together. 'Oh, I see it all,' she flung at him, unable to prevent herself from pacing the carpet. 'Your mother must be beyond the age of raising infants. She will hand him over to servants. Brought up by none of his family.'

Sir Ranulph, his features rigid, rose, regarding the agitated pacing. 'I must beg leave to inform you, ma'am, that my mother *is* his family.'

'But not close.' She swung to face him. 'Not as close as I am.'

'You?'

'Of course.' Determination filled her. 'Whilst he is so young he must be given into my care.'

'I cannot permit it.'

Two pairs of eyes clashed. 'Oh, sir? Why not?'

'Because … because.' He drew himself to his full height which easily topped hers. 'I am not obliged to explain my decisions to you, ma'am.'

'In this instance you are. This is the son of a sister who was …' her breath came unevenly, 'was most dear to me.'

'Most dear?' Exasperation filled his voice. 'The woman who ruined you? Her disgraceful behaviour besmirched your own reputation beyond recovery.'

'Do you think I care for that?' she shot at him. 'Now?' She shook her head again. 'I have no wish to re-establish myself. I shall be more than happy to spend my days caring for my nephew.'

'I cannot —'

Outside the window, carriage wheels crunched over gravel.

'Ah.' Louise rushed to stare through the panes. The daffodils trembled in their vase as she leant on the table edge. 'My parents have returned. They will support me.'

When the couple who entered the room heard Sir Ranulph's news, and Louise's intention, Mr Devreaux, a thin-faced man of some fifty-five years, cast his daughter an amazed stare.

'Are you run mad? I will certainly not permit the issue of that disgraceful union to inhabit this house.'

'But Amelia was respectably married. In church. He says so.' A look of recrimination replaced her amazed expression. 'As you must have known. For it seems she wrote to you.'

Mrs Devreaux gasped. She staggered against her husband's arm.

'Louise,' she begged 'Pray do not speak to Papa in that manner. Sir Ranulph must be appalled.' She tottered to the chair Sir Ranulph had vacated. A trembling hand rummaged in her reticule. She dragged out a handkerchief and applied it to her moistening eyes.

Louise ignored her distress. 'No, ma'am? Not even when he informs me that Amelia wrote to me?' Her scornful gaze swept across her father's face. 'What did you do with her letters, sir? And mine to her? Burn them?'

'You forget yourself, miss. Do not presume to question me. Remember I am the only arbiter of your behaviour.'

'You are not, sir. I am of age. I may please myself.'

'Louise!' Mrs Devreaux resorted to her handkerchief again. 'I beg you to remember we have company.'

'Much do I care for that. I tell you all, I shall go to live in Amelia's home and take her son into my care.'

In the ensuing minutes not one of the arguments advanced by a furious father and a wailing mother moved her. Louise laughed to scorn Mr Devreaux's final threat of receiving the same treatment he had meted out to Amelia.

'Indeed, sir? Then I would welcome it. Knowing how much I missed her, you kept her from me. What duty do I owe you now?'

Sir Ranulph, finally entering the lists, looked down his aquiline nose at her. 'And how, might I ask, ma'am, will you support yourself? Not to mention Christopher and the household. Or do you expect my cousin's estate to fund you?'

Louise dismissed his objection with a sweeping hand. 'I have a legacy from my father's mother. I shall use that.'

'But dearest,' her mother sobbed, 'you will reduce yourself to poverty. You'll be ruined.'

'I'm already ruined, ma'am.' Her eyes switched to her father who appeared in imminent danger of an apoplexy. 'And that must be laid to Papa's door. It could have been avoided had he accepted her. But he turned his back on her instead. And forced me to do the same. She must have thought…have thought…' Her voice broke. A furious glance that sparkled with tears swept all three.

'I *shall* go to Christopher. He *will* have one close member of his family to care for him. To love him. I'll not betray Amelia. Even if she will never know of it.'

The sorely-tried mother groaned. She swabbed her eyes with the uselessly damp wisp of linen.

Sir Ranulph Trent surveyed the scene from wilting Mama, to blustering father, to determined beauty standing isolated in the centre of the room. Suppressing an inconvenient wave of sympathy for the bereft sister, he bowed.

'I regret, ma'am, it is quite impossible. I could never agree.' He bowed. 'I will not impose my presence upon you any longer.' With another bow to Mrs Devreaux he took himself out of the room before the bell could be rung for the manservant.

Casting a speaking glance at wife and daughter, Devreaux hurried after him. His distraught wife fell against the back of her chair.

'However came you to speak so?' she moaned. 'And in front of a stranger.'

'You expect me to stay silent ma'am? When your grandchild – your only possible grandchild – is to be abandoned to that…stranger?'

'He might not be the only one. It is –'

'Don't console yourself with any notion that *I* shall wed.' A scornful laugh burst from her. 'Society wrote me off as an old maid long ago. It might have been different had Papa not been so…so shamefully stubborn.' She paced to the window. 'Amelia and her child could have been welcomed back into the family. I could have…could have –'

She broke off, biting her lip. For several moments she stood motionless, her arms clasped about her, staring with unseeing eyes at Sir Ranulph climbing into his carriage. Eventually, she turned. 'Could you not have persuaded Papa? For my sake as much as Amelia's?'

Mrs Devreaux lost herself in a morass of phrases and half sentences. Louise raised a hand to stop her.

'It's of no use. Pray don't continue.' Her breath caught. 'I must be alone. I beg you to excuse me.'

She moved from the room, her mind in turmoil.

In the hall, her father closed the main door. The sounds of his wife's sobs reached him. 'Louise, stop. I will not have you distress your mother.'

At the foot of the broad stairs, she paused in her flight.

'I? *I*, sir?' She stared at him, astounded. The past minutes had strained filial duty to breaking point. Barely enough remained for her to close her lips against the accusation that threatened to burst from her. She struggled to hold onto the remnants of her self-control. 'I cannot stay. It's impossible. I must leave as soon as it can be arranged.' Her colour heightened and her head pounding, she turned and mounted the stairs.

'Louise!' Gregory Devreaux marched to their foot. 'Come down at once. I will not have you speak with such disrespect.'

She stopped at the half-landing. 'How should I speak *with* respect, sir, when I no longer feel any?'

Blood suffused Devreaux's face. 'You cannot leave. You? A girl alone? It's impossible.'

'I'm five-and-twenty. Well able to take care of myself.'

'But think what people will say,' he shouted.

Waves of anger resurged through Louise. 'I care not in the least what people may say. And if you had taken less note of it, we would have been spared today's news.' Bitterness smothered a sob. 'No, sir, believe me, whatever you say – or threaten – I shall find a way to reach Christopher and care for him.'

Chapter Two

*A*lone in her bedchamber, with the door closed against the curious and interested housekeeper, Louise leant against its painted wood and waited for her breath to steady. The room was her refuge. It was a simple space, devoid of affectation; of damasks and frills. Pale linen curtains hung round the bed, their only decoration the roses she had embroidered here and there. The quilt ... dear God, the quilt.

Every inch of fabric had come from the gowns Amelia had left behind in her flight. Had her father's orders been obeyed they would have been burned, but Louise had rescued them. Alone in her room, she had stitched away the hours, days and years, reliving the happy times she and Amelia had shared. The knowledge that she should have emerged to comfort her grieving mother had often wrenched her conscience. That she had needed every iota of her bruised spirit to steady her own distress had never eased her guilt.

Beyond the window the grey clouds had shredded into thin wisps. A watery sun sent feeble shafts into the room. Still leaning against the door, Louise waited for the tears to come. When her eyes stayed dry, the notion that she had no proper sensibility gripped her. She wrapped her arms about her and ran her hands up and down them. But then, she thought, tears were no solution; the ache in her mind and body was too deep for such easy relief.

She pushed herself away from the door. The room could no longer be her refuge. Now there was something – *someone* – outside it who needed her. The past was gone. Over. Finished. The future must claim her now. She sat on the bed and gave herself furiously to thought.

Sir Ranulph Trent. He was her only contact with Christopher. Or was he? Amelia had written to her. Had she also written to her mother? If the letters were still in the house . . . no, her father would surely have pitched them into the fire. But her mother? The floorboards of the landing creaked. A scratch sounded on her door.

'Louise? Louise, are you there?'

The brass handle turned, the door inched open, revealing her mother's tear-stained face. Mrs Devreaux crept into the room.

'Dearest, try to understand Papa. He only did what he felt was best,' she pleaded.

'Please, Mama, please. I shall never forgive him for the pain he caused Amelia. And us.' Her face hardened. 'How she must have hoped to hear from us. Did she write to you too?'

Her mother's face crumpled. 'She did. Papa would not let me read them.' A sob. 'At least not all of them.'

Louise gasped. 'Do you have one he didn't see?'

'You must not ask me.' Mrs Devreaux's damp handkerchief shooed the idea away. She sank onto the bed. 'It was dreadful to go against Papa's orders.'

Hope whirled into Louise's mind. 'You have one, don't you? One he didn't see.' She slid to her knees at her mother's feet, grasping at the agitated hands and staring up into her face. 'Oh, Mama, let me see it. Please, please let me see it.'

Mrs Devreaux twisted the handkerchief into a ball. 'Oh, no. You mustn't ask it of me,' she wept.

Louise rose. Between coaxing and demanding, she urged her mother to her dressing room. The elderly eyes lit immediately on an octagonal jewel case.

Louise followed her anxious gaze. 'In there?' She darted across the room to the dressing table, tugged at its drawer and rummaged inside for a small key.

'Oh, no, no. Pray don't.'

'I must, Mama. I must.'

She pulled the casket towards her. The brass banding in the mahogany surface glinted at her, promising secrets. The key turned in the lock; Louise's heart turned in her breast. Would Amelia speak to her after these lonely years? There was nothing among the brooches and gems on the top tray. She lifted it out. Hidden under the lesser items was a single sheet of paper. It had yellowed slightly and its creases had frayed. How many times had it been opened and re-folded? Her fingers trembled. Behind her, her mother groaned and sank onto her bed.

Amelia's words swam before Louise's eyes. Words in her sister's neat hand. She swallowed and forced herself to read the pleas they revealed. Each one pierced her to the centre of her being. The tears that had earlier refused to flow now coursed down her cheeks, so many that the frill round her neck grew damp and wilted where it brushed her jaw. Her hands pressed the letter to her chest. For several minutes she stood unmoving.

On the bed, her mother's sobs grew louder. The sound stirred Louise from her own grief. With careful fingers, she refolded the letter and locked it away. Seating herself by her stricken parent, she placed an arm round the quaking shoulders.

'I must go to Christopher, Mama. He cannot be kept away from us.'

More anguished sobs broke from her mother. 'If you go, I shall have no-one. I shall have lost both of my daughters.' The sobs transformed into a gale of weeping.

'No, Mama, no. I shall return to see you, I promise.'

Her mother's head shook. Red-rimmed eyes raised from the handkerchief. 'No. Papa would never permit it. I shall never see you again.'

Louise wrapped both arms around her mother's trembling frame. 'He shall not stop me. Believe me, Mama. I shall find a way to bring Christopher to you.' She kissed her mother's temple. 'I promise you. I promise. On my life, I promise.'

Her mother would not be comforted. 'You'll never find him. Not unless that horrid man permits it.'

'I shall. I know the name of his house – Crestings. In Gloucestershire, he said. He must be known there. I can find him.'

'No, please! You cannot go wandering around the countryside asking for a man. You must not. It would finish me.'

Louise's resolve wobbled in face of her mother's distress. Continuing to croon soothing words into the distraught lady's ear, she struggled to find another option. After several moments, her shoulders stiffened.

'I have it, Mama. Cousin Hugo will know of him. Such a dandified man as Sir Ranulph is bound to be well known in London.' She held her mother away from her. 'Yes. Hugo must have come across him. I shall write to him. All will be well, you'll see. I'll do it this very moment.'

Mrs Devreaux watched her daughter hurry from the room, hoping beyond hope that Hugo, Lord Marston was still on honeymoon with his new bride and the letter would be lost by a careless servant.

Luck did not favour Mrs Devreaux. Lord Marston had returned with his bride from a delightful stay at Chalfont Mote some four weeks previously. Nor had the letter been lost, as she desperately hoped. No sooner did he tear open the wafer and read it in the library of Otterdean Priory than he had his servants bestir themselves for his immediate departure. Folding the letter into his coat, he went to tell his bride.

Imogene Marston regarded him across the expanse of the drawing room hearth where he had seated himself in his favourite winged chair. 'Miss Devreaux? She is not in unhappy circumstances, I hope?'

'Louise has been unhappy for years.' Marston rose. He stared into the blazing fire for several moments before shoving a booted toe at a half-burnt log. It promptly collapsed onto its fellows in a spray of crimson sparks.

'I do so wish I could have met her. I only saw her that once at Lady Crewkerne's ball.'

'I know, my love. She rarely leaves home. It's a shame the weather was so awful that she could not come to our wedding.'

Imogene looked down and up, warmly aware of her own happiness. 'How noble of her to retire from town life to care for her parents.'

Hugo paused. After a moment he said, 'That was the story put about, but it wasn't true. You were too far buried in the country to have heard. Her younger sister ran off with a man her father would not countenance. I have no idea why he would not. The man was of decent birth – related to the Trents – and with no mean income. He was quite an eligible *parti* for her.' He gave a half-shrug. 'Just another of Devreaux's irascible notions, I suspect. He is known for them.'

'Oh, how ... how sad.' Imogene's mouth trembled. 'I have no sisters but I would hate to lose one of my brothers.'

'Indeed. Louise was heart-broken. She loved Amelia dearly and now ...' The news from his cousin was not happy. Nor suitable for the ears of a bride of some nineteen years who still blushed when introduced as Lady Marston. 'If you would not mind, I think I should go to her.'

'No, of course I wouldn't.' A pair of large brown eyes surveyed him. 'Should I perhaps accompany you? I have not met your aunt and uncle as yet.'

Mr Devreaux's temperament was well known to his nephew. 'Not on this occasion, my love. If you remember, Lady Harriette is to call next Tuesday. It would not do for us to put her off. Please make her my apologies if I am not back by then.' He smiled down at her in the way that always brought a delightful colour to her cheeks. 'It will be quite something for you to welcome her as mistress of the Priory.' Imogene gripped her hands. He laughed and moved to take one.

'I assure you, you will soon become accustomed to it. You can rely on Mrs Radcote and Ollerton to help until you do.'

The mention of the housekeeper and the steward did little to reassure her, despite the warmth with which they had welcomed her as his bride. Hugo, intent on further reassurance, pulled her to her feet.

Haxby, quietly opening the door to supervise the removal of the tea tray, had an excellent view of his master's back and of the two slim arms clasped round his neck. Much gratified by an unexpected demonstration of his master's happiness, he stepped back, obscuring the view of the footman hovering behind him, and silently closed the door.

A good thirty minutes before five the following day, Hugo Marston's curricle turned onto the gravel sweep outside the Devreaux's manor. The weather had not been ideal for travelling in an open carriage, but at least the strong wind had held the rain at bay. Thurnscoe, his head groom, sat beside him, wrapped in a thick coat and with a long muffler twined round his neck.

'Thank goodness we're here,' Marston said. 'Are you frozen to the bone? I daresay you'll find a warm enough welcome in the kitchen.'

'I shan't be stepping into any kitchen until I've seen to the cattle, m'lord.' Thurnscoe's words were as chilly as his fingers. 'They'll be in need of a good rubbing down, for sure.'

Drawing to a halt at the main door, Marston tossed the reins to him and jumped down. The door opened, flooding the steps with a golden glow from the candles in the hall. Dorkins hobbled out, followed by a manservant of considerably fewer years.

'Welcome, my lord, welcome. This is an unexpected pleasure, if I might be so bold. If we'd known you were coming, I'd have had the flambeaux lit.' He pointed at the empty sconces either side of the door. 'But come you in. Mr Devreaux is in the book room but the mistress and Miss Louise are in the drawing room.'

'I'll go straight in to them, please.' He waved a hand at his curricle. 'My baggage?'

'You leave that to Jonathan, my lord.' The butler scowled at the man hovering behind him who jumped forward, his eyes alight as he scanned the curricle's elegant lines.

'If you'll follow me, my lord,' Dorkins said, 'I'll announce you.'

His arrival in the drawing room produced flustered half sentences from his aunt, and a speaking look of gratitude from his cousin. Both ladies were gowned in black. The only relief was an upstanding frill of white lace at Louise's throat.

'Hugo,' she said, hurrying forward and holding out both hands. 'Thank you so much for coming. I was at a loss as to think who else could help.'

His lordship kissed each hand in turn, his eyes running over her black gown. 'I'll want to know more than your letter said before I do.' The distress on her face prompted further words. 'Not that it is in the least like you to fuss about nothing, my dear.'

Mrs Devreaux fluttered towards them. 'Hugo, I declare it is wonderful to see you. I had no notion you were coming. Is Lady Marston with you?'

He bowed over her hand. 'I regret not. Lady Harriette is arriving tomorrow so she could not leave. She asked me to say how much she had wished to meet you.'

'Mama, do you think perhaps you should see Mrs Franhope about a room?'

'What? Oh, yes my dear, I must. I'll do it right away.'

Barely waiting for her mother to depart, Louise dragged her cousin towards the sofa set close to the warmth of the fire. 'Hugo, I'm sorry to cause you to leave Lady Marston so soon but I need your help.'

'Never mind that, Lou, what's this is all about? There was very little in your letter other than a plea for information on Ranulph Trent.'

Louise seated herself. 'I know. I couldn't bring myself to ... to put it into words.' Her fingers knotted in her lap. 'It's Amelia.' Saddened eyes lifted to his. 'She's dead.'

'What?' Marston stared. 'How do you know?'

The next few minutes tried Louise's control severely. She explained all that Sir Ranulph Trent had told her, ending with her determination to go to Christopher.

The lines on her cousin's face softened into sympathy. He sat beside her, offering his handkerchief. 'I'm so sorry, Lou. How positively medieval of your father to ignore her situation. It's beyond belief.'

'Then you'll help me find Christopher?'

'Of course, I will.' He rubbed her arm while she wiped the few tears that had betrayed her. 'It's not in the least part difficult. His house is in Gloucestershire at Charlton Kings. I stayed there when they were trying to set up some proper racing at Cheltenham.'

'Is it a town?'

'Charlton Kings? No. More of a large village.'

Louise fell silent, regarding her fingers interlaced on his handkerchief. After a moment she raised her eyes. 'Do you think I would be able to find lodgings in it?'

Marston's eyebrows rose. 'Why on earth would you wish to do that?'

'So I can be near Christopher, of course.'

He leant away from her. 'But Trent will have a care for him.'

'That's not enough. The child is not even breeched. Much too young to be without female companionship.'

'He'll have a nurse. You can be sure she will be the best. He's not one to stint, you know.' He possessed himself of her hand again and squeezed it reassuringly. 'He is a good man. Believe me.'

'No, I can't. From what I saw of him, he places himself far above his company. Not at all the sort of person to concern himself with how a child is raised.'

'You seem to have taken him in aversion. You are quite wrong, I assure you.'

Suspicion mounted in her that Sir Ranulph was one of Hugo's friends. The improbability of persuading him that she must go to her nephew struck her. She forced a smile. 'I expect you're correct. We shall say no more of it. Tell me instead how you like being married? And when I may have the pleasure of meeting Lady Marston?'

Hugo Marston was more than delighted to describe his bride and the pleasure of his new life. It was a conversation he was obliged to repeat to his aunt and uncle over dinner and continue afterwards in the drawing room. When she trod up the stairs to her bedchamber, Louise owned herself to be pleased for him. He had soon convinced her of his happiness but he had fallen a long way short of convincing her of Ranulph Trent's ability to raise an orphaned three-year-old in a family's loving warmth. She lay her head on her pillow and deliberated through the long hours on how she could reach Charlton Kings and where she could live when she arrived there.

Chapter Three

Sir Ranulph Trent departed Crestings in his curricle, followed by a venerable travelling coach. A pair of admirable chestnuts were poled up to his curricle. They were lively, not having been driven since his return from the encounter with the Devreaux family the previous week. Their antics caused him no trouble and he handled them with ease, something Treffin, sitting up beside him, viewed with approval. The head groom cast a sceptical eye at the weather. The wind that had afflicted the country for the past few days had dropped, allowing steely clouds to gather ominously overhead. By the time the curricle had passed down the mile-long avenue and through the tall iron gates, their threat had materialised and the animals' coats were sleeked with a fine drizzle that soon obscured the fields and trees. Treffin folded his arms across his chest and stared stonily ahead, keeping his opinion of people who made unnecessary journeys on days when any fool could see it would soon be a-drenching everyone firmly unspoken.

Sir Ranulph, however, was well aware of the disapproval emanating from his groom, a retainer well-favoured enough to feel able to comment on his movements, even if those comments were nothing more than grumbling sighs and loud sniffs. He endured the waves of censure for almost a mile.

'For heaven's sake,' he said at last, 'come out of the sullens. If I'd known you would take such an aversion to a little damp, I'd have brought Josh Ribble instead.'

Treffin held to the belief that the recently-employed Ribble was not capable of finding his way to the local inn, let alone anywhere within the ten miles it would take to reach Stapley Hall. He sniffed loudly. 'If that's what you'd prefer, then I'm sure I wouldn't seek to change your mind. Allus assuming you want his heavy hand dragging at the cattle's mouths.'

Sir Ranulph sighed and gave up. He knew that when Treffin was set on preserving his dignity and being disobliging, the best, if only, solution was to leave him to simmer. His normal nature would eventually resurface.

The vehicle bowled along the road that rose and fell over gentle hills, soon leaving the coach well behind. By the time Sir Ranulph guided it over the stone bridge into the hamlet of Little Witcombe the skies had cleared, unlike Treffin's brow.

'Ain't this the place?' he asked.

'It is. A bare half mile to go.'

Stapley Hall came into view as they passed the final dwelling. It occupied a modest rise above the river, its pretty park boasting several fine, spreading oaks, each still bare from their winter sleep.

Sir Ranulph encouraged his pair up the final incline and through the entrance gates. Sheep and cattle wandered between the trees dotted across the swathes of green of the pretty park. Treffin examined the nearest.

'Oak before the ash,' he recited, 'we're sure to have a splash. Ash before the oak —'

'We're sure to have a soak,' Sir Ranulph finished. 'I know. I'm not sure I believe these country fables.'

'That's 'cos you spend so much time up in town where they don't know nowt. If you'd been hereabouts longer you'd know sun afore seven, rain by eleven.'

'We had no sun this morning so how do you account for the rain you so disliked?'

'This weren't rain, sir. 'Twas barely a March whisper.'

Sir Ranulph gave up the unequal task of winning Treffin out of his glooms and drew the curricle to a halt at the arched main entrance. The house was not of a size to match Crestings, no more than eight main bedchambers, but it was charming; neat and well-cared for, with a gratifying symmetry to its timbered façade and in the chimneys rising at each end of a tiled roof. Delightful gardens could be seen, protected by a shallow ha-ha from the livestock's depredation. All in all, it was an establishment to stir the heart.

The vehicle had barely stopped before the solid door opened, causing the laurel wreath of mourning suspended on it to sway across the panels. An elderly retainer sporting a black armband emerged onto the shallow steps.

'Sir Ranulph, sir, we wasn't expecting you.'

'I dare say not. Have the goodness, Jedburgh, to tell the housekeeper I'm here. I want to see my nephew's nurse.'

Passing the reins to an unbending Treffin, he climbed down.

'Yes, sir. O' course, sir. If you'll step inside I'll tell Master Philip you're here.'

Sir Ranulph halted on the stone steps. 'Mr Aveley? He's here?'

'He is that, sir. Come to stay so as poor Master Christopher has some family about him at this sad time.' The retainer's head wagged despondently from side to side.

The Trent family features were notable for a somewhat aquiline cast to the nose. When Sir Ranulph was annoyed, his sharpened into the acutely patrician.

'By all means inform Mr Aveley of my arrival.' He strode past the butler into the generous entrance hall, handing him his hat and gloves on the way.

Stapley's drawing room was a low chamber of faintly Tudor appearance to the left of the hall. Two wide windows pierced the wall opposite a carved stone fireplace that reached to the stuccoed ceiling. A venerable selection of chairs, small tables, a desk and two settees stood on patterned carpets. Ranulph threw open its studded doors, relieved to see several logs crackling in the grate. He deposited his damp overcoat onto the chair nearest to it, causing its several shoulder capes to ripple down like the pages of an abandoned book. He cast his gaze about the room. It had been several years since his previous visit. A vague awareness of subtle changes washed over him. A silk shawl lay in soft folds over the back of the sofa. An open sewing box of padded cotton with colourful silks drooping from it rested on a table in the window embrasure. An embroidered fire-screen stood between the button-backed chair beside him and the fire.

A sudden image of the fair-haired girl Gerard had once brought to see him at Crestings assailed him. Whatever her actions, deplored as they must be, two-and-twenty was a desperately unkind age at which to die.

The door opened and a faintly harassed-looking woman of middle height, middle years but substantial width bustled in.

'Sir Ranulph, pray forgive me, sir. I wasn't expecting you and it's been ... it's been such a sad time.'

'No-one was expecting me. Mrs ... Mrs Nairn, isn't it?'

'Oh, how kind in you to remember me, sir.' The housekeeper dropped a curtsey. 'And you here not but a couple of times all them years ago.' She cast a swift glance around the room and advanced on the driving coat. 'Now, if you'd be so obliging as to be seated, I'll take your coat to the kitchen to dry properly and bring you some wine and fruit.'

'I don't need any refreshment, thank you. I'm here to collect Christopher.'

'Collect?' The small eyes above rounded cheeks blinked. 'Collect the young master, sir?' The damp coat was clutched to a wide bosom. 'But why?'

'He'll be living with me now. At Crestings. You should know that Mr Aveley's Will named me as guardian.'

'But sir, there's Master Philip. He's brought all his traps and has taken the Green bedroom.'

'So I understand. At least, that he is here, not where he wishes to lay his head.'

A worried frown crumpled the housekeeper's face. 'Oh, sir, you'll be taking the poor little lamb from the only home he knows.' The eyes moistened. The lips above an accumulation of plump chins trembled. 'And him so sad, sir. Always asking when his Ma and Pa are coming home. He's looking for them everywhere.'

Yet another repetition of the notion that the child should remain in his parents' home roughened the edge of Sir Ranulph's temper. 'If he lives with me, he won't be looking for them, will he?' He tried to quell the astringency of his tone. 'Now, please see that his clothes and...and whatever else a child needs are made ready to go. My coach will be here soon – at least it had better be – and I wish to reach Crestings before dark.'

Mrs Nairn, twisting her hands into the coat's collar, backed towards the door.

'Where is Christopher, Mrs Nairn?'

'Master Philip has taken him to look at the ducks on the river.'

'Then send someone to fetch him, please. I wish to see them both as soon as possible.'

The housekeeper nodded and disappeared. The coat, longer than she was tall, trailed its hem across the floor to be trapped in the closing door. Sir Ranulph frowned. The door opened a fraction, the hem disappeared sharply, the door closed. Satisfied his coat was released, he occupied himself flipping the pages of a week-old newspaper and wondering just how long it could take to find a child in a park of less than three acres.

Eventually, sounds of domestic upheaval drifted under the door. In the few breaths before he decided to instruct the household to cease its argy-bargy and produce greater efforts, it opened. A young man of little similarity to his late brother walked in, pulling a dripping and reluctant child by its hand. The unbreeched child's dress clung wetly to its small limbs. Its face was crumpled and tear-stained. Its breath came in gulping sobs.

'Trent,' Philip Aveley said, pushing the door to in Jedburgh's face. 'I wasn't expecting to see you.'

Sir Ranulph's teeth clenched briefly. 'I'm given to understand no-one was. And I can return the compliment. I did not expect to find you here.'

The younger man coloured to his fair hair. 'I've come to look after Christopher.'

Sir Ranulph regarded the gradually increasing puddle round the child's feet. 'So I see.'

'He fell in. Only a little. He was chasing a duck and toppled over. He hasn't even grazed his hands.'

'Indeed? Well I am here now to relieve you of his care. You must know I am named guardian. He will live at Crestings.' He directed his gaze down to the child. 'Won't you Christopher?'

Hearing his name, the child, who had sought refuge behind his uncle's legs, emerged. He peered up at Sir Ranulph, his eyes enormous.

'You seen Mama?' The little mouth trembled. 'She not home.' A large tear bloomed the corner of each eye. 'She promised, but she isn't.'

The consequence of the disastrous accident struck Sir Ranulph. 'I'm sorry, but I haven't.' He bent down, crouching onto one knee to bring his face almost to the child's level. 'I have come to take you to live with me at my house. Won't that be exciting?'

Two small arms clutched damply at Philip Aveley's pale pantaloons. The small face turned up to his uncle. The tears trickled over the lashes.

'What are you thinking of, Trent?' Philip hissed. 'Can't you see how distressed he is?'

Sir Ranulph straightened, brushing his knee. 'Rubbish. He will have his nurse with him. It will take him no time at all to accustom himself. I —'

Raised voices beyond the door interrupted him. After a few rattles at the handle the door flew open and a dame of determined countenance and impressive proportions pushed the butler aside. Her bosom heaved under a starched pinafore covering a blue and white striped gown. She fixed a fierce gaze on Sir Ranulph from under a cap knocked askew.

'So,' she declared, 'you've come to take our poor lambkin away, have you? Well, you'll do so over my dead body, and so I tell you!'

Sir Ranulph eyed her frostily. 'You have the advantage of me, ma'am. Who might you be?'

The dame bristled. 'I'm Mabson.' She clearly decided no further information was necessary.

Jedburgh peered past her as much as he was able considering her bulk blocked most of the doorway. 'Mrs Mabson is Master Christopher's nurse, sir.'

The Trent features unfroze. 'Then, ma'am, I have every hope that you will be coming too. We must keep as many of his people about him as we can, mustn't we?'

The nurse contemplated him from under the frill of her disordered cap. 'Just me?'

'Is there anyone else you would like?'

'There's young Letty, sir. Her as is nursery-maid.' The suspicious eyes did not shift from his face. A mumble sounded somewhere behind her. 'And what about the house?' she added.

'What about it?'

'There's folks who live here aside the little Master. Is it to be shut up and them turned off?'

'Of course not. But this is not the time for such considerations.'

From the mutterings emanating from behind the nurse, Ranulph concluded that his response was less than reassuring. He drew a deep breath. 'I see no need to shut the house up and let it go to ruin.' The murmurings achieved a somewhat lighter tone. 'I might consider renting it out. Whoever takes it is certain to need staff.'

From their softened expressions he decided the news had obviously pleased the nurse and the butler behind her.

Philip Aveley was not of their company. His face hardened. 'But what —'

A glance from Sir Ranulph silenced him. 'Now, ma'am, if you would see to preparing such of Christopher's things as you think fit and, er — find him some dry clothes. My coach is here for your convenience and — who else was it? — Letty's.'

The nurse subjected him to a studied gaze before she sniffed and nodded. 'Aye, then.' Snatching Christopher up onto her ample hip, she swept from the room, clucking nonsense to him.

The moment the door closed Philip Aveley burst into speech. 'You're being excessively high-handed, Trent. Not that it's a surprise. We had things nicely arranged here for the boy. There was no need for you to interfere.'

Ranulph extracted a gilt snuffbox from his pocket. His thumbnail flicked it open. He scrutinized the contents before closing it and returning it to his pocket. His eyes settled on Philip Aveley's flushed face. 'I am sure things *were* nicely arranged. But not, I think, for Christopher's benefit. More likely for your own.'

'That's exactly the sort of thing I'd expect you to say.' Philip took a quick turn about the room. 'You Trents are all the same. Because you're as rich as Croesus you assume everyone must jump to your tune.' He swung round to stare at him. 'Well, you're mistaken if you think I will. Christopher should be in his own home. He has inherited it, and he belongs in it.'

'Possibly. But you do not. Nor do you have the right to any part of it. It is, as you say, his and I expect to hear that you have returned to town in the very near future. Now, I have a letter to write, and, since I doubt Mistress Mabson will be ready in under an hour, I intend to write it while I wait.'

He walked to the desk at the far end of the room and sat down. Philip Aveley stared at his back for several moments with undisguised loathing before he wrenched the door open and stalked out.

Sir Ranulph had more than enough time to complete his letter and inscribe Miss Devreaux's name and direction on it. He also had time to drink the wine Jedburgh had brought up from the cellar and complete a disinterested survey of the newspaper before Mabson declared herself, her junior, and, more importantly, her charge ready to depart.

Gaining the hall with impatient steps he found Jedburgh waiting, his face drooping into sorrowful lines. He held out Sir Ranulph's driving coat, now dried by the efforts in the domestic regions. Sir Ranulph shrugged himself into it and handed over the letter.

'Have that despatched, please.' He donned his hat and gloves and stepped out into the inclement weather. Aware that Philip Aveley was glowering at him from one of the drawing room windows, he raised his voice. 'I shall return in a week to tell you what has been decided about the house.' He mounted into his curricle and took the reins from Treffin. 'Ready,' he called to his coachman, and started down the gravel sweep ahead of the lumbering vehicle.

Several pairs of critical eyes watched his diminishing figure from various other windows and vantage points. Few of them followed his departure with cordiality.

The household at Crestings was waiting for its new inhabitants with mounting curiosity. Everyone who could find even the slimmest of reasons to be in sight of the entrance hall when Hoarwithy opened the main door to his master had stationed themselves there. Drawing the curricle to a halt, Sir Ranulph alighted and stood by the door watching the coach crunch its tedious way up the avenue. Treffin took the reins, his face decidedly smug. Master Christopher had not proven to be a good traveller. He was not surprised. It was something he could have told his master would be the case had his opinion been sought. Young'uns very rarely travelled well.

'That was the slowest I've ever known you drive,' he said, struggling to keep the glee from his tones.

'You couldn't expect me to do anything else, could you?' came the tart response. 'Not with those women wittering away and demanding to stop every mile.' He turned to his butler. 'Is everything ready for them?'

'It is, sir. There's been fires in the nursery wing all day. Mrs Crowcroft has put spare linen in there and made up beds for the child and his nurse.'

'Then have her make up another. There's a maid come too.'

Hoarwithy bowed. 'Certainly, sir. Lady Trent instructed me to tell you she would wait in the Yellow drawing room for you. With Mr Trent. She told us to hold dinner until you had arrived.'

Sir Ranulph would have preferred time to recover his humour with a reviving burgundy and some cold game pie in his library before meeting his mother and uncle. Marius would scarcely be exercised about a three-year-old but Lady Trent was a woman of charm and sensitivity. She would be wishful to know as soon as possible how the day had gone and how much the child was suffering.

Resigning himself, Sir Ranulph told the butler to see the newcomers safely installed and entered his home. His extensive glance swept the hall. An unusual number of maids were bent over various items of furniture and the mahogany banisters, polishing furiously, aided by all four footmen currently in his employ. A reluctant smile played at the corner of his mouth but he refrained from comment. Mounting the stairs and nodding to the industrious staff on his way, he went to change out of his travelling clothes before repairing to the inquisition in the Yellow drawing room.

Chapter Four

Mr Gregory Devreaux, being of economical habit, had always declined to pay for letters to be delivered to his residence. He much preferred to send one of his few servants to collect them, usually the unfortunate but grandly-named footman, Benedict. Today Benedict had woken up with streaming eyes and an inability to enunciate his words in a comprehensible fashion. The housekeeper had taken one look at him across the small servants' room and packed him off to bed before he could infect the rest of the staff. What little sympathy the young maid-of-all-work, Ettie Tilbrook, felt for him soon vanished after Mr Dorkins informed her that hers would be the pleasure of hiking two miles through the damp lanes to collect the post.

By the time Ettie had the four letters stowed in her burlap bag and had trudged back to the gates of Dernstone Grange the morning's all-pervading drizzle had soaked through the shawl clutched over her head and shoulders, and drenched her to the skin. Her mind, though, was not on regaining the warmth of the kitchen and a possible cup of tea made from the mistress's used tealeaves. Rather it was on one particular letter in her care. Ettie's fourteen-year-old soul was one of romance and the letter occupying her thoughts was addressed to the young mistress. By rights, it should go first to the master. Only with his approval would Miss Louise be permitted to read it. In the three years that

Ettie had slaved in the scullery she had gathered, through the medium of incautious gossip delivered when her presence was overlooked, all of the misfortunes poor Miss Louise had been obliged to endure.

Perhaps, she thought, the letter was from an admirer. Ettie would have liked an admirer of her own but as she was rarely permitted to leave the scullery and the back stairs area she had very little chance of acquiring one. Moved by wondrous dreams of hidden love, she drew the letter from the bag and hid it down the front of her gown. Several minutes later, Lizzie Sutton was in receipt of a warm, and slightly damp, fold of paper.

Lizzie, forbearing to frown, examined the smudged superscription and promised to hand it direct to her mistress. Alone in her room some few minutes later, Miss Devreaux's furious expression would have told Ettie the letter came from no secret admirer.

'How dare he?' Louise demanded of her bed hangings. 'How very *dare* he?'

She flung the letter away. It fluttered onto the pile of clothes laid out on the bed.

Lizzie, entering the room with a large and dusty portmanteau, halted on the threshold. 'Miss?'

'That dreadful man has taken Christopher to his home already. Just as he said he would. He's given the child no time to recover at all. He informs me … he *begs* to inform me that the child is well and that my presence is therefore quite unnecessary. Unnecessary!'

The maid closed the door hurriedly and swung the portmanteau onto the bed on top of a particularly charming pleated muslin gown. 'So will you still be leaving, miss?'

'Of course I will.' Quick paces took Louise to the window and back. Her clasped hands flung apart; she shook an admonitory finger. 'He needn't think he's going to have his own way in this, for he isn't. Not by a long way.'

Lizzie kept her opinion to herself. If Miss Louise wanted to leave, she knew her too well to believe there would be any other outcome. Miss Louise was a sweet young lady, kindness personified to the staff but when fired up she could be excessively stubborn. Anyone who knew her would vouch for that. Even the master – though he failed to approve of his elder daughter's character – knew it. As did poor Mrs Devreaux. Fortunately, for the peace of the household, it was rare for Miss Louise to be so moved. Today was, of a certainty, one of those times.

Louise pulled her pelisse out of the wardrobe. 'Did you call for the carriage?'

'Yes, ma'am. Midgham will bring it round as soon as he has the horse poled up.' She eyed her mistress who was pushing her arms into the coat sleeves. 'Will you be wishing me to accompany you?'

'Certainly. I can hardly visit Mr Clampett on my own.' She snatched up her hat and tied its ribbons under her left ear with more vigour than style.

Dismissed to find her cloak, Lizzie was much of the opinion that a young lady should not visit the family lawyer, accompanied or otherwise. Sighing, she wrapped the heavy wool more tightly about her disapproving frame and stomped down the back stairs to join an impatient Louise in the hall.

Mr Clampett ushered the fierce young lady into an office that boasted a low ceiling, dark linen-fold panelling, a small diamond-leaded window and a polished oak floor. Closing the door upon her maid, he settled Miss Devreaux on a padded chair close to his desk.

'And how may I be of service, Miss Louise?'

The lawyer's paternalistic smile and tone chafed her bruised feelings so she spoke more abruptly than she intended. 'I wish to have access to my grandmother's legacy.'

Septimus Clampett blinked. 'The legacy?'

'Immediately, please.'

'Er ... I trust, ma'am, there is no trouble at Dernstone Grange?'

'Not at all. It is merely that I shall be moving to Gloucester in the near future and require access to funds.'

'Moving?'

'Yes.'

'But ...'

'No buts, please, Mr Clampett. I wish you to acquire ...'

She paused. Figures rattled in her head. She had long ago taken the household responsibilities from her mother's shoulders but she had never yet been required to arrange for transport. That had been her father's task. And he had paid the bills for it. Not that they ever travelled post; they always used their own carriage and horses, even if it meant journeys dragged out for more days than necessary. Hiring post-boys and paying for changes of horse would be something quite new. To add to her uncertainty, Gloucester was more than a day's journey away which meant she must find an hotel. Louise's teeth caught at her bottom lip. The best she could do was to hazard a guess. She settled for a nice round figure, certain it would see her through any exigency.

'A hundred pounds should suffice. And please make arrangements for me to draw upon whichever bank there that you think fit.'

Mr Clampett, unable to produce any sort of comment that would be anything other than an impertinence — something he declined to offer the flushed young lady before him — nodded.

Louise rose. 'I shall call again tomorrow. Please have the ... the money available. And the name of the bank you have chosen.'

The lawyer found himself rising from his chair, too stunned to cross to open the door. Her hand halfway to the doorknob, Louise paused, the second of her hurdles pushing itself to the front of her mind.

'Mr Clampett, how does one hire a post-chaise?'

The question had him sinking back into his chair. His most recent, and indeed longest journey since returning from London as a newly-qualified lawyer some twenty years ago, had been when he had conveyed his wife a similar number of miles to her mother's funeral in a gig borrowed from a client of more obliging disposition than Gregory Devreaux. He hemmed and hawed and gobbled slightly before advising her that he didn't rightly know. All he could do was direct her to the landlord of the Duck and Drake at the far end of the High Street.

Midgham, diverted from his observations of the comings and goings outside, stared down from the box. 'The Duck and Drake, miss?'

'If you please.' Louise climbed into the carriage, trying to look as if entering a public inn without male escort was a task in no way different from her usual practice.

Midgham raised his bushy eyebrows at Lizzie. He received nothing more than a furious glare in response as the maid flurried her skirts up the step and into the carriage. He shrugged and flicked the reins, encouraging the animal to plod the few hundred yards to the long, timbered building at the town's southern entrance.

Warmly aware of her retainer's simmering disapproval, Louise descended, directed Lizzie to follow and crossed the threshold with her chin determinedly high. Mine host, when summoned, managed to contain his curiosity, unlike his helpmeet whose bustling figure, scurrying up behind him, fairly quivered with it. Some few minutes later, Louise emerged into the street, satisfied and with her cheeks only slightly pink.

The thing was done. Seated in the carriage, she gripped her reticule to stop her fingers from trembling.

Two days later, when she was sure her father had walked along the lane for his customary chess game with old Mr Witherly,

Miss Louise Eleanor Devreaux commanded Midgham to load her trunk, a large portmanteau and two bandboxes into the carriage. She wrenched herself from her distraught mother's arms, and delivered the lady into those of her housekeeper gawping with every other servant at the door. With a roll of flimsies tucked firmly into her reticule, she mounted into the carriage. A defiant and dismissed Lizzie Sutton climbed in after her, clutching her mistress's dressing-case.

Mrs Devreaux's frantic entreaties almost gave Louise pause but the thought of a lonely, bereft child drove her on. 'Look after Mama, Mrs Franhope,' she called, her voice not completely steady. 'I'll write as soon as I'm settled.'

The promise did nothing to allay her mother's fears, or reduce her tears. 'What will Papa say? What am I to tell him?' she lamented.

Louise cast a look at the hovering servants. 'I don't expect you will have to tell him anything, Mama.'

Midgham, owing to some concern for his future employment, pulled away and a short while later delivered Louise and her worldly possessions into the care of the Duck and Drake's host. A yellow post-chaise was drawn up to the inn's door. The post boy lounging beside it showed no inclination to remove his shoulder from the wall and help transfer the luggage from carriage to chaise. Sighing, Midgham clambered down and did it himself, labouring breathlessly under the weight of the trunk. With the final strap buckled, he handed Louise up the step.

'Be you sure about this, miss?' he asked as she settled herself inside.

'Yes, I am.' Louise, belatedly, recognised the concern in his face might not be entirely for her. 'If Papa should ... should be minded to blame you, you must tell him I ordered you to bring me here and said I would drive myself if you did not. He would have had to recover the carriage if that had occurred.'

'You can't drive the carriage, miss. You ain't never learned. You'd have broke your neck. And the horse's legs.'

'There you are, then. You were protecting Papa's horse, if not me. He will approve of that.'

She patted his arm, suddenly aware that he was the final link with her home. Shaking the thought from her, she arranged the skirts of her pelisse with more fuss than was necessary while a scowling Lizzie took her own place.

The post-boy tugged his smock over his head revealing a clean uniform. Midgham, who might have wished him a safe journey, remembered the weight of the trunk and slammed the chaise door instead. The sharp sound made Louise jump. Her breath caught and her hands clenched. This was it. No going back now.

The post-boy sprang to his place, nudged his mounts and the chaise moved off so abruptly the occupants were flung back against the squabs. Lizzie grabbed at the strap hanging by the window with one hand, clutching the dressing case to her thin chest with the other. She cast an anxious glance at Louise.

'How far is it to Oxford, miss?'

'I couldn't quite tell from Papa's atlas, but I think it's about fifty miles.'

'Further than London, then?'

'Twice as far. And nearly the same again to Cheltenham. It will be a pleasant journey.' Louise forced more conviction into her tone than she felt. She nerved herself to preserve a confident air as best she could. 'I've brought the travelling chess set so I can teach you how to play.'

Lizzie regarded her straightly from under the rim of her plain bonnet. 'Oh, thank you, miss. That will be a treat.'

Unprepared for the failure of her pupil to comprehend the difference between a knight's move and that of a rook, Louise could hardly suppress a small sigh of relief when the coach finally passed along St Clement's Street in Oxford some weary hours later, and The Old Black Horse came into view. It appeared to be a perfectly respectable establishment. The discovery some time later, after mine host's good lady had curtseyed her up to her bedchamber, that the sheets were all one could wish wiped the small frown from between Louise's eyebrows. She had accomplished her first journey alone. It proved she need not rely on the protection of her father or of any other family member. She could take care of herself.

The night passed peacefully in a high, four-poster bed hung with green drapes. She woke refreshed and poised. Lizzie who had lain awake in a cramped truckle bed by the fireplace was somewhat red of eye and snappish of temperament.

'Do hurry Lizzie.' Louise rose from the table in her private parlour. 'I want to make good time today so we reach Charlton Kings while there is still light enough to see.'

'Light enough to see what, miss?' Lizzie snapped shut the clasp on the dressing-case she refused to let out of her sight.

'To see Crestings, of course.'

The eagerness on Louise's face was not reflected in Lizzie's. The novelty of travelling post with the unending sight of fields, trees, villages and the post boy bouncing in the saddle on the nearside wheeler before them had soon worn off. Nonetheless, she too watched out of the window as they wound along the London Road through the Cotswolds. When the Chelt river at last emerged from a stand of bare trees, Louise said,

'It can't be much further.'

Lizzie leant forward for a clearer view through the side window. 'Look, miss, look.' She pointed. 'Is that it?'

It was an imposing mansion of rectangular proportions crowning an extensive rise above the river.

'Oh.' Louise drew back against the squabs. The house was much finer than she had expected. Doubts that had been annihilated by her consuming anger at Sir Ranulph's high-handed assumption that she would bow to his command, surfaced. Perhaps she had been unwise to be so determined to confront him. She peeped out of the window. His home dictated that he was rather more above her touch than she had assumed.

The remaining few miles passed in silence. At the Plough Hotel in Cheltenham, she was forced to draw heavily upon her reserves of composure to accept the greetings from Joseph Whinton. That his wife showed more curiosity than the new arrivals found comfortable did nothing to improve her shaky equanimity. Deciding to quell interest, she managed to convey, discreetly and without precisely saying so, that she was a widow. Her intention of finding lodgings in the immediate area she kept to herself. She also resolved to search in her dressing-case for a ring that would serve as a wedding band before she appeared without gloves.

Sadie Whinton descended the stairs in her heavy-footed manner, and informed her husband that their guest had had the misfortune to lose her spouse. ''Tis a shame for one to be left so young,' she said, seating herself by the roaring fire in the kitchen grate and resuming her abandoned dish of tea. 'Not that she's draped herself in black, unlike some I could name. That I don't care to see. Far too imposing on a person's sympathies. It's not as if we don't all have our crosses to bear.'

Joseph Whinton eyed the now-stout frame of the slip of a girl he had married and was much inclined to agree. He sighed and re-applied himself to removing the muslin from a wheel of cheese. 'Don't you be sitting too long, love. I don't doubt the young lady will be wanting some tea for herself.'

Barely had he spoken when knuckles rapped on the kitchen door. It opened to reveal Lizzie Sutton with a pelisse folded over her arm.

'Miss – ah, *Mrs* Devreaux's coat needs hanging by the fire. There's a puddle by your door and the hem caught in it.' Her tone fully indicated her opinion of those who permitted a puddle to form at their entrance.

'Dear me, miss.' Joseph Whinton flung the muslin aside and dropped the heavy cheese onto the table with a thud. 'We'll see to it straightways. The missus will take the coat for you.' His eyes dwelt on his wife who was rather slower to deposit her tea cup on the hearth than he liked.

Lizzie sniffed and handed over the coat. 'And Mrs Devreaux is wishful to know the name of the parish incumbent.'

Sadie Whinton's face that had assumed an affronted expression softened. 'Ah, she'll be wishing to visit the church. A prayer for her dear departed, I'll be bound. Well, there's the Minster, of course, in the city, but we prefer St Mary's at Charlton Kings. It's only a step down the road and the Reverend Mr Gallin is a pleasant young gentleman.'

'Great heavens, woman.' Joseph's head lowered. 'It's a good two mile from here. The young lady won't want to go trudging like that.' He directed a conciliatory smile at Lizzie. 'You tell your mistress I'll be only too pleased to have our eldest drive her there, if that's what she wishes.'

Lizzie's head inclined a fraction. 'I'll tell Mrs Devreaux. No doubt she'll call for him when she's ready.'

With a final glance at the pelisse, now being clasped to the landlady's ample bosom, she departed.

'Don't forget it's Mr Gallin,' Sadie Whinton called. 'He'll have the right words for your lady.'

The comment echoed after Lizzie along the passage. She hoped the reverend gentleman would have the right words, though she was in no way sure. If he could not bring this excursion to an end, she feared what Miss Louise would do next.

Chapter Five

The Reverend Augustus Gallin was a tall young man of lanky form who looked decidedly underfed. He was not. The elderly Mrs Oldenshaw who cooked, washed and occasionally dusted for him, saw to that. He could, as she was apt to say, have broken his fast with a pig and dined on a cow and still not have widened by so much as a whisper. Unmarried, he rattled around alone in an ancient vicarage of decent size. Had he not known the Diocese would have frowned on it most severely, he would have filled its empty rooms with families plunged into poverty when the father lost his income due to enclosures by greedy landlords.

Every Sunday morning he occupied the hour before Matins in reviewing the presentation of St Mary's church. When he was sure no weed marred its gravel path and no dead leaf had invaded its sanctity, he turned to laying out prayer books in the front two pews. Unusually, this morning the heavy door creaked open behind him and an elegant visitor of obvious gentle birth entered, followed by a maid of slightly older years and sterner countenance.

Mr Gallin was a helpful young man, as Mrs Whinton had declared. He was also a polite one and managed quite adequately, after inviting his visitor to sit in a pew, to hide his surprise at the gentlewoman's request. 'Lodgings, ma'am? Well…'

He sank down beside her, propped an elbow on the book ledge backing the pew in front. His chin came to rest on the heel of his hand. To judge from his troubled expression, no ready solution occurred to him. He shifted uneasily. The head rose and his hands caught together. 'I'm not sure there are any … or any you'd care to take.' Colour rushed from his chin to his brown hair. 'There *is* the vicarage, of course, ma'am, but as I'm unwed it would hardly be proper for you.' The presence of Lizzie Sutton's dour faced and crossed arms three pews away bore in on him. 'Even with your maid. I'm sure you would not care for it.'

Only with the greatest difficulty could Louise keep her lips from twitching. 'Of course not, sir. I should prefer an establishment with a female.'

The vicar's tense pose slackened. 'Naturally, ma'am.' He took a few seconds to continue. 'The only suitable place that occurs to me is Mrs Fearnley's. She has one of the houses on Church Street. Not large of course, and I dare say not what you are accustomed to but …'

'That is of no consequence, Mr Gallin, as long as it is clean and decent. And Mrs Fearnley undertakes to feed us.'

'Oh, I'm sure she will. When would you wish to remove to her … assuming all is agreed?'

'As soon as possible. Do you think Mrs Fearnley would prefer to discuss a suitable recompense with you or with me?'

The vicar's flush returned at the mention of money. 'Oh.' He fiddled with the edge of his cassock. 'I, um …' His back straightened. 'I think with me, ma'am.'

Louise rose and held out her hand. 'As you wish. I shall await your instructions with confidence. I am staying at the Plough in Cheltenham, if you would be so kind as to write to me there.' She rose and held out her gloved hand. 'Now, I have interrupted you for far too long.'

The vicar backed unevenly out of the pew before her, hampered by the length of his cassock. Several mumbled words suggested that he was not in the least inconvenienced by her request. More tangled words indicated how honoured and happy he would be to address it.

Passing down the aisle and out of the door, Louise found the young Mr Whinton bending over one of the venerable head-stones standing in a row beyond the yew trees lining the path through the graveyard. His concentration was entirely on the process of rubbing a green-stained handkerchief over the lichen covering it. He looked round suddenly at Louise's approach and straightened, shoving the soiled cloth into a pocket.

'This be where Great-uncle Swithin is buried, miss,' he said, by way of explanation.

Conscious of her Christian duty, and ignoring Lizzie's ful-minating eye, Louise joined him to discover from the chiselled letters that Great-uncle Swithin had died at the august age of eighty-seven and was now joined with his beloved wife, Sarah, in God's Great Mercy. 'It must be a comfort to you to know you are of such a long-lived family, Mr Whinton.'

The concept was clearly new to him. He blushed, declaimed and hurriedly offered to untie the horse tied to one of the stone pillars supporting the barred gate.

Squashed uncomfortably in the gig, Lizzie managed to con-tain her comments until she was back in Louise's hotel bedcham-ber, relieving her of her hat.

'How ever can you agree to stay in some poky little cottage, miss? It's not at all what you're used to. Just as the vicar said.'

'Small matter.' Louise untied the ribbons of her bonnet and handed it to her irritated maid. 'The only matter of importance is that I find my nephew.'

'But how can you do that? If that house we saw was Crestings, you can be sure Sir Whatsisname won't be the kind to go visiting no small cottage by the church.'

'He might not but he said his mother resided with him.' Louise pulled off her gloves. 'She will attend church, I'm sure.

St Mary's being the closest, it must be there that I'll find her.' She unbuttoned her pelisse.

Lizzie all but snatched it. She flung open the wardrobe door. 'And how do you know she don't have her own chaplain? The house looked big enough to have its own chapel.'

Louise's face crumpled. 'Oh, I hadn't thought of that.' She slumped onto the bed and stared at the floor. 'Do you think it will?' she asked after a moment, raising her head.

Guilt washed through the maid. In a flash, she switched from the role of Job's comforter to one of a stalwart supporter. 'I'm sure there'll be a means to meet her. You're such a delight, miss, she's sure to beg for your company. I doubt there's much opportunity round here for any as would amuse a lady of standing.'

A thumbnail found its way between Louise's front teeth. She stared back at the floor.

'Don't you fret, miss. You leave it to me. I'll find out from this Mrs Fearnley how we can meet her ladyship.'

Mrs Fearnley – a motherly woman of some fifty years – proved only too delighted when the vicar asked if she would welcome a paying guest into her home. Poor Mr Gallin, elated to have agreed a solution to the charming young lady's problem, felt obliged to sit in Mrs Fearnley's small parlour, clutching a steadily cooling cup of weak tea, while she regaled him with all the preparations she intended to make. Her major concern was not for the style of food she should serve, nor for the narrowness of the stairs, nor even of the lack of lace on her best pair of sheets (the only ones not turned sides to middle to overcome the wear down their centres), but on how long the young lady intended to stay.

'I'm afraid I cannot help you there, ma'am. Mrs Devreaux was uncertain herself.'

The plump face sagged a little but Hannah Fearnley was of resilient nature. Her mouth soon lifted into a smile that had her eyes sparkling. 'Well, I dare say a few days, or even a sennight, will be better than none.' She peered at the vicar's cup. 'Now that's sure to have gone cold. I'll put some fresh water over the leaves and you can take some more.'

The sorely tried Mr Gallin hit upon a means of escape from the twice-used tea leaves. 'Thank you, ma'am, but no. I must send a note to Mrs Devreaux to let her know all is arranged.'

Mrs Fearnley heaved herself up from her chair. 'Then I'd best see to airing the sheets.' She beamed down at the vicar and pulled the cup and saucer from him with both hands. 'I can't have you delaying me any longer. I'll have to chase you out.'

Augustus Gallin rose from the chair with no regrets at all at being bustled out of the front door.

Two days later a faintly blushing reverend gentleman drove a smart dog cart through the Cheltenham streets and drew up at the Plough Hotel. The vehicle had been borrowed from the stables at Crestings. Lady Trent had been only too pleased to oblige the young vicar in the matter of assisting a widow much younger than herself but he had declined the offered curricle since he doubted his ability to handle a pair let alone a team. Her ladyship had suppressed a smile. She was fond of Augustus for his own sake, not just because she had counted his mother, Susanna Richmond, her closest friend. The boy had arrived within the year of her marriage to the handsome Rupert Gallin, and Stephanie Trent had happily agreed to stand as his godmother. It had taken no more than a word breathed into the local bishop's ear to assure young Augustus of the place at St Mary's when the living had fallen vacant shortly after he had gained his doctorate. Mrs Gallin could breathe easily knowing Stephanie Trent had her beloved son under her eye.

Conversation during the ride to Hannah Fearnley's abode could scarcely be said to flourish. Louise tried to introduce several topics, especially those touching on the Trents, but the vicar's attention was so fixed on guiding the horse away from the worst of the ruts in the road that she eventually abandoned the effort.

At their destination his shoulders relaxed and he sighed on a smile. With the reins wrapped around the end of the foot-guard, he hurried from his seat to assist Louise to alight. Lizzie, perched on the bench in the rear with the trunk beside her, the dressing-case clasped under one arm and the strings of the two bandboxes over the other, was left to her own devices.

'I hope, ma'am,' he said, 'that the journey has not been fatiguing.' He cast an eye over the cart. 'I would have preferred to collect you in a carriage but I –'

Louise cut him short. 'Pray think nothing of it. I am not so feeble as to find two miles in your dog cart in the least fatiguing. And it was most kind of you to collect me.'

'Oh, it's not mine. I begged Lady Trent for the loan of it.'

His comment met with an eager response. 'You are acquainted with her ladyship?'

'I am.' A trace of pink coloured his thin cheek. 'I hesitate to mention it but I have the honour to be her godchild.'

'How very fortunate – for you,' she added quickly, her mind whirling at the unexpected opportunity.

There was no chance for further comment as he had opened the gate to her new lodgings. Stowing the information in her mind, she regarded the neat house with approval. It was larger than the cottage of her imagination and stood tidily symmetrical behind a picket fence guarding a small garden. A single sash widow graced each side of the central door and three smaller ones brushed the roof tiles above.

'How charming. You have found me an excellent place to stay.'

Mr Gallin blushed. 'Giles Fearnley was the Squire's younger brother. When he died, the Squire let his widow move in here.'

'How generous,' Louise murmured, seeing a curtain twitch in a downstairs room.

Moments later, the door was flung open and the short figure of Mrs Fearnley, garbed in her best gown, flurried across the step.

'Why, ma'am, here you be at last.' She bobbed a shallow half-curtsey. 'Come you in now.' A hand swept towards the door. 'I've had the kettle on the hob waiting for you. You'll take a dish of tea, I'll be bound.' She barely cast a glance at Lizzie, being far too eager to usher Louise into her home.

The inside was not as dark or confined as Louise had feared. She was shown straight into an apartment that could only be the pride and joy of her new landlady. She cast a quick eye around the room. Of modest size, it was equally modestly furnished. Two chairs with padded seats and backs but wooden arms stood by the fireplace. Two straight chairs and a bench were drawn up to a square dining table that supported a bowl of quite hideous glaze upon its centre.

'This be the best parlour, ma'am. I've set it aside for you. And if you be wanting a glass of water or such and I'm not about, well, your woman can come across the hall to the kitchen.' She beckoned Louise with a waved arm and another half-curtsey.

Louise retraced her steps into the tiny hall and peeped through the door the woman had indicated. The room was a trifle brighter than the parlour, having a door at the rear that stood open onto the garden. A low, arched fireplace with a cheery fire burning in the grate occupied the inside wall. A kettle hissed on a circular hob swung over the flames. Two stick-backed chairs of simple design and a deal table, scrubbed to whiteness, encroached upon a dresser standing against the opposite wall. Several plates of eye-catching floral pattern stood on their rims along one of its shelves with tea bowls and saucers below. A curious chicken ventured across the far threshold, its feet stepping high and its head bobbing.

Louise ignored it. 'What pretty china you have, Mrs Fearnley.'

'Well indeed I have, ma'am,' she said, hurrying to shoo the creature out of the door which she then slammed shut. 'It were a wedding gift from my husband's brother – him that is squire over at Great Witcombe.'

'I collect you are yourself a widow.'

'I am that, ma'am, so you've no need to tell me how you're doing. And no need to fear I'll be treading on your corns about it.'

Behind Louise, Lizzie sniffed. A disbelieving 'Huh' breathed across Louise's shoulder. She turned, frowning.

'Lizzie, please take my dressing case upstairs.'

'It's the room above the parlour, miss,' Mrs Fearnley said. 'The one with the green patchwork quilt.'

Lizzie disappeared from sight up a set of narrow stairs taking no notice of the Reverend Augustus Gallin struggling to drag Louise's trunk into the tiny hall.

'Would it be convenient for me to carry this upstairs, ma'am? I mean, it would needs to go to your bedchamber ... though I could leave it outside the door if you ... well, it might be for the best. Your maid could carry it inside ... if she could. I mean ...' He gulped. 'It is a mite heavy.'

Louise's smile threatened to reappear. 'I'm sure there can be nothing improper in you depositing my luggage in my room, Mr Gallin, if you would be so kind. After all, my maid is there to watch over you.'

She stood back and allowed the Vicar, Lizzie and Mrs Fearnley to settle her things and herself into her new home.

The following Sunday, a day marked by a sharp, blustery wind that tried endlessly to snatch her hat from her head, Louise walked swiftly along the road for matins at St Mary's church. Lizzie traipsed behind her, muttering darkly about colds and rheums. Louise smiled to herself, her eyes bright with anticipation. The

Reverend Gallin's connection to Sir Ranulph's mother was a godsend, one she intended to make full use of in her quest to reach Christopher. She hardly dared hope that Lady Trent would be at church that morning for she must be quite elderly, being close to fifty summers at least. That made her older than Mama and Louise well knew how much Mama's ailments bothered her in weather like today's. She was not mistaken; Lady Trent did not appear.

After the service, Louise paused in the arched porch, waiting for the vicar to shake her proffered hand. 'Your Godmama must be pleased to have you so close, Mr Gallin. No doubt you take Communion to her – unless, of course, she has her own chaplain.'

Four paces behind her Lizzie Sutton snorted.

'Oh, no, ma'am,' Mr Gallin said. 'Her ladyship always attends Evensong. We have ...' here he blushed, '... one or two excellent singers in the village and have managed to get up a small choir. The two Mincham boys still have unbroken voices and when Squire Fearnley drives over, why, he has an excellent baritone.'

'How wonderful. I'm sure it must be your efforts that have achieved such a success.'

The vicar's ready blush deepened. He stammered on until Louise took pity.

'I shall give myself the pleasure of attending Evensong today.'

She nodded and returned to Mrs Fearnley's house to consume a small slice of ham from an overloaded plate, and read until it was time to set off back to the church though the fading March evening.

Chapter Six

The wind had subsided into little more than a chill breeze when the carriage from Crestings drew up at St Mary's gate. Lady Stephanie Trent descended from it, supporting herself on her footman's rigidly elevated arm. Planting both feet on the ground, she released her grip and steadied herself with her ebony cane before attempting the path to the church. Faines, a stick-thin maid of almost the same advanced years as her mistress, exited the carriage without help and pattered after her, clutching a large cushion of forest green tapestry to her bosom. Jupp, rubbing the circulation back into his forearm, pulled a fur rug from where it had been thrown aside on the carriage seat, slammed the door and hurried after them, attempting to fold the spread of chinchilla into some sort of order.

Augustus Gallin waited under the pointed arch of the porch, his nose and fingers pinched blue with the cold. He bowed and escorted his patroness straight into the church, knowing far better than to detain her outside with any lengthy greeting. Lady Trent processed along the aisle, her cane tapping on the flagstones at each slow step. Around her the congregation had risen. Those nearest the aisle bowed their heads or dropped a shallow curtsey as she passed. She inclined her own head fractionally to the few she had occasion to meet at somewhere other than a Crestings' open day. Drawing level with Louise, she paused, her eyes noting the fashionable sapphire blue pelisse with a sable collar and pillow muff of the same fur.

'Mrs Devreaux, my lady,' Mr Gallin whispered.

My lady inclined her head graciously and, receiving a similar accolade in response, continued on her way to her personal pew overlooking the chancel steps. Faines inched sideways round the vicar and scurried ahead to position the cushion on the wooden seat. Giving it a final plump, she eased herself to the far end of the long seat, so avoiding any suggestion that she was a companion rather than a maid.

Lady Trent's knotted hand grasped the barrier enclosing the front of the pew and she eased herself onto the cushion. With her skirts arranged to her satisfaction, she permitted Jupp to drape the rug over her knees. He retreated to the rear of the church; she lifted her hymnbook from her reticule; the vicar nodded and the service began.

Louise had taken as much notice of her ladyship as was possible in the brief glimpse afforded her. She was of medium height, or must have been when younger, as age had stooped her a little. Her slow progress to her pew and the tap of her cane indicated that she suffered from her joints as Louise had expected. Her features, being fine-boned and faintly patrician, clearly showed from which parent Sir Ranulph had inherited his own. Her eye colour Louise could not decide for they were hidden behind round spectacles, and the little of her hair that was visible from under the frilled cap inside her bonnet was coloured between grey and steel.

Rather than attend to the words of the penitential prayers, Louise pondered the various possible comments she could make if she were granted the opportunity to address her ladyship. The modest choir sang out, recalling her to the present. A deeply satisfying baritone betrayed the presence of the local Squire. The words of Psalm 121 bounded up to the beamed roof.

I will lift up mine eyes unto the hills: from whence cometh my help.

Louise clasped her hands tighter and hoped the redoubtable-looking dowager would prove to be her help.

In the silence following the final prayer, her ladyship rose, pushed off the fur rug and tip-tapped her way down the aisle with Augustus Gallin hovering at her elbow. She halted at Louise's pew. Her eyes behind the spectacles were brightly piercing.

'Good evening, ma'am. I collect you have lately arrived in Charlton Kings.'

'Indeed, Lady Trent. Only this week.'

The sharp eyes regarded her thoughtfully. 'Then, you must pay me a visit. No doubt there is still some life outside Charlton Kings. I shall be pleased to hear of it.'

Spared the necessity of creating an opportunity of her own to call on her ladyship, Louise thanked her and sent a thankful prayer towards the rafters.

Warmed, changed, and followed by her maid clutching a shawl, Lady Trent descended from her apartment in Crestings' west wing to join her son and her brother, Marius, in the smaller of the house's dining rooms. They rose as she entered. Hoarwithy, standing by the sideboard with three footmen and Jupp in attendance, readied himself.

'Well Mama, how was the choir this evening?' Ranulph walked forward to help her to her chair at the end of the table. 'In good voice?'

'It was. Squire Fearnley was present as usual, though we had a pretty soprano join us in the congregation today.'

'Oh? Who was that?' He eased her chair in for her. Lifting the shawl from Faines' hands and nodding a smiling dismissal, he draped it round his mother's shoulders.

'A Mrs...oh, dear, my wretched memory, I've forgotten. Never mind, it will come to me.'

'Memory?' Marius grunted, slumping back down in his chair. 'You never did have a good memory, Stephanie. Never known such a scatterbrain.'

Ranulph and his mother exchanged knowing smiles. 'I expect you'll remember with the second course,' he said. 'Particularly if Domfort has made you an orange cream.'

'Jacques is particularly brilliant at orange creams,' his mother replied. 'I think they are always the highlight of any meal.'

'Mama, you've forgotten his Porc á la Boisseau. I seem to remember you spoke highly of it at Christmas. Not to mention his Chartreuse of Partridges. A particularly colourful edifice as I recall. And of course –'

His mother broke in on him, laughing. 'You are calling me a gourmet, Ranulph.'

Hoarwithy, permitting himself a hint of a smile, nodded to the blank-faced footmen. The men hurried into action and carried a dozen or so serving platters to the table. He himself lifted the claret jug and approached his mistress.

She held her hand flat over the nearest of the three wine-glasses. 'Not for me, thank you. Some water will suffice.'

The butler bowed and proceeded the length of the table to pour a glass for his master who was peering at the platters as they arrived.

'Jupp,' Sir Ranulph said to his mother's footman who had taken position behind her chair. 'Carry the chicken to her ladyship, please.' He indicated a dish of fricassée bordered with darioles of rice.

Lady Trent permitted Jupp to help her to a portion of poultry and a single dariole. 'You take far too great a care of me, Ranulph. In every way. I think you will not find it so easy now dear little Christopher is with us.'

'Of course he won't,' mumbled Marius, chomping furiously at the first of five lamb cutlets. 'It's a fool's game to load an infant onto you at your age. He was fine where he was.'

His comment pleased neither his nephew nor his sister. It brought a frown to Sir Ranulph's brow. Pushing a morsel of chicken into the spreading sauce Lady Trent said,

'He is terribly sad, you know. It is so hard for him in this enormous place. He is accustomed to a much smaller home.'

'Told you so,' Marius added.

Sir Ranulph ignored his uncle but experienced an unusual spurt of irritation with his mother. Neither her comment nor his uncle's had shaken his conviction that the child must be brought up at Crestings, if for no other reason than should he fail to set up his own nursery Christopher would become his own heir. The realisation gave him pause. His fork descended to his plate. If a couple so young as Gerard and his wife could depart this life so unexpectedly, then perhaps he should give some thought to marriage. A quiet, obliging woman of quality would suit him very well. Perhaps –

'Ranulph?' his mother queried. 'What are you thinking?'

He blinked and applied himself to spearing a portion of rare beef. 'Only that he will soon be accustomed to life here. You'll see. He has his nurse with him.' He smiled reassuringly. 'I doubt if he saw much of his parents anyway. Most children don't.'

Cutting a second bite of meat, he missed the shaft of pain that crossed his mother's face.

'My dear, I hope you don't include me in that condemnation.' Her voice was not quite steady.

Sir Ranulph stopped chewing and swallowed. 'Of course not, Mama.' Tenderness lit his smile. 'You were … are the exception. That is why I am sure Christopher will be happy here.'

'You must remember, dear, to make allowances for my years. When you were young, so was I. I cannot play with a child now as I played with you.'

He lay down his fork. 'Do you wish me to hire a companion for you? Or a tutor for him? I can, quite easily – I'm returning to town tomorrow.'

'Good heavens, no. I should hate a companion of all things. And he is far too young to have a tutor. Why, he will not begin his alphabet for at least another year.' She studied her son. 'He is only three.'

'Ah, you will have to acquit me, Mama. I have no experience of children.'

'Perhaps you should have, my dear. You are past thirty ... perhaps –'

'No, Mama.' He raised a hand. 'I am nowhere near minded to take that route,' he said, banishing his earlier deliberations. 'Papa didn't wed until he was past forty.'

'No, he didn't. And I had too few years with him because of it.' Her mouth trembled. She looked down, blinking.

Her son cast a rapid glance round the servants' faces. To a man they were staring fixedly into the middle distance. He could feel their disapproval like a chill mist. He stared at his plate for several moments before cutting into another slice of beef.

Lady Trent passed a sleepless night and an anxious day. Up and gowned by an anxious Faines, she sat at an elegant table in her private sitting room and made poor work of her breakfast.

'Is there anything else your ladyship would prefer?' the maid asked, eyeing the abandoned bread and fruit.

The grey head shook, fluttering the lace edging the wisp of muslin that formed her cap.

'No thank you, Faines. I have had sufficient.' She pushed her plate away and placed her napkin beside it. 'Just ask Mabson to bring Master Christopher to me, please.'

The maid creaked an awkward curtsey and left. Some minutes later the nurse appeared carrying the child on her hip. His arms clung tightly around her neck, his eyes wide and staring.

'He looks so angelic,' Lady Trent said, regarding his fair curls and blue eyes. 'His mother must have been a beauty.'

'She were that, ma'am. Real pretty. Mr Gerard was devoted to her. And to this little darling too.' She ruffled the curls. The child's thumb crept into his mouth; she pulled it out and gripped his hand tightly.

'Bring him here, please.'

Mabson plodded forward and set him down on his sturdy legs. Her rough hand straightened the white dress he wore. 'Here's your Grandmama, Kit. Say good morning, like we taught you.'

The blue eyes widened even further. The thumb crept back into his mouth.

Lady Trent reached a hand out and smoothed a curl at his temple. 'Good morning, Christopher. Have you found lots of nice toys in the nursery?'

The child stared.

'Say yes, Kit. You loved that little horse on wheels.'

'Oh, did he?' Stephanie Trent looked up, her face softening into a smile. 'That was always Sir Ranulph's favourite.' She directed the smile back to Christopher. 'Did you have a pony of your own? A real one?'

The little head shook.

'Master Philip was going to give him one,' Mabson said. 'He promised. But then we had to come here and...' Her words faded away.

'I think we shall go down to the Blue salon. Have...what is the nursery-maid's name?'

'Letty, ma'am.'

'Bring Christopher down with me, please, and then ask Letty to bring him some toys. If she plays with him there he might become used the house, and to seeing me.'

'If'n you say so, ma'am, but –' The plump arms folded across the starched apron top with vigour. 'I must say as I think the angel would be better off at the Hall.'

Stephanie Trent swallowed her own opinion. 'I'm sure Sir Ranulph is well aware of what is best for his ward,' she said, rising from the small table.

Mabson hoisted her beloved back onto her hip. With disapproval writ large on her face, she followed her ladyship out of her sitting room and down the stairs.

In the tiny parlour of her new home Louise sat by the fire, her brows drawn together. Her ladyship had invited her to call, so call she would, but when? Would today be too soon? Would it make her appear encroaching? But Christopher was Amelia's child and she longed to see him. The ache to do so gripped her heart. She pulled her watch out of her reticule; Mrs Fearnley's establishment did not run to a timepiece. A half hour after two o'clock. She rose and rubbed a finger over the window glass to peer out. The sky was almost clear. Only some high, fragmented clouds marred its blueness. Her teeth caught at her lower lip. Would she? Wouldn't she? Yes, she would. She would go now, on her own and leave Lizzie engrossed in the laundry.

Five minutes later, with her bonnet on and grasping the umbrella Mrs Fearnley had pressed on her, she set off on the two mile walk along the footpath her landlady had assured her was the quickest route to Crestings.

Lizzie had refused point blank to allow her to walk out unaccompanied. Muttering, the maid traipsed after her over several stiles and along a hedge-side path through a field containing a herd of curious cows. Keeping her hem clear of the damp ground, Louise hurried on. The path led, eventually, to a stand of bare elms, their branches half-concealing their first, close view of Crestings. It was a property to fill any owner with pride. Wide and elegant, its proportions and symmetry could only be admired. Four pillars at the centre of the principal façade supported the impressive triangular pediment at roof level. The lower rank of tall sash windows bespoke a life of refinement and ease.

For a moment Louise's steps faltered, but only for a moment. Lifting her chin, she continued across the park to reach the gravel sweep that led to the front of the mansion. Coming closer, she could see the restrained decoration on the stone façade more clearly. The carved pilasters interspersed between the many windows gave the appearance of the roof being supported by Corinthian pillars.

Her footsteps slowed again as she neared the main door. She had been invited but she was certain few of the Trents' visitors arrived on foot. Relieved that Lizzie was with her, she mounted the shallow steps in some trepidation and knocked.

For several embarrassing moments nothing happened. After what felt like an eternity, the massive door opened and a liveried footman, complete with powdered wig, gazed down at her.

'Lady Trent invited me to call,' Louise said, holding out one of her cards with the 'Miss' neatly amended to 'Mrs'.

The footman took it, regarded its inscription then stood aside to permit her to enter the lofty hall.

'If you'd condescend to wait, ma'am, I'll apprise her ladyship of your arrival.' He waved a hand at one of the straight chairs that bracketed a console table at one side of the hall, appearing not to notice Lizzie at all.

Louise, who had never before been invited to wait in an entrance, cast a hasty look at the elaborate mirror above the table and sat down. Her fingers tightened round the umbrella. Lizzie hovered by the door.

Several minutes passed before the footman reappeared. Looking somewhat less starched, he bade her follow him up the sweeping staircase. Lizzie received nothing more than a pointed finger indicating that she should stay where she was. He mounted the stairs at a stately pace. At the top he traversed a galleried landing of spacious proportions and opened a pair of double doors.

'Mrs Devreaux,' he announced.

Louise entered into a pretty drawing room to see Lady Trent rising from a sofa near the fire. She opened her mouth to express her thanks when sight of the stunning fireplace arrested all speech. A pair of shoulder-high marble caryatids with their heads bowed bracketed the hearth. Turned towards each other, they supported the mantelpiece on their linked arms. Their chaste gaze was directed to the grate between their bare feet.

'Quite,' said Lady Trent, a laugh in her voice. 'Why my husband's grandfather should think two barely-shrouded females were an appropriate addition to the room I have never been able to imagine.' She moved forward.

'My dear Mrs Devreaux, how delightful to see you again. Pray come and be warm.' She held out her hand.

Louise dropped a brief curtsey then shook her ladyship's proffered hand before seating herself on one of the pair of armchairs opposite the sofa.

'How are you finding our little village?'

'Quite charming, ma'am.'

'I hope you are comfortably settled?'

'Mrs Fearnley has been kind enough to let me stay with her.'

Stephanie Trent wondered why her guest had removed to Charlton Kings, which was hardly the centre of the world, but was far too polite give way to such crass curiosity. She put it down to the young woman's recent bereavement.

Louise herself was very conscious of the lie that had gained her admission to Crestings. She hovered on the brink of admitting the deception but Lady Trent moved to discuss the recent cold spell and the state of the roads and the moment passed. Before she could summon up her courage again, the door opened and a magnificent personage entered followed by a maid bearing a tray of china and cakes and another carrying a silver kettle and stand with great care.

'You'll take some tea, Mrs Devreaux?' Lady Trent asked.

Discomfort gripping her, Louise accepted the cup and saucer the younger of the two maids carried to her. 'Lady Trent, I must explain –' she began. Behind her the door opened again.

'Mama – oh, I beg your pardon. I hadn't realised you were entertaining.'

Ranulph Trent, dressed in a flowing greatcoat with multiple capes, walked to his mother. 'Pray forgive me. And your guest too, I hope.'

He turned, half-bowing.

All movement froze. After a second he straightened.

'You!' he said, without bothering to conceal his anger. 'What the devil are you doing here?'

Chapter Seven

'Ranulph!' Stephanie Trent looked aghast from her son to her guest. 'Do you know each other?'

'We most certainly do.' Sir Ranulph continued to glare at Louise. 'Perhaps you would be good enough to explain how you've been able to trick your way into my house.'

'Ranulph!' his mother said again, casting a troubled glance from him to the servants.

The butler, rigidly concealing his curiosity, unlike the two gawping maids, ushered them from the room and closed the door. Sir Ranulph's face turned increasingly livid during the process.

'What, Mama?' he snapped when they were alone. 'When I last saw this lady I expressly forbade her to come here.'

Louise sat very erect, the cup and saucer trembling in her hands and her cheeks burning. 'I was about to explain matters to you, ma'am.'

'Amelia – Christopher's mother – was my sister. My very dear sister. As your son knows I too was named as guardian. And as he further knows, I wished to have Christopher in my care while he is so young.' Mounting rage stopped her hands from shaking. Her eyes flashed at him. 'He would have none of it. He forbad me to see him. He's my only ...'

Her words faltered. The fire drained from her in a breath. 'Christopher is the only thing I have left of Amelia. Ma'am, I cannot ... I cannot let him go. And I have yet to see him. I must, ma'am.' Her imploring eyes rested on Stephanie Trent. 'Indeed, I must.' Despite her every effort her throat caught. She looked away, blinking rapidly to preserve her countenance.

Lady Trent rose from her chair. The look she cast at her son was not one he had seen before. He recoiled from it.

'My dear girl, of course Christopher must be with you, and he shall be. I'm sure your parents will welcome their grandson.'

'Ha!' Ranulph flung his hat and gloves onto the empty chair beside Louise. She flinched.

'Explain that to my mother if you please, ma'am.'

Louise put her cup onto the table beside her. She fought to control her voice. 'I've no wish to deceive her. If you had not been so unreasonable, there would have been no need for me to act as I have.'

'Really? It seems to me, ma'am, that deceit runs in your family. Your sister practised it, and so it seems do you.'

'Ranulph.' Lady Trent, leaning heavily on her cane, moved unevenly towards him. Louise rose and stepped forward, steadying her with gentle hands. 'Ranulph,' repeated her ladyship, 'whatever the cause of this situation, I will not have a guest in my home spoken to in such a fashion. Beg Mrs Devreaux's pardon at once.'

Her son bowed. 'I would beg her pardon, ma'am, were she here but this is not Mrs Devreaux. This is *Miss* Devreaux.'

Puzzled elderly eyes moved from a furious man to a young woman whose expression varied fleetingly from distress to determination and back again.

'I beg your pardon, ma'am. I styled myself as a married lady so I could travel to Gloucestershire and find lodgings. I could not comfortably do so otherwise, even though I've gained my majority.' She looked down for a moment. 'Please understand, ma'am, I *must* follow my sister's wishes and be near her son.'

'Of course you must, my dear.' Stephanie Trent patted the hand still supporting her arm. 'Now I shall send Ranulph away and you shall tell me all about it.' She turned a cool gaze upon her son. 'You are still minded to go to town?'

'No, ma'am, I am not. Not now. I shall stay here until this ... this *situation* is resolved.' He snatched up his hat, bowed to his mother and stormed out of the room.

Thirty minutes, two cups of tea and a borrowed handkerchief later, Louise wiped away a final tear and looked at her hostess.

'You have been so kind, ma'am. I must thank you.'

'Not at all. From what you have said I can only offer you my heartfelt sympathy. And for your Mama. It must be so difficult to lose a child ... and to lose one that is not dead ...' Her gaze strayed to her son's gloves tumbled forgotten on the floor. 'You must understand that Ranulph is my only child. Sir Lawrence and I had hoped – had prayed for more but it was not to be. I fear we both doted on him too much. Indulged him too far. Now he has become too accustomed to having his own way.'

'Oh, no, I'm sure, ma'am ... at any other time ...'

A thin hand rose. 'No, no. I am not so advanced in years that I cannot recognise a fault in me ... or in others. Even in my son.' She tilted her head and smiled. 'Your only fault appears to be letting a deep devotion to your sister dictate your actions.

'Ma'am ... I –'

'Do not apologise, my dear. There is no need. I must own that in your situation I would do the same ... at least, I hope I would find the courage to do so. Now,' she drew herself upright, 'we must find a way to let you be with Christopher that will save Ranulph from storming about and glaring at us. But for now you must be aching to see him. I shall ring for you to be shown up to the nursery.' She reached for the cord. 'Take your time, my dear. I shall await you here.'

It was some little time before Louise re-entered the drawing room. It was obvious to the meanest intelligence that the sight of her nephew had tried her to the extreme. Stephanie Trent forbore to comment. Instead, she smiled most gently upon her guest.

'I have a solution which will suit us all very well. You shall move into the Dower House with me and Christopher.'

Louise gasped in horror. 'Oh, no, ma'am, no. I cannot be the reason for you leaving your home.'

'Nonsense. I should have gone there years ago. And must certainly do so when Ranulph weds. No, it will be no trouble to me. It will let you see Christopher, and it will be more comfortable for him. You will not have seen your sister's home, but I believe it to be of a similar size to the Dower House. This huge pile,' her hand swept an encompassing circle, 'is so unlike his home, it cannot be other than unsettling.'

Louise tried for quite some time to dissuade Stephanie Trent from her plan. She failed. Her ladyship was determined. Reaching for the bell-rope, she rang for her carriage.

'We shall go there immediately. There are bound to be things that need setting to rights before we can move in. Come along, my dear. You will want to see where you shall be living.'

The Dower House needed rather more setting to rights than Lady Trent had expected. It had stood empty, save for a housekeeper and her husband, for several years. All the rooms a dowager might inhabit were shrouded in Holland covers. In the late winter day the air struck chilly and damp. Mrs Lanthwaite pattered behind the ladies, twisting her hands. Her jumbled words sought to explain how impossible it was for one person to keep a house that boasted six main bedrooms properly cleaned. Or dusted and warm. Bert Lanthwaite, hurrying ahead of them to fling open the window shutters, supported his wife with doom-laden comments about the state of the roof. Were they not depressing enough, he feared the garden and lawns in which the building sat were beyond help.

'Never mind why,' Stephanie Trent said, 'the important thing is to determine what needs doing and how quickly it can be done. Do not fear I expect you to do it unaided. I will send Pembridge to see to it.' She turned to Louise. 'He's Ranulph's steward. Well, steward, cum agent for the estate. Wonderful man. My husband found him, you know. He's been with us for years.'

She led the way out of the house and stepped into her carriage. Turning on the seat beside her as the horses pulled away, Louise looked back at the pretty house.

'Queen Anne,' her ladyship said. 'Always so pretty a style.' She balanced her cane by her side. 'It was the Queen who created the baronetcy for Bernard Trent. He distinguished himself particularly well at Blenheim, you know. 1704, if I remember correctly. All very noble but terribly bloodthirsty, from the account he wrote of it.'

Louise, though a well-read girl, had not previously interested herself in battles that occurred over a century before. She murmured politely and limited her comment to the Dower House's pleasing façade.

The drive through Crestings' park was agreeable but not overlong. One bend in the path afforded a view of Charlton Kings.

'Ma'am, if you'd be kind enough to stop, I can easily walk down to Mrs Fearnley's house from here.'

'Nonsense, my dear.' Lady Trent's eyebrows rose. 'You'll stay in Crestings until the Dower House is ready.'

'Oh, no. I couldn't. It would be too much of an imposition.'

'Well, if you think getting to know Christopher is an imposition...'

'Of course not. Only Sir Ranulph...ma'am you must know he will not like it.'

'After his comments today I dare say that is true but Crestings has been my home for over thirty years. I think I may be permitted to invite a guest to stay.' She patted Louise's hand. 'You shall have an apartment in the east wing. It is not an area Ranulph frequents and you will be close to the nursery...if you wish it.'

Louise felt herself in danger of drowning in embarrassment. By the time she had expressed her thanks three or four times the carriage had reached the main door.

'Now, my dear, we shall summon your maid and Crooch will drive you down to Mrs Fearnley's for you to collect your things. Then you can come back here. Do you hear, Crooch?'

The middle-aged coachman turned on the box and tapped his head. 'I hear, my lady.'

'Good. And take Jupp with you. I'm sure Mrs Devreaux will have a trunk to bring with her.'

After an embarrassing wait for Lady Trent's footman to appear with Lizzie, Louise was conveyed to her lodging. A curricle she recognised was standing outside in the care of a groom. Her heart shuddered down to the soles of her half-boots. Please, she whispered to herself, let there not be more argument. Today had stretched her emotions more than she had expected; she doubted her ability to endure another scene.

Jupp opened the carriage door and unfolded the step. Only too aware of Sir Ranulph's stony-faced groom and a similarly stony-faced Crooch, her hand trembled on Jupp's arm as she stepped down. Once she had two feet on the ground, he trod forward and opened the picket gate. Its squealing hinges made her wince but she managed a fleeting smile and a slight nod of her head. Swallowing, she trod up the short path and rested her hand on the latch of the green door. The urge to fling it open and immediately flee up the stairs gripped her. She could not.

With her head high and a hand clutched on her reticule, she lifted the latch.

Sir Ranulph stood in the middle of the parlour. He overwhelmed it. Not by his height, nor by the many-caped driving coat that swirled round his ankles as he gesticulated. It was the cold fury in his face.

Backed into the fireplace corner, Hannah Fearnley was wringing her hands and blinking rapidly. 'Oh dear, dear. Oh, dear, dear.'

She saw Louise. 'Oh, Mrs Dev–... oh, no, Miss Dev–... oh, no. Oh, dear, dear.'

'Ah.' Sir Ranulph swung round. 'There you are.'

'Indeed, sir, here I am. I see I am interrupting your... your *conversation* with Mrs Fearnley.' Scorn quelled the nervousness she had felt.

'Yes, you are. And I may say she has been much distressed to find she's been harbouring a liar.'

Louise's grip on her reticule tightened. Though the top of her bonnet barely reached his black hair she found it easy to meet his eyes. 'Not as distressed as she must be by your bullying.'

'Bullying?' The coat swirled again. 'I'm not bullying anyone.'

'Not me, certainly. I would not permit it. But if you are not in a rage, how did you fail to hear the carriage arrive? Or the gate squeak?'

'Carriage?' Sir Ranulph looked sharply at the window. His sparking eyes turned back to Louise. 'That is of no consequence.' He pulled in a deep breath and held it for a moment. When he spoke again his voice was icily controlled. 'I trust you will be leaving Mrs Fearnley's now.'

'I shall indeed.' She felt an unaccustomed delight at his presumed superiority, knowing she was about to banish it.

'Lady Trent has invited us – my maid and me – to stay with her so I may come to know Christopher.' The thunderous change in his expression gave her pause. Her assurance wavered. She forced herself to speak calmly. 'If you wish to discuss it with me further, I suggest you wait until I have acceded to your mother's wishes. I would not wish to delay acting upon them.'

With an incensed glare that promised more hot words, Sir Ranulph Trent bowed to the cowering landlady and stalked out of the house.

The front door slammed. Louise sank gratefully onto the nearest chair. She was pleased with herself. Pleased not to have been overborne by Sir Ranulph. A few steadying breaths restored her composure. She turned to the shaking woman still hovering in the corner. With a quick scan of her distraught face, she said,

'I am so sorry to have brought that scene upon you, Mrs Fearnley. Sir Ranulph's quarrel is with me, not you.'

'Oh, no, miss. He weren't quarrelling with me.'

'It sounded as if he were. He certainly looked very angry.' She unwound the strings of the reticule that had unaccountably knotted themselves round her fingers until they bit into them. 'I must apologise for my small lie to you. He has obviously told you of it.' She looked up.

'Well, yes, miss. He did say as you weren't a widow.'

'Did he also say I am joined in guardianship with him of my dead sister's son?'

A frown pleated the landlady's forehead. 'No, ma'am. No. That he did not.'

'Then I see I shall have to tell you all.'

Hannah Fearnley clucked and sighed. At the end, she lifted a corner of her apron to wipe a tear. 'And her so young, miss. How your poor Mama must be grieving.'

Louise gulped. A small stab of conscience nudged her; not all of the story had been told. Her father's expulsion of her sister had not been owned to. Nor her mother's pleas to turn from her own intention. 'Now,' she said, 'I'll put my things into my trunk and be gone in a moment.' She rose, pausing on a thought. 'I believe the Reverend Gallin said I might be here for one or two weeks.' Mrs Fearnley nodded. Then I'm sure you must have gone to some trouble for me. If you are agreeable, I shall give you the full two weeks rent.'

Mrs Fearnley, after some mild protests proved eagerly agreeable. Louise dug in her reticule for her purse and placed the money discreetly on the solid wooden mantelpiece.

'He's not such a harsh man, you know, miss. By all accounts he's a good master, but ... well, I don't envy you your place.'

'I shall be fine. Lady Trent has decided to remove to the Dower House and it is there I shall stay.' She forced her voice to lighten. 'I'm sure Sir Ranulph would never knowingly distress his mother,' she added with far more confidence that she felt.

Chapter Eight

Ranulph Trent was at that moment staring at his steward in amazement. 'A hole?'

'Yes, sir. Quite a large one.' Pembridge held his hat in front of his coat. His fingers shuffled the brim round in a circle. The late sun shafting through the library windows served only to highlight his discomfort.

'Why did no-one tell me?' Sir Ranulph rose, scowling, from behind his wide mahogany desk. 'A chimney doesn't fall through a roof without somebody noticing.'

'It was when you were in London, sir. In that terrible storm last November.'

'But you were here.'

Pembridge shifted his weight from one foot to the other. 'I'm sorry, sir. My wife was lying in with our fifth and it didn't go well. I was that put about that Martha Lanthwaite wouldn't let her Bert tell me.'

Ranulph dredged his memory to recall what, if anything, he knew about his steward's wife and their fifth child. Vague hints of some unspecified difficulty drifted back to him.

'Of course,' he said at last. 'And how is Mrs Pembridge now?'

'A trifle weak, sir, thank you. We're hoping she'll improve once the weather lightens.'

'Of course. Please give her my best wishes. Let me know if there is anything her ladyship and I may do for her.'

'Thank you, sir.' The steward's head tilted and his gaze wavered. 'Lady Trent sent some fruit down from your succession houses.'

'She ... what? Oh, of course. I'm pleased her ladyship thought of it.'

The anxious expression that had printed a deep furrow between the steward's brows and turned his mouth down lifted slightly. Sir Ranulph failed to notice.

'Now,' he continued, 'what are we to do about the Dower House's roof? Can they get up there and repair it? And what of the rooms underneath? Are they damaged?'

'One of the attics'll need new floorboards, sir, but the main bedchamber which is beneath it isn't hurt, as far as I can see. The Lanthwaites collected as many buckets as they could put their hands to and set them under the hole. With their tin bath, too. I must say, sir, they did their very best to keep the place dry.'

Sir Ranulph quelled his irritation. Pembridge and the Lanthwaites were not its cause. He knew perfectly well whose behaviour was disrupting his humour. His forced his features to relax. 'It was very good of them. I'll see to some sort of recompense. It cannot have been easy carrying buckets of water down the stairs.'

'Oh, they didn't do that, sir. Lanthwaite put a bench by the nearest dormer window. He climbed on it emptied the buckets down the roof.' He cast a quick look at his master. 'Not but what it did Lanthwaite's back no good at all.'

A frown flickered across Ranulph's face at his own stupidity. 'Of course. How sensible of them. I hope he is recovered by now.' He thought for a moment, tapping his fingers on the side of his jaw. Pembridge kept silent, waiting. 'Set some men to repair what they can from inside the attic. Don't let anyone onto the roof until this rain has stopped. It will be far too dangerous and I want no accidents.' He walked back to the chair at his desk and sat. 'I shall want to know how long the repairs will take. Her ladyship cannot move in until they are done.'

'Yes, sir. I'll see to it myself. With Hitchin. He's never failed us yet.'

Ranulph's face softened at the name. Hitchin. The estate's head carpenter. More than twenty years ago he had enchanted a lonely six-year-old with a rocking-horse. What a birthday that had been, and how Ranulph had loved the horse with its dappled grey paint and real horsehair mane and tail. Hitchin, now grown old in service to the Trents, was one of the few servants he held in especial regard. 'Very well, but don't let him exert himself. He's well past the age of mending roofs.'

'No fear I'll let him do that, sir.' The tension left Pembridge's shoulders. He took himself away to reassure the Lanthwaites that their efforts had met with praise, not with dismissal without a character.

It would have been difficult to say who was the most disconcerted by the news of the damaged roof. Reporting it to his mother that afternoon Ranulph recognised her deep disappointment.

'Mama, please reconsider. There is no need for you to remove to the Dower House. You have your apartment here. There is everything you need. Why unsettle yourself so?'

'You know why, dearest. Miss Devreaux cannot stay in the same house as you. It would not be in the least part proper, even if I am here too. She is not a governess or servant.'

'Miss Devreaux may return to her father's home. There is no need for her to be here.'

'I agree.' Marcus Trent bestirred himself from his somnolent doze by the fire. 'The lad has his nurse. And that girl she brought with her. It's not as if they'll need any help. Not from her, and not from you either, Stephanie.'

'No.' Lady Trent's voice brought the men's heads up sharply. 'I will not deprive the child of any member of his family remaining to him. And such a close member too.'

She rose more abruptly than her aging joints made wise, and grimaced with pain. Her son saw it and unfairly added it to Louise's account.

'You will have to excuse me,' his mother continued. 'I must see that Miss Devreaux has everything she needs.'

Sir Ranulph moved to open the door for her and she passed from the room without another glance at him. He shut the door with a snap.

'Women,' Marcus Trent exclaimed. 'Dashed if I know why they get so worked up about the wretched little creatures. It's not as if they have anything to say for themselves before they're able to go out to shoot.' He shifted in his chair. 'And not even then, most of 'em. More likely to put one across the line or wing a beater.'

Sir Ranulph ignored his uncle. He strode to the nearest of the tall windows and stood looking across the sloping lawns to where the river had been widened into an ornamental lake. It was a view his father had particularly liked; one several dozens of men had laboured over a year to produce. When the trees planted in clumps around it grew to maturity it would indeed be something to be admired. His mind wandered to his father. Memories of him were few, and faint. The baronet had been a distant figure, standing beyond tutors, schoolmasters and university dons. He had given him some words of caution before setting him up in rooms in London, words that had been blunt and very much to the point on card-sharps, horseflesh and the muslin company.

No, if Sir Ranulph remembered anything from his youth and childhood, it was his mother's affection. The reminiscences lifted one corner of his mouth. How she had protected him from his sire's version of justice. Not in a dishonest way, her explanations had simply omitted part of the truth. Not as open as they could have been. And her scent. He remembered that. She still wore the same one. The merest trace of it summoned memories of her warm embrace and her smiles.

Perhaps...perhaps Miss Devreaux did have something to offer Christopher. He could not deny she was a woman of character. Would her pretty face form the same memories for the child as his mother's did for him? Pretty? She was pretty, at least when sadness or temper did not inform her features. When anger overrode it, he had to admit she was quite the most magnificent termagant he had ever encountered. One who could put any avenging Greek goddess to shame. There would be no fear of her failing to manage a household, or being an insipid wife.

He gasped. One hand reached for the window-frame to steady himself. Wife? What a ridiculous thought. The hand fell. He squared his shoulders. Ridiculous.

Slumped by the fire, his uncle snored.

The prospect of residing under Sir Ranulph's roof for an indeterminate length of time filled Louise first with trepidation, then embarrassment, and finally with fury. What a quandary to find herself in. She had left Mrs Fearnley's home in a ruffled frame of mind, half anxious, half elated. How that had changed. The temptation to return there and avoid the fuming Sir Ranulph alternated with a determination not to. The hole in the Dower House's roof had trapped her. She did not feel able to return to the cottage and beg to resume her room, despite having parted with the extra rent. Nor would she return to her parents. In that house she would be subject to a barrage of tears and moans from her mother and unending recriminations from her father. At the moment it seemed as if every route led her to affronts or problems.

She sat in the bedchamber to which she had been shown, bit
on her thumbnail and stared with unseeing eyes at Lizzie who
was putting away the contents of her trunk in the wardrobe. A
tap sounded on the door of the pretty parlour that adjoined the
room. Lizzie paused, two folded shifts in her hands.

'Miss? There's someone knocking.'

She lowered the garments onto the bed and went to open the
door.

Louise rose and followed her, fighting to appear serene.

'My dear,' said Lady Trent when Lizzie opened the door to
her, 'I am sure you must be disconcerted by the news of the roof.
As indeed was I.' Her head tilted enquiringly.

Recalled to herself, Louise gestured to the chintz-covered
chair by the fire. 'Please, ma'am.'

'Thank you.' Lady Trent nodded to Lizzie, who curtseyed
backwards out of the room, and walked unevenly to seat herself.
'This is such a pretty room. I hope you like it.'

'Thank you, ma'am, but I hardly feel able to stay. Not now.'

'Of course. That is why Ranulph will be leaving for London
tomorrow.'

'Leaving? Oh, ma'am.' Louise sank down on the chair opposite her hostess. 'It will enrage him further to be driven from his
home and it is scarcely becoming in me to do so. It is bad enough
that you are leaving it.'

'You have not driven either of us out. He had already planned
to go to town this week. He wants to make sure the house is
ready for me to go up for the Season.' She leant forward smiling
confidentially. 'I have no wish to stay be immured in the country with no news of life, except what I learn from letters.' She
noticed the shadow that crossed the young face opposite. 'Oh,
my dear, how thoughtless of me when you have endured just
that. I do beg your pardon.'

'It's nothing, ma'am, really. After Amelia . . . after she . . .' She strove to collect herself. 'I had no wish to return to town. And no interest there.' She pleated the folds of her gown. 'I believe . . . I intend to abjure society completely now I have Christopher to care for.'

'It would be society's loss if you did.' Lady Trent laid a hand over the fidgeting fingers. 'As we shall be companions in that, my dear, I'll not stand on ceremony with you. You should be thinking of a family of your own. An accomplished woman like you would be an asset to any man. And to his children. I hope, my dear, when you have recovered your equanimity you will reconsider.'

'No, ma'am. I have no intention of marriage. From what I have seen of it, it does not ensure happiness.'

'Not everyone is fortunate, I agree. Not in our world.' Lady Trent said, her mind casting over her own marriage and coming to rest on her son. He was no rigid tyrant, yet he was not predisposed to the tender emotions. He would need a wife of character. One who could warm his cool nature. Her eyes rested, without any degree of calculation, on the young woman opposite.

Ranulph Trent left Crestings at ten o'clock the following morning, wrapped in his greatcoat, wearing his gloves and hat and with a fur rug over his knees. Rather than take the tree-lined avenue to the main gates, he tooled his curricle along the drive that took him to where the lake narrowed to the original river. The Dower House overlooked it from the other side. He crossed the bridge that rose and fell on three arches, and drew to a halt by the entrance.

Pembridge was awaiting him in the tiled hall with Hitchin at his side. He did not introduce the gangly lad hovering in the background.

'Good day, sir.' He bowed his head briefly. 'Hitchin's here as you asked.'

The head carpenter knuckled his forehead but Sir Ranulph reached out and grasped his hand.

'I hope you are well, Hitchin. Only yesterday I was thinking of that rocking horse you made me.'

His words brought a smile to the old face before him. 'Ah, well, it were a fine beast if I do say so myself. I thought I might give it a look, see if it would do for the young master. The maid says he's mad for horses.'

'I dare say he is. Thank you, I'm sure he'll love it as much as I did. Now ... this roof?'

'I've took a look, sir. It's a mighty big hole. Hasn't gone through to the floor below but I'll wager the ceiling's damaged. Can't tell just now for all the rubble lying around. Bricks and tiles and such. A fair splintering of wood too. And the roof laths will need replacing, sure as eggs.'

Sir Ranulph sighed. 'It sounds serious. I'd better see for myself.' He stripped off his gloves, dropped them into his hat and looked around. The only item of furniture was a table replete with a thick layer of dust.

'Look lively there, Mat,' Hitchin commanded. 'Take Sir Ranulph's hat.'

The boy swallowed, stepped forward and took the hat held out to him.

'And if you'd hold my coat too, please Matthew.' Sir Ranulph's smile was encouraging. Relieved of his encumbrances, he followed his steward up four flights of stairs with Hitchin slow pacing bringing up the rear.

'It's just as well you took off your coat, sir,' Pembridge said. 'It's way grimy up here.'

Grimy was a flattering description. The floor of the middle attic resembled the aftermath of an artillery round. Chunks of demolished brickwork mingled with stone cappings, terracotta chimney pots, broken slates and strips of wood. A space had been cleared among the debris to permit the establishment of an ancient tin bath and an assortment of buckets and bowls, including an old cracked chamber pot. The roof above the devastation was rent with a gaping hole. Above it pale grey clouds raced across the sky.

'Well, Hitchin?' Sir Ranulph said, waiting patiently for the older man to arrive. 'How long to repair it?'

'If it just be the roof, sir, I'd say a good fortnight. But there's no telling how safe the rest of it is to crawl across. And then there's the chimney to put up.'

'I don't want anybody up there until you're certain it is safe. No injuries at all, if you please.'

'That be alright, sir. We'll make a frame and put it across the rest. No-one'll be in danger. I'll see to that.'

'Very well. Make a start as soon as you can, and you, Pembridge, keep me informed as to progress. And how much longer it will take. I'll be at the town house.'

With a last look at the gaping hole, he picked his way across the attic to the door and disappeared.

'He's a good master,' Hitchin said. 'Not many 'ud be as bothered as him about their people.'

Chapter Nine

Lady Josephine Varennes's laughter tinkled around her exquisite London drawing room.

'My dear, Ranulph, you don't mean to tell me that you are become an infant's guardian?' She laughed again. 'How delightful.'

Sir Ranulph shifted on the satin chaise he was occupying. 'I fail to see what is so amusing about it.'

The faint petulance in his tone registered with her. 'Only that you have never shown any interest in setting up your own nursery,' she said, recovering her position. 'Let alone taking charge of anyone else's.'

'I haven't a choice. The duty was laid upon me.'

'But did not this cousin of yours first seek your permission?' A shake of the head answered her. Her ladyship permitted a slight frown to crinkle her brow. 'Aveley,' she pondered. 'Isn't – wasn't – Philip Aveley his brother?'

'He was. Is.'

'How very odd. One would expect a brother to be first in line as guardian.'

Her words chimed with Ranulph's own thoughts, something to which he would never own. 'Presumably,' he countered, 'Gerard believed him too young for the task.'

'Or unsuited.' Sir Ranulph's face closed stiffly at her words. Seeing it, Lady Josephine decided there was little purpose in continuing her probing. 'Well,' she said, plying her fan between the glowing fire and her delicate complexion and seeking to desert the topic, 'no doubt you will soon find someone to take charge of the infant. Other than Lady Trent, of course. She would surely find it a burden.'

Her eyes flickered. There had been a flash of anger on Sir Ranulph's face. Storing it in her memory and resolving to discover from elsewhere what had caused it, she turned the conversation to the state of the dear King's health.

'I wonder which has affected it the most. That dreadful Walcheren Campaign or the Prime Minister's distaste for hunting.' Her laugh tinkled again. 'Or of course it could be that Monster rampaging around the Continent,' she added, only too aware that she had lost his attention.

Since Sir Ranulph never showed any interest in the prevalent gossip, and held to the opinion that the establishment of a Regency was only a matter of time, as was the defeat of Napoleon, her suspicion was quite correct. He failed to respond, saying only, 'I regret I must leave you, ma'am. I have business in the City that must not be delayed.'

Lady Josephine was a little surprised and much offended at him taking his leave without seeking any of the private moments they had frequently shared. Raising her hand for him to bow over, she smiled in her most winning fashion, a smile which lasted until her butler had closed the door behind him. She flung down her fan and proceeded to wrinkle her brow. So the magnificent Sir Ranulph had tired of her, had he? Then she must let it be seen that she had tired of him first. There must be no question of permitting public speculation that she had received her *congé*. Discovering a means of doing so occupied her for the remainder of the afternoon.

The result of her cogitation convinced her that whatever had caused Sir Ranulph to cool towards her was, in some way, connected with his new guardianship. Discreet enquiries disclosed that Philip Aveley was not at his lodgings in London. He was said to be lingering at Stapley Hall. Consequently, some few days later, Lady Josephine, took a trip into the wilds of Suffolk to call, quite casually of course, upon the bereft uncle.

The Hall was a charming residence set on a gentle rise in a small but elegant park. The gravel carriage drive to it passed along a short avenue of sturdy beech trees before opening into a generous circle. A ha-ha protected house and gardens from depredation by the sheep and cattle wandering across the swathes of green surrounding it. The building itself, of mellowed stone, showed a symmetrical arrangement of refined windows ranged about an arched central porch. All in all, it was an establishment to stir the heart.

Philip stood, hands on hips, in the neat garden trying to estimate the income from the five farms the estate owned. His ride about them showed them to be in good order with tenants who appeared to care for their jurisdiction rather than to be milking it for every half-penny. He fairly itched to have the command of it, even if only until Christopher came of age. That, since it was set at five-and-twenty years, was a considerable distance in the future. If Gerard had not been so ridiculous in his Will, he, Philip, would already have control of this for the next two decades. Such means of adding to his own modest competence could not but please. Not that he would sink to any unscrupulous method to achieve it only …

A maid rejoicing in the name of Angelica dashed across the lawn from the house calling to inform him of a visitor. He followed her back at a more dignified pace while admiring her flashing ankles revealed by her lifted skirts.

Lady Josephine Varennes was seated in the drawing room, holding her fingers to the fire. She rose, extending a hand gloved in ruby kid.

'My dear Mr Aveley, how delightful to see you again. I declare it has been an age.'

'Indeed, ma'am. A pleasure.' Philip was far too well-bred to enquire why a woman he had not seen for months, and who was credited with being his cousin's latest flirt, should have called upon him.

'I expect you are a little surprised to see me,' Lady Josephine supplied, 'but I was on my way to town from a family visit in Norfolk and felt I must call – since I was so close – to express my condolences for your loss.' She permitted her voice to lower to sympathetic volumes and painted a suitably doleful expression on her face. 'Such a young age to pass from us.'

'Thank you, ma'am. It was.'

He ladyship drifted back towards her chair. 'This is a charming room, Mr Aveley. Indeed I found the approach to the house to be singularly picturesque.' She sank onto the chair at Philip's gesture. 'No doubt you will be eager to take up residence here.'

'Alas, ma'am, it is not my property. My brother had a son and the estate has, of course, passed to him. As it should.'

'Oh, yes,' said Lady Josephine. 'But as his guardian, you would be expected to –'

'I am not his guardian, ma'am. My cousin Ranulph Trent is. He has taken the child to Crestings.'

'Has he? I *am* surprised. I have not had the time to see Sir Ranulph for some weeks,' she said, sowing the seeds of her departure from his protection, 'so I had not heard.'

Philip successfully hid his surprise. If anyone was to know of Trent's opinion it was she. He himself was not numbered among Lady Josephine's admirers. He could, and did, appreciate how she managed her career without attracting the least whiff of scandal but he had never been tempted to join her court. Nevertheless his current irritation led him to own to a degree of surprise that she had not broken her journey at Crestings.

'Oh, but I find it so gloomy,' said one who had cherished hopes of becoming its mistress. 'And Lady Trent is such a high stickler. Quite old-fashioned enough to make any visit a bore.' She covered her mouth briefly with gloved fingers. 'Oh, forgive me, I should not speak so of your aunt.'

Philip, still standing, bowed. 'Perhaps you are wise to avoid Crestings. There is sure to be talk about it now that the child's aunt is staying there.'

'Aunt?' The word came sharply.

'Miss Devreaux. Gerard married her sister Amelia.'

'Devreaux? Amelia Devreaux. I seem to recall there was several days chatter about her, was there not?' She tilted her head in thought. 'Oh, I have it. She ran off with him. Then the child...' She allowed her unspoken question to hang in the air.

'Gerard and his wife were married in Derbyshire. He had a friend there. They spent their honeymoon at his house.'

'Ah.' Lady Josephine leant back in her chair. 'I am surprised the older Devreaux girl – if one can still call her that – has emerged from her seclusion. So sad for her to have withered away because of her sister. Perhaps I shall call at Crestings after all. It would be only charitable to offer support if she is desirous of reappearing.'

Josephine Varennes was not renowned for her charitable instinct. It took Philip very little time to realise that her ladyship was intensely annoyed by the turn of events. She might even be as annoyed as he. If she arrived at Crestings, Ranulph would be far from pleased. The possibility of annoying and embarrassing his cousin held a fair degree of appeal to Philip at that moment. He made his decision.

'Are you particularly in haste, ma'am? We could go there together if you would permit me to settle one or two matters here first. Allow me to summon some refreshment for you.'

Stapley Hall was treated to the Varennes' laugh. 'That would be delightful, sir. Thank you.' She rose. 'Perhaps the housekeeper would conduct me upstairs to remove my coat.'

Philip bowed. 'Of course.'

The refreshments, which took the form of wine, cold meat and fruit served in the small drawing room on the other side of the entrance hall, passed in a spread of polite chatter which almost but not quite failed to cover the fell purpose which underlay it. Josephine Varennes was keen to know if the Devreaux girl had excited any response in Ranulph Trent and Philip was curious to see if his cousin could be thrown sufficiently off balance to be driven to change his mind about housing Christopher.

By the time her ladyship had finished dissecting the apple which was all she had chosen to eat, drunk a second dish of tea, ascended the wide stair to don her coat and hat, and had entered her carriage belatedly summoned from the stables, the daylight was fading. Philip, knowing his aunt was more kindly than she was a high-stickler, rode beside the carriage with his portmanteau strapped to his saddle. He had every confidence that they would be invited to stay overnight. Stephanie Trent would never fail to be less than a gracious hostess, even if she knew that her son and Josephine Varennes were not exactly strangers. And he, Philip, could not be expected to allow a lady to travel at eventide without a male escort. No gentleman would be guilty of deserting a lady in such a manner.

Jostled inside her carriage, Josephine Varennes was assaulted by doubts. Contrary to her usual caution, she had allowed the news of the Devreaux girl's presence at Crestings to trip her into an action that could quite easily be to her disadvantage. One hand plucked at the satin lining of her sable muff. Why on earth had she left London in the first place? True, Ranulph's coolness had annoyed her. She had been almost certain he was in earnest, and would eventually beg her to become his wife. After all, it was well over a year since they had become such dear friends. Perhaps she had misinterpreted his demeanour at their last meeting. Perhaps he was fonder of his cousin than she had allowed. Or more unsettled by the sudden burden of guardianship.

She pulled her fingers from the satin, annoyed with herself for losing her poise. Refusing to own to any degree of anxiety, she spent the remaining miles constructing, and then abandoning, several explanations for her arrival at Crestings at an advanced time of day. To pass at least some of it off, she decided her maid sitting opposite without the benefit of a fur rug over her knees had been taken unwell. So unwell that she had begged her mistress to let her lie down at Stapley Hall, thereby delaying her departure until a protracted hour.

Her ladyship's carriage passed between the tall iron gates that guarded the entrance to Crestings' park as the last rays of weak sun threaded through the avenue of trees. She had still to hit upon a reason for her visit that would convince Ranulph Trent in the slightest. Unless of course he had not yet returned to his estate.

She sat up suddenly. Perhaps he was not there. Perhaps he was still in London. Why had she not discovered it before she had left? His absence would make her arrival all the easier. She could claim to have called at Crestings to express her condolences to his mother. She leant back against the velvet squabs. Yes, that solved the matter. She need worry no further.

Chapter Ten

The nursery apartments at Crestings occupied the entire third floor of the east wing. Their simply-furnished bedchambers could easily have accommodated eight or nine children, together with their nurses and maids. A larger apartment positioned beside a schoolroom allowed for the presence of a governess and provided her with a small sitting room. The largest of all the rooms served as a day nursery. Its furnishings were worn, originating as they had in earlier decades, if not centuries. Not all of the rooms were occupied, the only residents of the floor being the new arrivals, Christopher, Mabson, and Letty. Under Mabson's firm instructions the day room had been rendered warm and cosy. The comfort of the several chairs scattered about it had been much improved by the addition of cushions and rugs folded onto their uncompromising dimensions.

Louise had taken to visiting the hallowed ground in the early afternoon. In the few days since the nursery party had arrived she had quickly discovered that Mabson was least likely to resent her appearance if it occurred after Christopher had eaten his noontime bread, milk and egg but before she deposited him in his bed for a post-prandial rest.

As had become her custom, she occupied the chair drawn up to the waist-high metal fireguard curving around the hearth, watching Christopher examine a set of blocks painted with pictures of animals he was never likely to see crossing Crestings' green acres. The one bearing an E and a depiction of an elephant rested near her foot. She reached beyond it for the one showing an H and a horse.

'Do you know what this is, Christopher?'

The face turned up to her struck at her heart. The child was angelically fair, like his mother, and being as yet unbreeched his appearance in his little white dress was so close to her memories of Amelia at that age she could barely restrain a sob.

'Horsie,' he said with a degree of scorn. 'It's a horsie. Uncle Flip was bringing me one 'til Uncle Raff took me 'way.' The zebra brick he held was thrown to the floor. 'That's not horsie. I want my horsie.'

Mabson put down the shawl she was folding on the scrubbed pine table and bustled across the room. 'Now then, my lambkin, 'I want' never gets.' She swooped down and picked him up. 'Time for your nap.'

She disappeared out of the room disregarding the youthful protests, leaving Letty twisting her hands beside the table.

'Are you comfortably settled in?' Louise asked.

'Yes, ma'am, thank you, ma'am.'

Louise nodded and turned her attention to the pair of dresses spread over the fireguard's top rail to dry. Letty shot across the room.

'I'll see to them, ma'am. I doubt they're dry yet.'

'Doesn't Mrs Mabson make use of the laundry maids?'

'Oh, no, ma'am. She don't know them much as yet. She says she won't trust them with Master Christopher's linen.' She turned one dress over. 'Apart from the bedding, that is.'

'What are you gossiping about?' Mabson demanded entering the room.

'Nothing in particular, Nurse. I was asking Letty if she had settled in.'

'She's settled in just fine, thank you, ma'am.' The nurse's strict eye fell on the blushing maid. 'Get yourself along to Master Kit's room and watch over him.'

Letty dashed to the doorway, only remembering to bob a curtsey to Louise in the second before she disappeared through it.

'You are both so devoted to Master Christopher,' Louise said. 'It must be a comfort to him.'

'I hope it is, ma'am. It don't become me to question the actions of my betters but I still hold to the notion he'd be happier in his own home than in this great pile.' She waved a scornful hand towards the walls.

Louise shifted in her chair, very conscious that she held the same view. 'I believe Sir Ranulph thought there would be no memories here to distress him,' she temporised. 'As there is bound to be at Stapley Hall.'

'Yes, well...' The nurse swished the dresses off the fireguard and folded them against her wide bosom. 'There might be a word or two in that.' She eyed Louise. 'I dare say you find the little lambkin very much like his Mama.'

'Oh yes.' The words came on a sigh. 'He looks just as I remember her at that age.' Her lips trembled and her eyes prickled. She swallowed and blinked.

'You'll stay with him then, ma'am?' Mabson asked, her features softening at the desolation sweeping the face before her. 'If you don't mind me asking.'

'I hope to. I am his guardian, as is Sir Ranulph, but I fear – I think,' she corrected, 'the main decisions will be his.'

'Hmmm.' Mabson growled in her throat. 'Then I hope he makes himself agreeable. This nursery's far too big for one child on his own. He needs company. Someone his own age to play with and the Lord knows who he'll find when the time comes. Unless of course his mightiness weds.'

She bustled across to continue folding the child's linen on the table, leaving Louise thunderstruck by a possibility that had not previously troubled her. Being retired from society she knew little of Sir Ranulph and his world. There might very well be a serious love interest in his life. Her hands twisted in her lap. What would that mean for her? Would his new wife be happy to have her living in the Dower House? She cast her mind back over the few days since she had removed to Crestings. Lady Trent had made no mention of any particular lady. Of course she would not do so to her — someone she barely knew. And Sir Ranulph certainly would not. She caught her bottom lip between her teeth. If there was someone...if Sir Ranulph did marry...Her fingers twisted and unwound. The sort of woman he would chose would surely be someone who matched his own autocratic nature. Such a woman would not be likely to tolerate her presence. Teeth worried at her lip until a happy thought struck her. If he did marry his wife might make him more will-ing — might even insist — that he let her take Christopher back to Stapley Hall. Her fingers and mouth relaxed. She leant back in the chair on a sigh. The happy thought cheered her for several moments until a frown pleated her forehead. For reasons she could not define, the prospect was not as completely pleasing as she would have expected.

The clock on the dayroom wall chimed. 'It be time for you to go downstairs, miss,' Mabson announced. 'Her ladyship will be waiting.'

The custom had developed for Louise to take tea with her hostess in the fading afternoon. She rose.

'Thank you,' she said, wondering how the nurse, who rarely left the nursery wing, would know that. 'I'll go down now.'

Ellen Mabson watched her leave and not with the narrowed eyes with which she had first inspected her. Everyone who came near her darling was viewed as a possible danger. She had thought the same when she had started as nursery-maid to young Master Gerard the best part of thirty years ago. Miss Louise, she decided, was a fit and proper person to be allowed near her present darling. Fitter than the cold-hearted Sir Ranulph, that was for sure. Her face flushed and transformed into a furious scowl. How dared he swoop on her baby the way he had. The little lamb had been on his knees searching under his bed and calling for his poor mama when he had demanded his presence.

No, she thought, carrying the dresses to the drawers, Miss Louise would do much better for her lambkin. She was no sweeping, vindictive termagant. A body could tell that easily from the tears that had spilled from her eyes when she had first seen Christopher. Why, the lass had sunk onto her knees and clasped him so tight the little darling had cried out. There was no doubt she'd turn out to be as sweet as her dear sister was. Mabson sighed. A lovely girl, Mistress Amelia had been. So much in love with Gerard it was beautiful to see. And he worshipped her. Miss Louise must have loved her too else why would she cry?

Louise found Stephanie Trent seated by the window in the smaller of Crestings' main salons. The prospect from the room encompassed a formal garden which gave onto to the park with its curving lake and spreading oaks. The garden was, according to her own account, her ladyship's delight. She had resisted all advice from her friends to have it dug up and replaced in the modern style. Beyond the low, clipped hedges and the geometric paths, steps descended to an ornamental pond boasting a fountain that could attain nearly fifteen feet when the water was turned on.

'Ah, my dear.' Lady Trent's gaze lifted from the classical temple her late father-in-law had commissioned across the lake. 'How is Christopher this afternoon?'

'Very well, ma'am, but somewhat disgruntled that he does not have the pony his uncle promised him.'

'Oh, dear. I expect he is. I must own I have never been comfortable with the notion of setting three-year-olds on horseback. Rather too young, I fear.' She lifted a hand to the matching armchair on the other side of the window. 'Ranulph has been mad for horses since that age, as was his father. I had many hours of anxiety about it but there were very few falls.'

Louise moved to the chair and sat. 'Perhaps, now he is living here he will forget about it. Especially if Sir Ranulph is not present.' She smoothed a finger over her gown. 'I collect he is much in London.'

'Indeed. Or staying with friends for the hunting. I shall be pleased if he prolongs his stay there.' She leant forward confidentially. 'He is much given to thinking I shall fade away if he is long between visits home.'

'Surely when he sees you, ma'am, he is reassured.'

Stephanie Trent chuckled. 'One would like to think so but he is as stubborn as his father. Let them but fix an idea in their heads and there it stays.' Her gaze drifted to the prospect outside. 'Though I must in all honesty admit they can be persuaded if sufficient evidence proves them to be in error.' Her face returned to Louise. 'He is only here for two days before he goes to Northamptonshire. The Wynchursts, you know.'

Louise gripped the arms of the chair. 'Sir Ranulph has returned?'

'Earlier today. He said he would join me for tea.' She smiled. 'I know he does not care for it but he thinks to oblige me. Which of course, he does.'

Louise rose. 'Then I shall leave you, ma'am, to enjoy his company.'

'No, no. Sit down, my dear. He will not be displeased to see you.'

'No, ma'am, I cannot help but be aware he does not approve of my presence here.'

'Then we must ensure he becomes better acquainted with you. I am certain Christopher will benefit greatly from your company. As shall I.'

The tension left Louise's frame. She sat again as directed, turning when the salon door opened. The butler entered, followed not by a train of maids bearing trays but by a stunning woman dressed for travel in a pelisse of crimson velvet with sable trimmings. A younger man entered behind her.

'Lady Josephine Varennes,' the butler intoned. 'And Mr Philip Aveley. They insisted on being shown straight up.' He bowed, his face immobile at the breach of custom, and withdrew.

'My dear Lady Trent,' Josephine Varennes advanced across the room's Aubusson carpet, extracting her hand from her muff and holding it out. 'Pray forgive me for calling so unexpectedly but as I was passing Stapley Hall I stopped to condole with dear Mr Aveley, and now I find myself in such a fix. I cannot hope to reach London tonight and there is no hostess at the Hall.'

Stephanie Trent rose. 'Then you must pass the night with us. We cannot have you wandering the countryside in the dark. Even if Mr Aveley is in company with you.'

'I'm not, ma'am.' Philip Aveley bowed. 'I only came when her ladyship entreated me to accompany her.'

'Mr Aveley has been so kind,' Josephine gushed. 'If it had not been for my maid declaring she was too unwell to continue I would not have had need of such a valiant knight.'

'Most kind of him. You must allow me to make Miss Devreaux known to you.'

Louise had risen, her eyes fixed on Lady Josephine's lush frame. 'How do you do, ma'am?' she said in her quiet voice.

'Devreaux? Devreaux?' Lady Josephine extended two fingers to be shaken. 'That name is familiar.' She smiled thinly. 'No doubt it will come to me.' She returned her attention to Lady Trent who had no doubts at all that the name was already known to her unexpected guest. 'I hope I find you well, ma'am?'

'You do, thank you. Pray let me summon the housekeeper to show you to a bedchamber.' She glided across to the fireplace and pulled the tasselled rope.

A bare minute later the butler reappeared, this time followed by the maids.

'Hoarwithy, please ask Mrs Crowcroft to conduct her lady-ship to the Primrose bedchamber. We are to have the pleasure of her company for the night.'

Hoarwithy, who had recognised her ladyship from his duties in the Trent townhouse, bowed. 'Yes, my lady. If your ladyship would condescend to follow me.'

Her ladyship did, only to arrive at the door at the moment Ranulph Trent appeared. He halted abruptly and stared down at her.

Very little ever disturbed her ladyship's composure. 'Sir Ranulph,' she declared in musical tones. 'How delightful to see you.' A gloved hand was extended to him.

Sir Ranulph, his face a mask, bowed over the slender fingers. 'This is an unlooked-for pleasure, ma'am.'

'I know. I have just been explaining to Lady Trent how it comes about.'

His gaze travelled from Josephine Varennes' charming features, to his cousin, his mother and finally to Louise. Her face showed none of the practised charm of his mistress's, only puzzlement.

Josephine Varennes watched him closely. His rigid features betrayed none of the thoughts behind his eyes. She had no idea that his overriding concern was, to his surprise, a wish to protect Miss Devreaux from what he knew to be the Varennes' spiteful tongue. It was no plan of his to have Miss Devreaux's character stained as her sister's had been. And certainly not by association with his name.

He quelled his irritation at finding his mistress in his house. 'You have met Miss Devreaux, I am sure,' he said. 'She is the late Mrs Aveley's sister. We are joint guardians of my cousin's son.'

'So Mr Aveley has explained. Such a tragic event.' Her ladyship uttered a sympathetic sigh. 'So young to be taken from us.' She brushed at a non-existent tear and glided past the butler with an expression of deep sorrow on her face.

Philip Aveley, who had been waiting in some agitation for his cousin to turn his attention to him, cleared his throat. 'I could hardly let her set off alone, Trent.'

'Indeed you could not, Philip. Miss Devreaux, I hope we may persuade you to abandon your apartment and dine with us this evening.'

'Oh, please do,' Stephanie Trent urged, well aware of the precise nature of her guest's relationship with her son. And of the danger her presence presented to Louise. Only a clear demonstration of her own delight in Louise's company would dull suspicion.

Succumbing to their blandishments, Louise found the means to escape from the room. 'Forgive me, ma'am. Pray excuse me, if I am to dine with you I must see if Lizzie has pressed my dinner gown so it's sufficiently uncreased to be seen.'

In her apartment with the dinner gown still in the wardrobe, she sat on her bed wondering quite why she had found the arrival of Lady Josephine and the familiarity with which she had greeted Sir Ranulph so deeply unwelcome.

Chapter Eleven

$\mathcal{D}$inner proved to be in every degree as hideous as Louise had suspected, a view shared, had she but known it, by Sir Ranulph and his mother and uncle. By the end of it, Lady Josephine had made her feel like some scheming mushroom of dubious virtue despite not having uttered a single word in her dispraise. She could only be grateful for the manner in which Lady Trent had conveyed the notion that she was a valued family member without whose aid Sir Ranulph would find the burden of guardianship intolerable.

She warned herself to ignore his expression as he bowed over her hand at her departure for the night. Had she been so minded she could have believed he was trying to convey his regret at the aspersions cast in her direction. She was not so minded – at least not so very much. It had felt quite strange to have someone protecting, not dominating, her, as her father so often tried. And as Sir Ranulph himself had attempted at their first meeting. Fully determined not to think of it, she fell asleep after a length of time, her mind still winding through every possible reason for his behaviour.

The morning brought little relief from the problems afflicting her. Barely had the grey light penetrated Crestings' many windows on the east façade than Lizzie scratched on her bedchamber door and opened it.

'Miss Louise,' she whispered, her voice urgent. 'Miss Louise.'

Parting the bed-curtains, Louise struggled up onto an elbow. 'What is it? What time is it?'

The door squeaked and the maid's head appeared. 'It's early, miss.' She pushed the door wider and shuffled in, her feet in her unfastened boots and a shawl dragged unevenly about her shoulders. 'Mrs Mabson's asking for you. She sent that nursery-maid – Letty – to have me wake you. She says the young master is not at all comfortable.'

'Oh.' Louise pushed back the bedcovers. 'Hand me my robe. I'll come at once.'

Decently shrouded and shod, she padded up the stairs to the nursery floor above her apartment. Mrs Mabson, her cap askew and her gown crumpled stood at the head of the small bed staring down at its feverish occupant.

'Oh, Miss, I'm right glad you've come. I've been up all night with the little lambkin. I can't get him soothed.'

Louise eased past the nurse and looked down at the restless little figure. His threshing limbs had tangled in the rumpled bed-covers. She placed her hand on his forehead. 'His temperature is raised.' She hesitated, unsure why she, a woman completely untried in nursing the young, should be able to help. 'Have you bathed him?'

'With vinegar and water, miss. I sent Letty down to the kitchens to fetch some during the night.'

'It were right dark, miss.' The girl stood at the foot of the bed, her shawl grasped tightly about her and her tousled hair devoid of its cap which now hung round her neck by its strings. 'Took me ages to find the right way.'

'I'm sure you were very brave,' Louise said, straightening. 'Mrs Mabson why don't you take some rest. I shall dress and sit with Christopher.'

'Oh, no, miss, what if – '

'I promise to call you if there is any increase in his fever. And if there is, I am sure Lady Trent will let us summon whichever physician she favours. Now, Letty can help you to your bed and if she can find her way to the kitchens again – which I'm sure she can for she is a very resourceful girl – she can have them brew some tea for us all.'

Followed by further reassurances but still muttering anxiously, the nurse departed. Louise forced confidence she did not feel into her voice. 'Watch over him, Lizzie. I'll be back in a moment.' She hurried from the room to dress.

Despite the attentions of his nurse, her helpers and Louise, and frequent applications of vinegar water, Christopher's fever did not abate. He tossed restlessly, wailing and kicking off his sheet, the only cover Louise would permit to cover him after forcibly removing two blankets and a small quilt. He could not be brought to swallow any drink. He wept so often salty tracks stained his cheeks. He moaned, 'Mama. Mama,' incessantly.

His distress brought tears to the eyes of his nurses until Louise decided he would only be calmed if some potion could be given to him. Having no laudanum with her, and not daring to use it if she had, she descended to the main floor in search of Lady Trent.

Her ladyship, on receipt of the news insisted on traversing the lengthy corridor to the east wing and climbing the flights of stairs to the nursery.

'My dear, you did very well to call me. I shall send Jupp to Doctor Garford at once. We must have his advice.' She scanned the drawn faces of the women about the bed. 'I am sure none of you has slept. I shall sit with him and all of you will lie on your beds until Dr Garford arrives.' She turned to Lizzie hovering in the background. 'Run down to the kitchens, please, and have them prepare some tea and toast for your mistress. They can serve it in her sitting room – with some fruit,' she called after the departing maid.

Sir Ranulph had the tidings discreetly whispered in his ear by Hoarwithy. Unwillingly engaged in ridding his home of both his mistress and his cousin, and hesitating to approach Miss Devreaux's apartment himself, he sent his housekeeper to enquire after the child. Her report did not please him. It did however provide an excellent reason for hurrying Lady Josephine from Crestings' elegant dimensions. Drawing heavily on the dangers possibly unleashed in the servants' quarters by the reported sickness of her maid in addition to the child's illness, he knew a feeling of considerable relief when the Varennes carriage disappeared between the trees of the avenue. Philip's suggestion that he remain until the cause of the child's distress were found earned him such a fierce stare and terse comment as to prompt him to discover an urgent need to hurry to the stables for his horse.

Doctor Garford, having received Mrs Mabson's stern opinion upon his arrival, followed Louise to the salon some time later to find Sir Ranulph waiting for news with his mother. Even Marius Trent had bestirred himself to attend.

'Well?' Sir Ranulph demanded his hand on the back of his mother's chair.

'Not at all, sir, ma'am.' The doctor bowed to her ladyship. 'The child has suffered much disruption in the past few days. He is, naturally grieving for his mother, something the presence of his nurse cannot relieve. I discover from her that he spent most of his days in his mother's company. The sudden lack of it is bound to have shocked him. And of course his surroundings are strange. I did not have the pleasure of waiting upon the late Mrs Aveley so have not seen Stapley Hall but his nurse assures me it is considerably more modest than Crestings.'

'It is. But surely that cannot account for his present state,' Sir Ranulph said.

'One never can tell with infants. So sturdy in some respects, so fragile in others.' He deposited his bag on the floor by his feet. 'From what I hear, he has not been in contact with any other children. Nor do I know of any epidemic afflicting this, or the Hall's vicinity.' He shifted his slight weight from one booted foot to the other. 'I can understand your wish, sir, to have the child under your roof, but I find myself much given to agreeing with the women who have cared for him so far in his life. I believe he would improve if returned to surroundings with which he is familiar.'

Sir Ranulph's expression froze. 'That is just female wittering. His nurse was never happy that I had brought him to Crestings.'

'It might well be the case, sir, but I feel it is a solution we must try. And try fast.'

Louise felt Sir Ranulph's eyes switch to her as an almost physical attack. 'I have no doubt you, ma'am, are in complete agreement with this.'

Her hands clenched at her sides. 'I have expressed no opinion at all today, sir. Other than to say Christopher has cried often for his mother.'

The doctor inclined his head to her. 'I assure you, sir, my opinion has not been swayed by pressure from any of the child's attendants.'

Sir Ranulph drew three deep breaths. 'Very well then. He shall return to Stapley Hall. May I assume, ma'am, that you will go with him?'

'You may, sir.' Louise quelled the desire to inform him that if he had listened to her in the first place the current situation might have been avoided.

'Then I shall arrange it. I shall, however, insist that you have a companion to bear you company. From what I have heard,

Aveley is given to calling and it will not do to have you receiving him alone.'

Louise's eyes flashed. 'I need no companion, sir. I am well past the age of requiring one.'

'You may think so but I do not. You will have a companion, ma'am, or you will not go.'

Faced with this stark choice, Louise took several moments before she could bring herself to agree to his command.

'Excellent. Mama, would you be kind enough to write to Mrs Henshaw and beg her to stand as companion to Miss Devreaux? I'm sure she will agree.'

'Of course I shall, my dear. And of course she will.' Lady Trent appeared amused.

'Who,' enquired Louise frostily, 'is Mrs Henshaw?'

'A second cousin of mine. Or is it a third?' Sir Ranulph said. 'Whichever, she is a lady of undoubted gentility and reputation. Her consequence cannot fail to prevent any adverse comment on your situation.'

Louise could only swallow the furious response that rose to her lips and accept, well aware that her sister's elopement had blemished her own reputation in many eyes.

Three days later, Mrs Cressida Henshaw swept into the salon after disposing of her coat and hat in the bedchamber to which she had been assigned. She was not the antidote Louise had feared. In fact the family likeness to Lady Trent was pronounced. She had the same open features but a less autocratic nose. She was younger than her ladyship by several years, and, her joints apparently unaffected by rheumatism, was capable of more active movement. There was a quiet elegance about her. Her gown and Norwich shawl, for instance, were more in fashion than Louise's own. She did not possess her ladyship's grace of manner but nonetheless she in no way resembled an impoverished relative, desirous of hanging on the sleeve of the better endowed.

She exchanged a kiss with Lady Trent and permitted Sir Ranulph to bestow one on her cheek before casting a seasoned eye over Louise.

'So you are the youngster's aunt,' she said 'I am very pleased to meet you.' She held out her hand. Her grip was firm. 'You look to be a woman of sense so I dare say we shall deal well enough together. I have no intention of entering the nursery, though I do not object to a child appearing in the drawing room from time to time. Mine were brought down every day after their nursery tea. Unless of course we were in town.'

'Then, ma'am, we shall see little of each other as I intend to spend as much time as I can with my nephew.'

'As you wish, my dear. All very right and proper, I am sure.' Her tone was remarkably undeterred. 'I apprehend that Mr Aveley is much given to calling at Stapley Hall. You may rest assured that I shall be in evidence whenever he does.' She seated herself beside Lady Trent. 'Now, Stephanie, tell me how you have been. Does this damp weather affect your joints as much as ever?'

Effectively dismissed, Louise inclined her head and moved to the door. Sir Ranulph opened it for her and followed her out.

'I trust my cousin meets with your approval, ma'am.'

'Would it matter if she did not?'

Sir Ranulph blinked. 'Not really. At least you will find her conversation something to be appreciated. She neither witters, nor moans of aches and pains, nor utters inanities.'

'That is something to be grateful for.'

'As, I would hope, is my care for your reputation.'

Louise halted part-way across the expansive marble hall. Common courtesy obliged her to respond. 'Then I must thank you, sir, for I know it goes very much against the nerve for you to have me staying with Christopher.'

'Not as much as it did, ma'am. No-one who has seen your care of him these past few days would be capable of less than gratitude and admiration.' He paused. 'I would still prefer him to reside at Crestings but as Garford recommends he return to Stapley for his health, so he must. I know I may repose complete confidence in you.'

He bowed and left her standing in the echoing hall, staring after him, more confused than ever.

Chapter Twelve

Marius Trent put down his teacup on the fragile table at the side of his chair in the Yellow drawing room and stared at his sister-in-law from under his bushy eyebrows. 'What do you make of all this?

'What do you mean?'

A pudgy hand circled. 'This notion of the girl removing to Stapley.'

'Girl? Do you mean Miss Devreaux?'

'Of course I do. Who else would I mean?'

'Then I think it is a good proposal for Christopher but perhaps...' She paused, her gaze resting on the flowered china on the tea tray.

'Perhaps? Perhaps what?'

'I find her a very restful person. Nor is she devoid of intelligence.'

'No, she's not. No rinnyhammer there.' Mr Trent eyed her. 'You match-making, Stephanie?'

'No, of course not. Only...'

'Only it's been your ambition to see Ranulph wed these past ten years.'

'Oh, no, not *ten*. I'd no wish to see him settled as soon as he'd gained his majority. No,' her head shook gently. 'It's only that time is passing and we're none of us turning any younger.'

Marius chuckled. 'And you want some grandchildren about you. I know.' He laced his hands over his portly stomach. 'If the girl removes to Stapley, there'll be less chance of his coming to like her.'

'Or she him.'

'She him? Of course she'd like him. Any sensible woman would. He's presentable. Well-born. And his fortune's nothing to turn up a woman's nose.'

Stephanie Trent frowned. 'I don't want him wed for his fortune. Nor for his face.'

'You women are all the same. Romantics to the core. There have been some perfectly good marriages where the couple were barely acquainted.'

'Then why haven't you wed?'

'Pooh, not I. Never saw a woman to take my fancy.'

'Now who's the romantic?'

'Bah! I'm not the problem. If the girl is at Stapley and he's in London, you may bet your best bonnet that he'll fall into the Varennes woman's clutches again.'

'Oh, no. She isn't the one for him. Why the *on dit* was that –' She caught herself up short.

'No need to turn all conscious on me. I know she was a friend of George Levington's mistress, and probably suspect herself. Everybody thinks so.'

Stephanie Trent failed even to blink. She had long since become accustomed to her brother-in-law's frankness. 'If you put it like that, then I must own to some concern.'

'Hmm.' Marius, his hands still laced across his waistcoat, twirled his thumbs and stared absently at the carpet beyond his toes.

'What?'

'Thinking. Just thinking.' His chin sank onto his chest. His thumbs continued to rotate. After several moments during which Stephanie Trent viewed him with some concern, he bent his arms and he propped his chin on his interlinked fingers. Eventually his head lifted and his eyes twinkled. 'Chaddington-Wye. The very chap.'

'Mr Chaddington-Wye? What has he to do with anything?'

'He's just sent his latest piece of the muslin company about her business.'

'Marius!'

'Well, he has. Sorry, but you know how these things go. Not that Lawrence ever gave you cause to blush, never looked at another woman after he clapped eyes on you.' He sat forward, the moistening of his sister-in-law's eyes escaping him. 'Now if I hint to him that the Varennes woman is…looking for a new interest shall we say, he might grab at the fly.'

'This isn't fishing, Marius. It's far more serious than that.'

'Nothing's more serious than that.' He stood up. 'I think I'll take a little jaunt up to town. See how things are going.'

'Now Marius, I really do not want you interfering. Ranulph is old enough –'

'Old enough, I grant you, but he's not quick enough to see when the ideal girl has dropped into his lap. No. I'll have a little ponder. See if I can't give matters a push in the right direction.'

With an absent wave of his hand, he strolled out of the room, leaving his sister prey to mounting apprehension.

Marius Trent did not enjoy travel even at the best times of the year. Still less did he enjoy it when the late March winds buffeted his coach from side to side and the wheels juddered him up over hard ground or down into that softened by squally rain. But he was of placid temperament and bore the trials well until he could deliver himself into the gentle hands of the management of Grenier's Hotel in Jermyn Street. He preferred Grenier's to Grillon's in Albemarle Street as it was closer to the clubs and therefore committed him to less exertion should he not wish to have recourse to a hackney.

Grenier's manager knew which bedchamber he preferred – most definitely not the one in which the Duke de Sicignano had shot himself – and which was his favourite wine. He was installed in a familiar and comfortable armchair with gratifying speed, a newly-opened bottle of claret at his side and his unbooted feet being warmed by the golden flames leaping in the grate. He wiggled his toes in the warmth and watched Rullick depositing a pile of shirts into the second drawer of a bow-fronted chest.

'Will you be needing your evening dress tonight, sir?'

Marius shook his head. 'No. No. I shan't bother going about. Apparently, there's a saddle of mutton tonight which they tell me the chef has a new way of fixing. Sure to please, they say. I'll take my time over it and retire early. No point in sitting up after twelve.'

The valet bowed and pushed the drawer shut. Picking a fresh-looking publication from the polished top of the chest, he carried it to his master.

'I've obtained a copy of The New Annual Register for you, sir, if it should interest you to read the account of Mrs Clarke's activities regarding the army commissions.'

Marius viewed it with a frown. 'Stupid man.' Seeing his valet wince, he said, 'Not you. York. He should have known that woman was trouble. Selling commissions? Pah! She'll cost him more money yet, you mark my words.' He took the publication and tossed it onto the table beside the claret. 'I'll ring when I need you.'

Doing his best to keep his face straight at the dismissal of the periodical he had taken some pains to acquire, the valet bowed himself out of the room, trying to decide if a heavy wet in the hotel's servants' quarters was beneath his dignity and, if it were not, would it restore his bruised spirit?

Marius did not call upon him until the manager's boast of the mutton's excellence had been proven to be well-founded. Relieved of his day clothes and gowned in his nightshirt, cap, slippers and brocade dressing gown, he sat by the fire with a decent vintage port at his elbow. He stared into the flames and gave himself to deep consideration of ways of achieving Chaddington-Wye's introduction to Josephine Varennes. It must not appear to have been engineered. Eventually the problem, combined with hours of travel, the excellent mutton and several glasses of claret and port weighted his eyelids beyond his ability to keep them open. Dropping his dressing gown on the floor, he clambered between the bed curtains and quickly fell asleep, disturbing the night hours, and his immediate neighbour, with stentorian snores.

The morning brought no solution to his problem. Rather it added another. It had not taken him many minutes at the hotel to realise his coat was no longer fashionable. Oh, he did not want the spreading lapels some of the other residents sported. Only some that were wider than the narrow folds that declared his present attire as out-dated. Nor did he care for the nipped waists some ill-advised souls had chosen; his innate honesty informed him that his own dimensions were considerably wider than nipped. A resolution hardened in his mind. Before adjourning to White's he would make a short tour of the shops he most favoured and rectify his appearance.

He rang for his valet and permitted him to shrug his great-coat up his arms. Contorting himself to see his image in the bedchamber's inadequate looking glass, he sniffed and pulled it tighter round his form to hide the coat's shortcomings before venturing out to descend the stairs.

The hotel porter leapt to summon him a hackney for the chance of a small coin. It delivered Marius, eventually, to Clifford Street and George Stultz's establishment at number ten. A short time later he was bowed out of the premises with the promise of a fitting for his new coat in a mere couple of days. At no time had there been any mention of such vulgar considerations as the hefty cost to his purse.

Returning to the hotel for a reviving tipple, Marius surveyed the sky through his parlour window. No grey clouds hovered. He would dispense with another odorous hackney and stroll down to Piccadilly, then cross to St James's Street and White's.

As usual, Piccadilly teemed with carriages, carts, riders, pedestrians and an unconscionable number of hawkers pestering any and everyone to buy their wares. Brushing aside a pale-faced purveyor with a tray of pies slung round his neck, he hopped as rapidly as his figure allowed between a phaeton, a small donkey-cart loaded with chopped kindling, and a widow's lozenge carriage to gain the safety of the flagway opposite.

At the corner of St James's Street, the window of Hoby's bootmaker brought him to a halt. He had worn his present pair of boots for at least a year. He lifted a foot to examine one only to be jostled so firmly by a hawker that his balance went and he threatened to fall. Glaring at the man, he planted his foot beside its fellow on the ground. It could not be denied: the morning's excursions had covered the toes with dust. Even before the desecration of Rullick's handiwork they were decidedly uninspiring. A new coat deserved new boots. Barely had his hand lifted to the shop door than a youngster pulled it open and scraped and bowed him inside. Settled into a chair and fawned upon, he submitted to having the despised boots drawn off and the shape of each foot drawn. Several minutes were needed to decide the vexatious choice between hessians or top boots, gold tassels or none. The matter settled, he emerged to round off his purchases at Lock's at number six. Coat and shoes he must wait for, but a new beaver with a particularly elegant turn to its brim could be selected and worn immediately.

With a contented swagger to his steps, he entered White's some few minutes later and made his dignified way up the stairs to the coffee room that overlooked the street. Various of the chairs were occupied, one in particular by a gentleman whose raised voice addressing his companion opposite he recognised.

'Why the deuce they need to change a perfectly good door, I have no idea.'

Marius strolled to my Lord Rangmoor. 'Now then, Chuffy, what has you in a tizz?'

The grizzled head swung round. 'Ah! It's you, Trent. Well I dare say you'd approve. Always wanting to be head of the fashion list.' My lord raised his eyeglass on its black ribbon. 'Not that you'd think it to see you in that coat.'

Marius tugged his waistcoat hem. 'That's as may be, but there's no reason to rip up at me because someone's salted your tail.'

'Bah! The fools here are talking of moving the door to the side so they can put some ridiculous window in the middle. Never heard anything so stupid. Who needs a bow window? Door did for my father where it is. Can't see any reason to move it.' He glared at Marius, almost daring him to disagree.

'If you say so.' He pulled the chair opposite to a more agreeable position and sat down. 'Have you seen aught of Chaddington-Wye? I thought he might be in town.'

'Saw him dining at Steven's Hotel with some Guards' major or other a couple of nights ago.'

'That'll be his second boy, no doubt.'

'If you say so. Makes no odds to me.'

Marius, deciding the rumours of a new door would impair his lordship's good humour for the rest of the day, if not the month, betook himself back to his hotel to try for some more of the mutton.

Harvey Chaddington-Wye was at last run to ground in his Albany set. Marius had once or twice toyed with the idea of removing from his existing apartment at the top of the Trent townhouse to a set of chambers there. The idea remained until he discovered there were none available in the central mansion that had once been York House. He could not bring himself to fancy any in the stucco additions around the rear garden so the notion lapsed. He strolled past the porter, heading for the building to the west of the garden. Several comprehensive thumps on the door of set D5 brought a pale-faced valet to open it. Bowing, the man ushered him into the hall. Marius lingered by the neat fireplace until he had been announced, then ambled into the living room.

'Well, Chadders, how do I find you?'

The tall, thin person of Chaddington-Wye rose from an embracingly comfortable armchair with an ease that belied his fifty or so years. 'In fine fettle, my dear. In fine fettle.' He waved Marius to the armchair's twin and despatched the valet for wine. 'What brings you to town this late? I must admit I'd expected to see you earlier.'

'Oh, this and that. You know.' Marius deposited his great-coat over the back of the chair and took his ease with barely a nod at the valet who returned with a small salver bearing a glass of wine. The words he had so carefully planned failed him. 'Bought a coat,' he said instead.

'I'll be doing that soon.' Chaddington-Wye settled himself down again. 'I dare say you've heard.' He paused until the valet had withdrawn. 'My flaxen beauty is now despatched so the dibs are in better fettle.'

'Ah, yes. A whisper had reached me. Unlike you to be without company.'

'Turned over a new page, dear boy. Going to save myself the expense. These birds of paradise can run through your purse like a wire through cream.'

Marius's plan fell about his ears. He sipped his wine then rubbed a thumb over the corner of his mouth. Chaddington-Wye watched him, his head tilted.

'Not feeling quite the thing?'

'Oh, no, I'm fine. Just debating whether to amble round to Almack's this evening. It is Wednesday, ain't it?'

'It is, but I don't recall you aspiring to tread around the floor. Not for the past twenty years.'

'No – gave that up long ago, as you say. No, I thought I might just take a turn and see who's who and what's what. Catch up, you know. Not been there since ... oh, whenever it was.' He took a casual sip of wine. 'Fancy coming along then toddling off to White's?'

Harvey Chaddington-Wye hitched himself upright in his armchair. 'Well, you could persuade me. Haven't anything else planned for tonight. A hand or two of piquet wouldn't go amiss.'

Marius's wine acquired a pleasanter flavour. 'Good,' he said, finishing it. 'I'll see you there.'

Chapter Thirteen

*L*ady Trent's carriage bearing Louise and Mrs Henshaw drew up at Stapley Hall's arched entrance. This close to the house, Louise's breath knotted in her throat. This was where Amelia had lived. Had spent her few happy, married years. Had borne her child. The thought made her fingers tremble on the reticule in her lap.

The footman jumped down from his perch and opened the carriage door. Louise found herself unable to move. Behind her Cressida Henshaw, already risen to alight, was balanced unevenly between the seats.

'Are you quite well, Miss Devreaux?' she said at last.

'Oh, yes, quite. Thank you, quite.'

She grasped the loop of corded silk hanging by the door and pulled herself to her feet. With a hand on the footman's arm she stepped down. Before her an elderly man, stooped and anxious of expression, hovered in front of the entrance flanked by two females, a girl to his left and a woman of middle years on his right. His hands twisted together and the girl's apron was knotted into a lump in hers. The woman regarded the newcomers steadily from under the drooping frill of her cap.

Louise moved forward. 'Good morning. I am Miss Devreaux, Mrs Aveley's sister.'

The man's face softened with relief.

'Jedburgh, ma'am. I'm Jedburgh, as was the master's butler.'
He pointed to the older woman. 'And this be Mrs Nairn, the
housekeeper. And Sal – Sally – the housemaid.' He swallowed
and his Adam's apple bobbed above his narrow neckcloth. 'Can
it be you can tell us what's happening about the house?' He drew
a shaky breath. 'If you please, of course. Not meaning to be
prying.'

'Certainly. I am removing here with Mrs Henshaw and
Master Christopher. He is following with his nurses. And my
maid.' The three faces before her brightened. 'They have been a
little delayed. I expect you know that Master Christopher is not
a good traveller.'

The housekeeper stepped forward, grabbed Louise's hand
and shook it vigorously 'I'm that pleased, ma'am, that pleased.
We were all over worried that the house might be shut up or
sold.'

Carefully detaching herself, Louise patted the woman's arm.
'I'm sure you must be very relieved. Now, shall we go inside so
you may show us round?'

'Oh, yes, ma'am. Whatever am I thinking of?'

The housekeeper led her into the pretty entrance hall. 'This
is the hall,' she declared, unnecessarily, 'and this be the sitting
room. The master and mistress liked this room. It gets the sun
for most of the day. But not,' she added quickly, 'so much as to
make it hot in summer.'

Chattering about the painting of Gerard Aveley above the
carved desk on the far wall, Mrs Nairn realised the young lady
was not listening. Louise had halted by the sofa, her eyes pinned
to the shawl cast over its back. The housekeeper's words dwindled into silence.

A sewing box stood abandoned on a table by the window.
Cressida, gesticulating firmly to the wide-eyed Sally that she
should remove it, stepped towards the shawl.

'I dare say we shall see many of your sister's belongings, my dear. Would you prefer to remain here while Mrs Nairn and I undertake a survey?'

Anxiety replaced puzzlement on the housekeeper's face. Her hands sought the comfort of each other. 'Oh, miss, I'm right sorry. I never thought.'

Louise took uncertain steps to the sofa and sank down. 'Pray do not fret. I am sure I shall accustom myself to ... to ...' Her fingers slid over the silk shawl.

'Perhaps a dish of tea,' Cressida said, looking severely at the butler. 'I assume there is a cook who might prepare it?'

'Yes, ma'am.' Jedburgh rushed into speech. 'Bella Farrow. I'll see to it now, shall I?'

'If you please, Jedburgh.' Cressida's eyebrows rose. 'Mrs Nairn, if you are ready?'

'Oh, yes, ma'am, yes.' The housekeeper cast a worried look at Louise then followed Mrs Henshaw out of the room.

Left alone at last, Louise gathered the shawl in her hands. She raised it to her face and sat motionless while hot tears dripped onto it. This she had not expected. She should have. All her thoughts so far had been on reaching Christopher. On taking him into her care. None had been on what she might find when she did. Her teeth caught at her lip. She should have realised that the house where Amelia had lived would be filled with her echo. It must do. She had been such a lively girl. Full of smiles and laughter. Rare was a day when Dernstone Grange had not rung with it. Until Papa had banned Gerard.

Then Amelia's smiles had vanished. More than once Louise had discovered her crying in a secluded corner of the garden. The pain that marred the pretty face had driven her to beg their father to let Amelia follow her heart. A sob broke from her at the memory. His comments had been fierce and annihilating. Gregory Devreaux had never been known to change his mind and he had not done so then. His word was the law and look where that had landed them.

The door behind her opened. She scrubbed the tears from her cheeks with the shawl and turned. A well-padded woman of some fifty years was crossing the floor, a tray of crockery held high.

'Tea, miss.' She advanced. 'I'll put it here.'

She lowered the tray onto a table by the sofa. Straightening, she took in Louise's moist eyes. 'Oh, miss. Sad, is it?' she asked, completely overstepping the bounds of propriety. 'I dare say you are. But the young mistress was that happy when she was here. Her and the master. Think on her happy days.'

Louise recovered herself under the kindly words. 'Thank you, Mrs ... Mrs?'

'Farrow, miss. Bella Farrow. Now you just tell me what you'd like for your dinner and I'll set about making it.'

'Thank you, Mrs Farrow, but I'm not terribly hungry at present.'

'Now that will never do, miss. You'll be needing your dinners if you're to keep up with Master Kit. He's a proper caution at times. Always running off from Letty as soon as he sees the chance. Game little pullet, Mr Gerard used to call him.' The happy reminiscences faded. 'A sad business it is. Sad, sad, sad.' She rallied. 'But we mustn't let that get us away from bringing up Master Kit as his Pa would have wanted. Now,' she looked sternly down, 'you set off your coat and bonnet and be drinking your tea and I'll put my mind to making a dinner to tempt your appetite.'

With something that might have been a shallow curtsey but probably was not, she bustled from the room, leaving Louise prey to the notion that, whether she wanted it or not, she was going to be well looked after by a kindly domestic tyrant.

The Trent travelling chaise had wheeled onto the neat carriage sweep and pulled up outside the door before Louise had drunk her tea or Cressida Henshaw had returned from her tour. Happy squeals emerged from the vehicle. Setting her teacup down with more speed than care and rushing to the window, Louise watched as Letty jumped out before the step was let down. Turning, the nursery-maid held out her arms and Christopher's little figure launched itself into them.

'Mama. Mama,' he cried struggling to the ground. His sturdy legs carried him to the door before Letty could reach it. His hands reached for the doorknob but he had not the strength to turn it.

Louise hurried into the hall. 'Christopher,' she called dropping to her knees and holding out her arms.

He catapulted into them as fast as his little legs allowed. 'Mama here?' A hopeful face lifted to hers.

'No, dearest.' There were no words to tell him his Mama would never again be here. 'Not yet. Now, come with me. I have something for you.' Untangling her hem from her heels, she rose and took him into the sitting room. 'First we must find my reticule. It's a pretty green one. With pink flowers on it.'

The item was found on the sofa by a determined child. Beside it lay an oddly-shaped, brown paper parcel tied up with string. A pair of young eyes fixed on it. Young hands trembled towards it. A young face turned with a query.

'I wonder what this is,' Louise said, lighting her own eyes with fun. 'Can you lift it, do you think?'

Two little hands struggled to do so.

'Will the string and paper come off?'

Eager fingers pulled one end of the string bow. It unravelled to be dragged off and dropped onto the floor. A crackling paper flap that fell back revealed two red wheels joined by a wooden dowel. The rest of the paper, speedily torn away, revealed two more wheels and small cloth horse.

'Oh.' The blue eyes widened. 'Horsie.' The toy thumped onto the floor. Christopher dropped to his knees. A hand gripped its back. Balancing on knees and his free hand, the other propelled the horse a few inches backwards and forwards with great enthusiasm. 'Horsie,' he repeated.

The red cord tied to the front axle had wrapped itself around one wheel. Movement stopped. Two eyes stared at it. A finger pulled at it. The head looked up.

'Oh, dear,' Louise said. 'Let me untangle it for you.' On her knees beside him, she unwound the cord, explaining that she had carried the toy all the way from her own home and kept it for him for a special occasion.

Christopher listened gravely. 'Uncle Flip has pony for me. He promised 'fore Uncle Raff took me away.'

'I dare say he will come to see you soon.'

'Now then, Master Kit, you shouldn't be in here.' Mabson's stern voice cut into the shared confidences.

'I don't object to him, Mabson. I'm sure his Mama had him in here as often as she could.'

The nurse's bosom heaved. 'Well … well, yes, she did. Didn't hold with having him upstairs. Many's the hour I've sat and watched her play with him.' Her face grew quickly red around the eyes and nose.

'It will be good for him to be in here again. And if we can keep his thoughts occupied, he will become used to it and perhaps – in time – learn not to miss his … her.' Louse quickly corrected herself from using a word that would certainly cause the child to repeat his earlier question. 'Now,' she said to him, 'you go with Mabson. I'm sure there will be tea in the nursery and Letty will want to see your horse.'

With his new toy clutched in his arms and telling his nurse he would call it Fire, he allowed himself to be carried from the room.

Left to herself, Louise rose to her feet. She gathered up the shawl and hugged it. 'I'll care for him, Amelia,' she promised. 'I'll care for him.'

Three days later, after Stapley Hall had adjusted to its new inhabitants, and they to it, much assisted by Jupp's continued presence,
the sound of hooves on gravel made Louise lift her eyes from the
hem she was stitching on a new shirt for Christopher. She looked
out of the sitting room window.

'Visitors, my dear?' Cressida asked.

'I think ...' She leant forward the better to see who was riding up the short carriage sweep with the reins of a skittering
pony in his hand. 'I think it must be Mr Aveley.'

Dropping the shirt into the sewing basket, she hurried to the
front door, pulling it open before Jedburgh could arrive.

'Good morning, Mr Aveley.' She regarded the lively little animal. 'This must be the pony Christopher speaks of so
endlessly.'

Philip swung his leg over his pommel and slid down. 'It is.
Good day to you, Miss Devreaux. I hope I find you well and
settled.'

'Thank you, yes. The people here are most kind. And of
course Mabson is pleased to be back ruling her own domain.'

'I am sure she is.' He looped the reins together and held them
out to the butler who had arrived. 'Walk these round to the
stables. Tell – I can't recall the groom's name – tell him I'll call
for them when I'm ready.'

Leaving Jedburgh holding the reins in his limp hand, he
flashed his most charming smile at Louise. 'You will permit me,
ma'am, to impose on you until I can show Christopher his new
possession?'

'Of course. Please come in.'

She led him into the sitting room where Cressida Henshaw
was standing by the sofa. 'Ah, I think I need not present you to
Mrs Henshaw. You are cousins I believe.'

'We are,' Cressida said, her face stern. 'But only by the grace of our great-grandfather.'

If the frigidity of her welcome surprised Louise, it did not unsettle Philip. He advanced and bowed over his cousin's extended hand.

'I should explain, ma'am,' he said to Louise, his bow completed, 'that my cousin undoubtedly remembers the follies of my youth. You will understand that green young men newly come to town can fall into unwise ways. Until they are old enough to know better, of course.'

'Indeed, I must say not, Mr Aveley. I had only a sister, not a brother.'

'Of course.' He eyed the severity of her black gown. 'Your appearance, ma'am, reminds me of your grief. I apologise.' He bowed again.

Much moved by his sensitivity, Louise indicated that he should be seated. 'Thank you. If you will wait a moment I shall see if Christopher has finished his nap. I am sure he will be eager to greet his pony.'

Philip, caught halfway to seating himself, straightened quickly and moved to open the door for her. When he had closed it behind her, he turned a pleasant face to Cressida. 'Let me see, ma'am, are we third cousins or second cousins once removed?'

'The latter.' Cressida sat down. Her gown rustled about her.

'Oh, come, ma'am. Let us be reconciled. You cannot still begrudge me my green stupidities. They are all at an end, I assure you.'

The Henshaw face did not soften. 'I wish I might believe that. I wish Gerard might have believed it too. Then he would have made you guardian.'

'Gerard,' Philip snorted, his amiability vanquished. 'As you well know, ma'am, he was much given to pomposity.' He took three hasty steps forward. 'Thought himself head of the family and sought to force everyone into his mould.'

'Pomposity? Gerard? When he ran off with an under-age girl barely out of the schoolroom?'

'A fall from grace, I grant you, but his only one. And one that was forgiven by the rest of the family, including you and Trent.'

'By our family, yes, but not by Miss Devreaux's. That wound has not healed.'

Philip was spared any further condemnation by the door opening and a small figure hurtling into the room on unsteady legs.

'I saw him. I saw him, Uncle Flip. Is he mine?' The child arrived panting at Philip's knees. 'All mine?'

'He is indeed.' Philip ruffled the blond hair. 'But he's a she and hasn't a name. What shall you call her?'

'Oh.' The excitement vanished into deep thought. 'I'll call her … um …'

'She has a star on her forehead. A white one. You could call her Star, if you wished. I'm sure she would like that.'

'Oh, Star. Yes. I ride her now, Uncle Flip?'

'If Miss Devreaux does not object.' Philip looked up as Louise entered the room followed by an indignant Mabson.

'He be too young, Master Philip,' the nurse declared before Louise could speak.

'Oh, I think not. His father and I were both thrown into the saddle by the time we were his age.'

'I don't like it.' Mabson folded her arms and drew her brows together.

'Miss Devreaux, I appeal to you. I promise to do no more than lead him round the south lawn.'

'Well … if you take great care and keep a firm hold on the bridle then –'

'Excellent woman.' He scooped Christopher up. 'I promise to follow your every command. Come, my little cavalier. Let's to the stables.'

He marched out of the room, followed by the muttering nurse.

Louise resumed her stitching by the window. Her stitches faltered. The coolness between Mrs Henshaw and Philip Aveley troubled her. She lowered the material into her lap, gazing unseeingly out of the window. Did something other than his former behaviour lie beneath it? She could hardly ask either of them, nor would she ever consider questioning a servant. But...Mabson might know. She might tell. The freedom with which she expressed herself about anything that affected her *lambkin* was quite improper for someone in her position, as Louise had discovered. But propriety did not seem to weigh with her when she considered his well-being at risk.

She lifted the shirt and threaded her needle into in the hem only to become aware of another horse crunching across the gravel. Ranulph Trent was approaching the house. Her heart lurched. The needle pricked her finger. What would he find to criticise this time? And why had he come? She watched him walk the horse towards the corner of the house on his way to the stables.

Under her amazed eyes, he raised his arm, shouted and spurred his mount to the gallop. His hat flew off behind him, bouncing on the ground. Riding *ventre-à-terre* he hurtled from her sight.

Chapter Fourteen

*L*ouise dropped her sewing, snatched up her skirts and ran from the room. She sped through the hall and burst through the servants' door at the rear. Seconds later the kitchen staff were stunned to see her race past them and out to the spread of flagstones that separated the stables from the house.

Halfway across she rocked to a halt, her hands clasped over her open mouth. The pony with Christopher on its back had broken free. It was bolting down the lawns towards the shallow ditch that kept the cattle from the garden. Christopher, bent forward, was clinging to its mane, one foot in a shortened stirrup and the other shaken free. His terrified screams echoed back to her.

Hideous visions of a child fallen from the saddle and trapped to the animal by his foot drenched Louise's imagination. If that happened, his curly head was certain to crash on the ground with each of the animal's strides. Louise's senses spun. She raised a hand to her forehead. She was too far away to help. Who could? Philip Aveley — clearly injured — hobbled after them clutching at his leg. He could not possibly reach them before the animal plunged into the ditch killing them both.

Ranulph Trent careered round the corner of the house, heels and whip urging his horse to its utmost speed.

'Make haste,' Louise called uselessly. 'Oh, make haste.' Her hands flew to her mouth.

Sir Ranulph was too far away to hear. His attention was all on the screaming child. He raced across the grass to curve in front of the thundering pony. It shied as his stallion cut it off from the ditch. Its headlong race faltered. He dropped his reins, reached out and hooked his fingers into its bridle. His free arm grabbed Christopher and shook the little body until the trapped foot cleared the stirrup. The child, screaming, clung his arms round his rescuer's neck.

Louise swayed with relief. An unknown arm grasped her round the waist, steadying her.

'Thank the Lord,' Jupp said, revealing his presence. 'The boy's a game one to hang on so well.'

Louise tried to steady her racing heart, too shaken to realise Lady Trent's footman had raced from the house. 'Yes,' she croaked.

'Beg pardon, miss, but you looked to be faint.' He eased her away from him, slightly. 'Are you well now?'

She still could not drag her eyes from the scene. 'Er...yes. Yes, I am. Thank you.'

'Right you are, miss.' Jupp removed his arm. 'No offence meant.'

'Indeed. No, I thank you.'

Louise became aware of the other servants clustered round her. 'Please go back inside.' She forced a calmness into her voice that she did not feel. 'There is no need to worry. Master Christopher is quite safe.'

With the servants and their mutterings receding, she tuned to watch Sir Ranulph approach. With Christopher held close, he kept his horse to a slow walk. He spoke briefly to Philip on the way but did not halt. As he drew closer she could see him talking brightly to the child whose little face was turned up to him, streaked with tears. He stopped beside her.

'Take him in while I dismount.' He bent forward, lowering Christopher into her arms. 'I shall join you presently.'

Obeying what could only be described as an order, she did as she was bid, murmuring nonsense words of 'great adventure' and 'brave horseman'. She carried him into the sitting room, advising him to tell Aunt Cressida, who looked up enquiringly, how wonderful the jaunt had been, while she settled him on her knee.

Sir Ranulph entered the room some moments later. The fury on his face cause her breath to catch. 'Whatever made you think you could care for him?' he demanded. 'Even a fool would think him too young to sit on a horse.'

Louise tried to keep her voice level, aware of the tension that had returned to Christopher's body. 'It was not to be desired but he has taken no harm.'

'No. No thanks to you and Aveley.' He swung round to Philip who had limped in behind him.

'It was an accident,' he said.

'An accident?' Sir Ranulph's blazing eyes swept him from his head to his boots. 'Thank God I was here or it would have been much worse.'

Christopher trembled, his face puckering at the angry voices.

'Control yourselves,' Louise hissed. 'You are causing him more alarm.' She wrapped her arms tighter about the child seconds before Mabson arrived in a flurry of skirts, pinafore and copious tears. Louise fended off her attempts to snatch Christopher from her.

'He isn't hurt, Mabson.'

'Nor would he have been,' Philip said. 'The pony would have stopped at the ha-ha.' He appealed to Louise. 'She trod all of her weight on my foot, ma'am. God knows why she bolted. If she hadn't surprised me, I would never have let go of the bridle.'

'Don't seek to cast blame on the creature,' Sir Ranulph snarled. 'You were the one responsible.'

'I've said he was in no danger. I called to him to keep tight hold of its mane. And he did.'

'He's three, for God's sake —'

Cressida's quiet voice cut through the angry exchanges.

'Shall we all stop shouting? It is only alarming the child further. Miss Devreaux, perhaps it would be sensible to take him to the nursery. He should be less troubled there. Especially,' she continued, looking severely at Mabson, 'if the people about him stay calm.'

Louise was only too pleased to absent herself and Christopher from what bore every sign of becoming a family feud. She led the way to the nursery, clutching the shaking child close.

Mabson dogged her steps. 'You best let me take him, miss. He knows me.'

'He knows me too,' she spoke over her shoulder. 'He is quite happy with me.'

Mumblings not quite loud enough for her to distinguish followed her. She entered the bright nursery. 'Now, what would you like to play with first, Christopher? Or would you like a drink?'

The child raised his head from where he had buried it in the side of her neck. 'Shugplum, please.'

'Shugplum?'

'He means sugar plum, miss,' Letty said, catching sight of Mabson's uncooperative face. 'Mr Aveley gave him some. I'll fetch them.'

She hurried across to a painted cupboard let in to the space by the chimneybreast. The door opened to reveal various nursery necessities and a blue and white striped paper box. She carried it forward and lifted the lid.

'Oh.'

Mabson's head turned. She reached out a hand and grasped the box.

'Is something wrong?' Louise asked.

'There be only one left.' The nurse rested her stern gaze on her charge. 'Where are the others?'

The little face bowed. A thumb crept into a rosebud mouth. 'You've been stealing them, haven't you?' The Mabson bosom inflated. 'No wonder you was sick in the carriage. And at your uncle's.' She scowled heavily. 'And we know what happens to them as steal, don't we? The devil creeps in and takes them in the night.'

'Mabson, really! Hasn't he had enough of a scare for one day?'

'But –'

'No. No more. Here Letty, I think his clothes need changing. Mine certainly do. Keep him happy for the rest of the day. And no more threats.' This last was directed at the nurse. Holding her gaze for a moment, she walked out of the nursery to change her dampened gown.

A strained silence filled the sitting room when she entered it. Seeking to introduce a lighter note she informed Philip that only one plum remained of his gift. 'I fear you will have Mabson after you. She is convinced you are to blame for his nausea and fever at Crestings.'

'I'm sure I'm to blame for every misfortune,' he said, a trifle sulkily. 'I wouldn't be surprised if he –' his head jerked towards Sir Ranulph, 'holds *me* to blame for the drowning too.'

Louise gasped.

He was immediately contrite. 'Oh, Miss Devreaux, I do beg your pardon. Pray forgive me. I wasn't thinking.'

'You don't think, that's your trouble,' Sir Ranulph informed him. 'A moment's reflection would have prevented today's fiasco. That pony was far too big for the child. He's not to ride it again.'

'How can you be so unkind?' The words burst from Louise before she could stop them. 'He was thrilled to have it. Now he will be so disappointed.'

Sir Ranulph's icy regard switched to her. 'Indeed, ma'am? Better disappointed than lying with a broken neck.'

She would not be browbeaten. 'If you prevent him from riding after today's … episode, you may well turn him afraid of horses for life.'

Their eyes met, his cool and grey, hers so deeply blue with emotion they looked violet. He would not give way.

'I doubt it, ma'am. Children are soon enough moulded.'

'How typical of you, Trent.' Scorn filled Philip's voice.

'And how typical of you to set the place in a stir. I think we can manage without the pleasure of any more of your company today.'

The cousins glared at each other.

'I think,' said Cressida Henshaw, 'we may do very well without *both* of you.'

'As you wish, ma'am.' Sir Ranulph bowed. 'I came merely to deliver a letter to Miss Devreaux. It arrived this morning.'

He drew a fold of paper from his pocket and held it out.

'Thank you.' Louise examined it. 'It's my mother's hand.' A lowering thought occurred to her. 'You must have been obliged to pay for it. I beg you will –'

'If you are about to offer me a sixpence, ma'am, I take leave to tell you I shall be highly insulted.'

She swallowed. He bowed. 'I bid you good day.'

He stalked out in silence. Philip limped forward. He took her free hand. 'Pray forgive me for causing you distress. Such was very far from my intention.'

'Do not concern yourself, sir. It was an accident. Such things may happen to anyone.'

'But to cause my cousin to rip up at you so … it was quite inexcusable of me, ma'am. I do apologise.'

She withdrew her hand. 'There is no need. I am becoming accustomed to Sir Ranulph's manner.' She stopped and cast a glance over her shoulder. 'I am sorry, ma'am, to comment so upon your cousin. It was not well done of me.'

Cressida inclined her head. 'Let us all forget these events. You have your Mama's letter to read and I'm sure Mr Aveley would be best advised to seek his own home to rest his injury.'

Philip bowed. 'Very true, ma'am.' He turned to Louise. 'I shall ride over tomorrow to see if our nephew has taken any lasting harm.'

Bowing, he withdrew. With a low growl, Cressida returned to the sofa by the fire and took up her book. Louise seated herself at the table at the window. She slid a finger under the wafer sealing the letter. Her mother's recriminations brought a flush to her cheeks. Mama was missing her dreadfully. Mama had not been able to leave her room. Papa was in a fury. He would not permit her name to be mentioned. Mama had been forced, most disagreeably, to deceive him and beg the vicar's wife to carry this letter to the post. Why would Louise not return home? Surely she must be assured by now that the child was being well cared for.

Louise smothered a bitter laugh. Well cared for? By a man whose every action showed the coldness of his nature? Saddened as she was by her mother's obvious distress, she would not serve the dead Amelia such a dreadful turn as to leave her child to the mercy of a man who could destroy his joy in his pony.

The drawer at the table contained paper, quills and ink. She pulled them out and began to pen an answer. Within a paragraph, her anger was spilling onto the page so fiercely the quill spluttered ink in arcs of tiny blots. Sir Ranulph was never to be trusted with Amelia's child. There was no gentleness in his nature. No accommodation for others' thoughts or feelings. He was so used to having everything his own way that even the slightest resistance brought the most hurtful, hateful words to his lips. And how they curled with his speech. And his eyes … they were never warmed by any degree of tenderness. Rather they held the cold immovability of steel at all times. Mama must understand how it was she could not leave the precious child to him.

She pulled forward a second sheet, too lost in her emotions to bother crossing her lines. Not even Papa was as authoritarian as he. How she pitied the woman who would become his wife. The poor creature would be downtrodden beyond belief. Her hand slowed. Her words were becoming difficult to read. So fierce was the force of her writing that the quill point had splayed. Her head bowed. She laid the pen down and drew a steadying breath. How very unlike her to give way to such passion. It was not at all in keeping with her nature ... or, rather, the nature she had constructed for herself since Amelia had run from home.

The pages ripped under her fingers. The letter must never be sent. No matter how difficult she found life in Sir Ranulph's vicinity, she would not demean herself by showing how much he riled her. Nor would she distress her mother further.

Allowing her gaze to wander to the prospect outside the window, she reflected upon his character. She found herself forced to admit that some ... much of her wrath came from his furious opinion of her own conduct. He had ripped her character to shreds in a way quite undeserved. There had been no reason she should fear Mr Aveley would not have a care for Christopher. So what prompted the strength of Sir Ranulph's anger? Surely a man raised by so kind and charming a lady as his mother could not be a complete stranger to the softer emotions. For several minutes, her thoughts ran over their meetings. She could detect no such side to his nature. Even the way he had announced Amelia's death had been cold and unfeeling.

Leaning an elbow on the table, she propped her chin on her hand. Outside the light was fading from the sky. She hoped Mr Aveley would reach home before the temperature plummeted. For Sir Ranulph she felt not the least iota of com-passion. Chiming with her meandering thoughts, the object of them cantered his horse round the corner of the house. He was looking down at a bundled blanket clasped tightly in one arm. Cuddled inside its folds, his face barely visible, was Christopher. She half rose in alarm. Was he taking the child away? As she watched a small arm emerged to clutch at one of the capes of Sir Ranulph's greatcoat. The horse circled round the carriage sweep. Christopher's face was clear to see. Delight formed every speck of his features. His mouth opened in a laugh. His enjoyment of the ride was obvious. And so, it seemed from the warmth and laughter on Ranulph Trent's own face, was he.

Under her amazed yes, he cuddled the child close and trotted out of sight.

Chapter Fifteen

Marius Trent was pleased to discover how easy it was to slip back into the sybaritic life he enjoyed in London. It being late March, many if not most of his friends had also returned. Emerging from his bed in Grenier's Hotel, he permitted Rullick to envelop him in a cosy dressing gown before he applied himself to the plates of cold meats the valet had caused to be delivered to the bedchamber.

'Shall you be riding this morning, sir?' the man enquired.

Marius peered towards the part-opened curtains. 'How's the weather today?'

'Fair enough, sir. Clouds but no rain. A slight breeze perhaps.'

'Hmm.' Marius pulled the dressing gown's collar closer. 'No. No, I think I'll visit that new place in Bond Street. Might have something to interest me. Chaddington-Wye spoke well of it. Said you could buy everything you need there. No reason to go traipsing around town from place to place any more.' He reached for the coffee cup by his elbow. 'Though I can't see how one establishment can provide for everything a chap might need.' He gulped the coffee then held the cup away, looking at it critically. 'Cold.'

The valet hurried to refill the cup. 'I collect, sir, you refer to *The Gentleman's Emporium*. Mr Neave's establishment.'

'Is that him? Hmm, a Cit, no doubt.'

'Made his money in the East, sir – or so it's said.'

'Ah, lots of 'em nowadays. I'll try it out. See how it does. It's not as if I'll have to speak to the fellow himself. I'll go there, then call at White's, then have a little snooze before dinner and toddle off to Almack's. See who's about.'

'As you say, sir. I'll see to pressing your evening wear after you've departed. Have it all in readiness for you.'

Marius swallowed his coffee and permitted Rullick to shave and dress him. Well-wrapped against the possibility of a chance wind, he set off on his planned excursion. The merchandise in *The Gentleman's Emporium* far and away exceeded his expectations. He had no trouble at all in discovering an enamelled snuff box, a very smart hip flask and a Malacca cane that absolutely demanded he purchase them. He also ordered two new waistcoats in a newly-arrived Chinese silk the style of which he had not seen before. Imperial yellow, according to the eager man who waited upon him.

Well pleased with himself, he exited the shop, only to be brought to a halt by the sight of Josephine Varennes entering her carriage at the adjacent *Ladies' Emporium*. Managing to spend no more time with her than politeness demanded, he took a hackney to White's where he whiled away a peaceful two hours snoozing off the bottle and a half of burgundy he had consumed during a modest – in his view – meal of white soup, a brace of partridges stewed in gravy, some carp in anchovy and lemon sauce, and sufficient vegetable dishes to fill any remaining empty corner.

His return to Grenier's saw him correctly attired in knee breeches, striped stockings, and a dark coat. With a *chapeau bras* under his arm, he entered Almack's hallowed ground at a quarter to eleven precisely. Mounting the stairs to the crowded and noisy ballroom, he bowed over the gloved hands of Ladies Jersey and Sefton, before greeting Hugo Marston and his bride. Uttering all the felicitations proper to the occasion, he bowed and eased his way through the crowds of gowned, jewelled and scented ladies fringing the dancefloor with either their attendant cicisbeos or their drooping, partnerless daughters. Safe from the exertions of the dancing couples skipping and hopping in the centre, he remained there nodding to sundry acquaintances until Harvey Chaddington-Wye hove into view. Abandoning his refuge he decamped to the door.

'Chadders, well met. Thought you might have changed your mind.'

His friend dragged his gaze away from a pair of young ladies who did indeed lack partners and who were therefore chattering brightly and plying their fans. 'That must be Dollwen's second girl,' he said, nodding towards the one in the primrose gown. 'The first 'un caught Beauworthy two Seasons ago.'

'It amazes me that you remember all these girls. Not something I've ever managed. Far too many of 'em thrust at us.'

'Like to watch the bloodlines. See how they fall out.' He indicated a vivacious brunette tripping enthusiastically down a set in the centre of the room. 'Now take her. One of old General Strathan's line. Well-known for producing sons.'

Marius surveyed him with raised eyebrows. 'You hanging out for a wife? Thought you'd abandoned that notion years ago.'

'I have, I have. Confirmed bachelor me. Just like you. Prefer my attachments without any attachment, if you take my meaning.'

Marius leapt on the opportunity to push his idea for Josephine Varennes. 'If that's your idea, then —'

A female voice cut through his words. 'My dear Mr Trent. And Mr Chaddington-Wye. How delightful.'

The men turned.

'Lady D'Arborough,' Marius bowed. 'Delighted, ma'am. Delighted. In town for the Season, I collect?'

'Indeed. D'Arborough has brought Maurice up for his levée so I am come with them.'

'Delighted,' Marius repeated.

'Your eldest's levée already, ma'am,' Chaddington-Wye pronounced. 'How time flies.'

'Indeed.' He ladyship's face stilled.

'Not that one would ever suspect him to have left the nursery as yet,' Chaddington-Wye bowed.

Her ladyship's face softened. She tapped his arm with her fan. 'You old flatterer, you.' With a gay laugh she drifted off.

'Another one of General Strathan's girls. Four sons to her name. All of 'em D'Arborough's too. Couldn't be anything else with that nose of his.'

Marius, finding his friend's interest in the bloodstock present in the room considerably less enthralling than that he would hear at Tattersall's, said, 'I don't have a fancy for the hideous orgeat they serve here. What say we toddle up St James's right away?'

Chaddington-Wye cast a look at the dancers and supporters thronging the ballroom. 'I'm with you, then. There's only so much a man can stand of those infernal violins scraping and twanging.'

They headed for the door. Reaching the safety of the ground floor, they collected their cloaks and had almost achieved their escape when a ripe figure gowned in the height of fashion emerged from the supper room.

'Why, Mr Trent, I do declare you might almost be my shadow.' Josephine Varennes tapped his arm teasingly with her fan and smiled up at him, her head tilting far too coyly for a woman of her years.

A blinding thought, ghastly in its implication, shot cold fear through Marius. It froze the smile on his lips, gripped his throat, slid down his chest and coiled hideously with the consumed carp in the lower reaches of his stomach. After two or three attempts he managed, 'Lady Josephine, ma'am. Delighted.'

His friend stirred himself to the rescue. He bowed. 'Ma'am, you cast all others into the shade.'

'Mr Chaddington-Wye, I had not expected to see you in town.'

'On the point of leaving, ma'am. Seen the new batch of debutantes and young sprigs. Saw no reason to stay.'

Lacking the expectation of any further comment from Marius, who was looking faintly stuffed, her ladyship laughed gaily and swept imperiously to the stair.

Making good his escape, Marius fairly dragged Chaddington-Wye out of the door and smartly rounded the corner into St James's Street.

'Steady on. Anyone would think you'd a pack after you.' He lengthened his stride. 'Mind, if she's got her eye on you as another conquest, you'd best rusticate for a couple of months.'

His words caused Marius to completely abandon any idea of encouraging him to avail himself of Lady Josephine's charms. He shuddered. 'I need a reviver. Let's call at White's.'

Approving the notion, Chaddington-Wye summoned the link boy who was cowering for shelter in the next doorway and they followed him up the street. Immediately they entered the hall, Marius found himself accosted by a lanky gentleman of predatory feature.

'Seen that nevvy of yours lately? He'll be green about the gills, the fool.'

'Ranulph? See him often. Difficult not to when we're living in the same house. I know Crestings is big, but it ain't that big.'

'Not him. Aveley.'

Marius's heart, already unsettled by Josephine Varennes, thumped. 'Him! Why should I see him? And he's not my nephew. Sort of cousin, if you must know.'

'He's your second cousin, once removed, I believe,' Chaddington-Wye informed him.

Complete disinterest in the meanderings of the Trent family left the lanky man unmoved. Intent on inserting salt wherever he might find a wound, he added, 'Ah, so you won't have backed him.'

'Backed him? Backed him to do what?'

The man snorted. 'The fool bet Trelowen he could make it to Brighton without being seen at any changing post.'

'How's he to manage that? He'd have to change four or five times.'

'I don't know. He's an idiot. Bound to lose if he's bet against Trelowen. The man's a charlatan.'

'So he is,' Chaddington-Wye agreed. 'Didn't know he was back in the country. Thought he was still hiding out in ... where was it? Italy? No ... can't recall.'

Marius, making a supreme effort, passed the affair off with a shrug. 'Aveley's nothing to do with me, thank God.'

'Ah, well,' the lanky gossip said, before strolling off, 'rather him than me.'

Marius and Chaddington-Wye continued into the establishment. Whatever his friend was saying as they climbed the main stairs and passed into the back-dining hall with its curved window drifted over Marius's head. He continued inattentive, quite failing to do justice to the rather fine burgundy and port Chaddington-Wye had commanded.

'That's set you about, has it?' Chaddington-Wye asked after fifteen minutes of continuous silence.

'What? Uh?' Marius dragged his preoccupied gaze from the fire. 'Oh. No. No. Well ... yes.' He swirled the dregs of burgundy in his glass, watching the ruby liquid rise, fall and circle. 'If you must know, I don't like the idea of debts so close to Crestings.'

'Then you'd best have your nephew tell him.'

'It's true then is it?'

'If you believe the rumours, yes. No proof as yet, as far as I know.' Chaddington-Wye eyed his friend. 'Worth looking into, wouldn't you say?'

Marius sniffed and lapsed again into his abstracted study of the fire.

The following morning failed to lighten his mood. Quite the reverse. Checking the bets recorded in Tattersall's, he discovered Philip Aveley had not only bet against Trelowen some four months ago, he had done so for one hundred pounds at odds of five to one. Marius Trent was no fool. Nor had he ever taken any particular interest in the dealings of his second cousin once removed but he was sharp enough to realise that the junior sprig of the Aveley family was unlikely to be able to put his hand to five hundred pounds with any great speed. Even if the bet had not been with Trelowen, it was a bet of honour and, as such, must be paid immediately.

The situation brought a frown to his plump forehead. Lack of the readies meant only one thing...a quick deal with the cent-per-centers. A deal with one of those gentlemen, none of whom were known for the charitableness of their nature, meant repaying considerably more than was borrowed. And the longer it took to pay off, the greater the amount the blood-suckers wanted.

He left Tattersall's deep in thought. So deep he failed to respond to at least two acquaintances, thereby giving rise to a small stir of gossip that he had run himself off his legs. Oblivious to the offer of a cheap journey to wherever he desired from a lingering jarvey looking frozen to the bone in a thin coat and long muffler on the box of his disreputable vehicle, he picked his way past those others foolish enough to be walking along Piccadilly in less than clement weather and entered his hotel in Jermyn Street quite lost to the world.

It was not only the news of the debt that filled his mind; he was certain that more lay behind it. Quite surprising Rullick by retiring to bed several hours in advance of his normal time, he lay in the flickering light of the fire staring at the four-poster's fabric cover high above his head debating his next move. Shopping, eating and conversing were things of the past. There was no enjoyment left in them. Nor could there be a retreat to Crestings. No, there was more to be unearthed. He had no illusions that it would probably produce a fair amount of mire for him to wade through.

After a night marked by restless tossing, he rose, dressed, and exited the hotel with as much enthusiasm as a French *aristo* mounting a tumbril. Forcing his shoulders back and stiffening his spine he set himself to unearth what, if anything, there was to discover about the finances of his second cousin once removed.

What he discovered had him setting pen to paper two days later, only for him to screw the missive into a ball and toss it into the fire in his room's narrow grate. He watched the paper blacken and burn. The news he had to impart should not be conveyed by letter. He knew beyond doubt that Stephanie was well aware of what post was delivered to Crestings for the butler would tell. And he would recognise Marius's scrawling hand. Nothing would stop Stephanie from asking Ranulph what her brother-in-law had to say. For a lady marooned in a country pile by age and infirmity, letters and news were the mainstay of her existence.

No, he must abandon his visit and return home. Suspicion was spreading like a fungus in his mind. It must be acted upon, and soon. He departed London at more than his usual speed.

Chapter Sixteen

Marius's words hung in the air of Crestings' handsome library with its ranks of bookshelves and plethora of bizarre items of furniture. Despite the mild weather outside its two tall windows, the atmosphere inside struck chill into his bones. He shifted uncomfortably under his nephew's grey eyes. Ranulph Trent's narrowed mouth stayed closed. Receiving no response, Marius blustered into further explanation.

'And debts of course. Not that there's anything odd in that – nobody pays their tailors on time. They don't expect it. His bets are a different matter, of course.' He eyed the decanters standing on a side table. 'Think I'll take a glass, if you don't mind.' Without waiting for a comment he hurried across the patterned carpet as fast as his stout legs permitted and slopped a generous measure of brandy into a rummer. The fiery liquid was gone in seconds. His hand lingered over the decanter until a single word from his nephew made him jump and turn.

'Bets?'

'Yes. Most of 'em lost.'

'Cards?'

'Faro. And with gaffed boxes, I'll be bound. He ran pretty deep and he's not the sort to spot a Captain Sharp or a Greek when he's in his cups.' He turned the empty glass in his hand. 'What shall you do? You can't let the child stay at Stapley now.'

'No I can't. He'll have to come back here.'

'It'll look mighty odd to drag them back so quick when you've only just let them go. Best pack him off to Bath. Or Brighton. Say it's for his health. That sort of thing.'

'No. Aveley would only follow them.' Sir Ranulph tapped a thumbnail against his teeth.

'What about the Dower House? Is the work on it done?'

A shake of the head. 'Not when I was there two days ago.'

'Well put a burr under them. Tell 'em you want it finished betimes.'

'I'll go down and see the Lanthwaites in the morning. I'll have them make ready as much as possible.'

'Will you tell Stephanie why she must move?'

'No.' Sir Ranulph studied the carpet for a few moments. 'No. It would only distress her.'

'She'll wonder, nonetheless. Whether you tell her or not. She's no fool, your Mama.' He paused, then chose his words with care. 'That girl will not want to come back.'

'I know.' Sir Ranulph walked to the nearest window and stood motionless, not registering the impressive prospect of the sweeping deer park where the evening mist was gathering under the wide oaks.

Reluctance was not the best way to describe Louise's reception of the decision in Stapley Hall's drawing room. She was incensed.

'You cannot intend to move him again. He is here on the doctor's advice.' She tried to calm herself. To reason more persuasively. 'One look will show you how very much improved he is.'

'Nevertheless, he must return to Crestings.'

'But why?'

'Because it is my wish.' His tone, his fierce expression, brooked no argument.

Louise took a quick turn about the room, her agitation evident in her twisting hands. Cressida Henshaw's eyebrows that had risen at Sir Ranulph's announcement drew together. She would not question him in Louise's presence but she surely would as soon as they were alone. Despite being a cousin, she was several years his senior and had no qualms about demanding the true explanation. Standing by the bureau where she had been penning a letter, she folded her hands and waited.

Aware that his immediate future included a sharp catechism, Sir Ranulph asked Louise to ascertain how soon Christopher's party could be ready to leave. 'For I intend to escort you home myself, ma'am.'

Unable to trust herself to speak further, Louise looked from one to the other. Obtaining no help from Mrs Henshaw, she turned and left the room without answering.

'Well, Ranulph?' Cressida said as soon as the door had shut. 'I trust you are going to give me the real reason for this change. I don't care to be fobbed off with some Banbury tale.'

The force of her words brought an ironic twist to his mouth. 'I would never try to flim-flam you. You should know that.'

'I do. Come...out with it.'

'The child is not safe here.'

'Really? I presume you have good reason for saying that.' She studied his face. 'It cannot be that Miss Devreaux is the danger. She is devoted to him. For her sister's sake at present, if not for his own, but that will soon change. He is a charming child.'

Sir Ranulph regarded her steadily.

'Not her then. Nor his retinue – that they would defend him with their lives I doubt not. So...' She met his gaze directly. 'The uncle. It can be no other.'

He continued to regard her. She applied her mind. 'The pony?' He nodded. His gaze did not waver. Her eyebrows rose. 'The illness at your house? How can that be? Philip was barely there.

Nor left alone in the child's company.' She walked to the settee. 'Surely you are not accusing him of some nefarious object with the sugar plums? They would do no more than turn him sick.' She sank onto the seat, her poise undisturbed. 'Why should he be doing it?'

Ranulph crossed to the fireplace and leant a shoulder against the carved mantelshelf. For several moments he watched the flames leap and the logs spark. 'Debts,' he said at last. 'Many of them. And he has made a bet I'm sure he cannot meet. He will have to go to the usurers, if he hasn't been there already. They will be more than willing to fund him. Especially if he leads them to believe he has … prospects. Whoever he chooses, the devil will let the interest mount until the debt is far greater. They always do if they have garnered the impression that it will – eventually – be met.'

She folded her hands on her knees. 'You are saying, then, that he will attempt Christopher's life so he may inherit?'

'Exactly so.' He kicked at a log that had almost burnt through. It collapsed into ash. 'So you see, he must be taken where Aveley cannot reach him. There is no other solution.'

'Shall you tell Miss Devreaux the reason? If you don't, she must think you wilfully capricious.'

'Unless I mistake, she already does. Not that I will that to weigh with me. I shall say nothing to her – and I wish you not to as well. It is a family matter … not something I care to have known by outsiders.'

'Is Louise not family?'

His head shook. 'No. Not ours.'

'I think you *are* mistaken. Informing her of your concern will put her on her guard. Keeping her in ignorance will not.'

'That is a chance I must take. Once they are installed in the Dower House I can be easy.'

Cressida regarded him levelly. 'Then it must be your responsibility.'

'I know. I believe I know what is best for the child.'

'I hope you are right.'

Some three hours later the party was waved off by tearful servants clustered at Stapley's main door. Cressida Henshaw rode beside Sir Ranulph in his curricle. Louise, who had barely favoured him with a word since he had issued his decree, travelled in the Aveley coach with Christopher on her knee, her maid at her side and Mabson and Letty crushed opposite. The nurse occupied considerably more than her share of the padded seat and her wrath filled the coach. From the moment she had heard of the move, she had not ceased to complain. The only pause had come when the horses had been given the office and the coach had lurched so much her head had been rocked forward then whipped backwards to collide ungently with the squabs.

Louise bore with the litany of complaints as well she could. They tried her self-control to the limit, reflecting as they did her own resentment. When the last vestiges of her restraint were in danger of expiring, she handed the child to his nurse.

'I think you had best take him. He looks to be falling asleep and I know how he likes to be with you then.'

'He most surely does, the poor little lambkin. All this to-ing and fro-ing will have his head in a twist. And he won't like that. He'll be off his food for days now. Just as he was before. You mark my words.'

'I believe we may lay that at the door of the sugar plums, Mabson. He hasn't any to eat this time so I'm sure your fears are unfounded.'

'You comfort yourself with that, ma'am, if you choose. But when you've known him as long as I have – and that won't be for years – you'll learn better.' She shuffled herself on the seat the better to accommodate Christopher's drooping head. The move squashed Letty into further discomfort.

'Come and sit this side, Letty. Mrs Mabson will find it easier if Master Christopher can lie on the seat.'

'Oh, no, miss.' Her eyes widened. 'It isn't fitting for me to face forward. And besides –' she cast a look at Louise's maid. 'You and Miss Sutton will be fearful squashed.'

'Nonsense. It will be better for you both – all, I mean.'

The girl wobbled across the bouncing coach. She did not presume to take Lizzie Sutton's window seat. Instead she edged herself gingerly between Louise and her maid with copious apologies. At any other time her attempts to keep her feet from everyone's toes and her slight frame from toppling into anyone's lap would have lifted Louise's mouth in amusement. But nothing could amuse her today. Today was not a day for pleasure.

The nursery party settled into the East wing amid complaints and moans and general dissatisfaction. Louise returned to her own apartment with less regret than she had expected. Crestings was a delightful establishment. The park was spectacular and the gardens charming. As was her ladyship. She caught herself up. She was not to be distracted – or appeased – by the beauty of her surroundings. She had been perfectly happy at Stapley Hall. Except of course that there were constant reminders of Amelia. That had not been easy to bear. Her honesty obliged her to admit that, apart from her dislike of his autocratic behaviour, she was not entirely unhappy to be back at Ranulph Trent's Crestings.

Preparing to dine with Lady Trent – an invitation she could not decline since it had been offered with such genuine pleasure – her mind drifted back to the sight of Sir Ranulph trotting Christopher on his horse at Stapley. Seated before her dressing table, she lifted her hairbrush to a ringlet. The expression on his face had been much softer then than any she had seen before or since. In fact, she had to admit, he had given every indication of enjoying himself. Why had he done it? Such an action did not

sit well with her experience of his temperament. It cannot have
been — could it? — her accusation of teaching the child to fear
horses. She lowered the brush. Could he have paid attention to
her comment? The thought lingered. He had never struck her as
a man to take instruction from a woman.

The ringlet twisting resumed in an abstract manner until
she snapped herself from her musings to collect her shawl and
descend to the small drawing room Lady Trent preferred. Passing
the bed, she realised she had left the book she had been reading
at Stapley Hall. It was one of the novels she and Amelia had
laughed over in secret at Dernstone Grange.

A flicker of irritation crossed her face. How would she pass
the quiet hours of the evening now? Lady Trent was a great
reader but she did not feel on sufficiently close terms with her to
ask to borrow one of her novels. There was, however, a library
at Crestings, one she had heard was renowned for the range and
excellence of it books. She knew it to be a large room of com-
manding proportions, glimpsed but never entered on her way to
the drawing room. There must be something in there to appeal.
As a sort of house guest she must be able to avail herself of a book
or two. Not even his high-and-mightiness could object to that.

She was accustomed to reach the drawing room by a small
flight of twisting stairs close to her bedchamber. Holding her
shawl close she hurried down them, her way lit by the fading
light through two narrow windows. She reached the passage at
its foot to find it brightened by a warm glow from the library. It
was no surprise. On her first day at Crestings she had learned that
Sir Ranulph had candles lit in all of the main rooms. And fires
too. It was a major extravagance, expended in case Crestings'
lord and master should perchance, wish to visit any of them at
any time. This time she was grateful for it.

At the library door she halted abruptly, barely across the threshold. Several branches of candles cast their flickering light upon the

red damask of the curtains, on the desk, chairs and tables positioned on Turkey carpets and on the ranks of leather-bound books in the cases that lined the walls. Their light also fell on Ranulph Trent, standing by a table in his shirtsleeves with his back to her.

'Oh!' she gasped.

He turned, revealing a strange device of furniture. The table top of polished yew had swung up pulling out a stepladder as tall as his shoulder.

'Good heavens.' She stepped forward, intrigued into forgetting her resentment of him. 'How ingenious. I've never seen anything like it before. It must be very useful.'

'It is, indeed, ma'am.' He held out a hand to her. 'Come and see for yourself.'

Entranced by the table she entered the long room, oblivious to everything else. He closed it down before she reached it.

'Watch,' he said. He lifted the top again and a ladder of some seven steps unfolded on brass hinges.

'Is it quite safe?'

'Perfectly.' The ladder clicked into place. He trod up the first few steps. 'See?' he declared looking down at her upturned face.

'A most excellent contraption.' She scanned the collection of small furniture items at the farther end of the room. 'Do all those things become something else?'

'Many of them.' His eyes brightened at her interest. 'I must own that you have discovered my secret obsession.'

'Library steps?' The question came on a laugh.

'No, ma'am. Metamorphic furniture. It means —'

'It transforms into something else.' A memory grabbed her. 'My grandmother Melthorpe has a table that does the same — or … I assume she still has it, I have not seen her for some time.' She saw a sceptical expression cross his face. 'Well, not quite the same. It merely became a larger table. But not in the ordinary way. It was a circle and opened like … like —'

'Ah – into segments. Like an orange. With extra pieces to slide in.'

'That's it exactly. Grandmama would let me open and shut it to my heart's content. Not that it was easy. The leaves were heavy and I was quite small. I spent hours on my knees underneath it trying to discover how it worked.'

Her delight and his enthusiasm banished their former constraint.

'That is not something I would have expected to amuse a girl.' The elation in her eyes prompted him to point at a globe standing waist-high on carved legs. 'What would you say that was?'

She walked forward to examine it, looking for joins in the wood. Straightening from the task, she tilted her head, her hand to her mouth. 'I think . . I think it is some sort of work box. Or does it hold wine?'

'Neither.' He had joined her. 'Not least because the wine would overheat.' He placed his hands on either side of the top hemisphere. Moments later the front half had divided to reveal a writing desk with several drawers and partitions.

A gurgle of laughter greeted the revelation. 'And this?' She indicated a low, fragile-looking armchair of tapestry slung between dark wooden sides formed of tilted crosses. It stood on the lower points with the tapestry joining the crosses' centres to form a seat. A shallow back and padded arms joined the upper points. 'You cannot claim that this transforms into a ladder.'

'Certainly not.' He gasped the back of the seat and pulled. The rigid arms were hinged at the front and they swung the back upwards to a fair height.

'A *prie-dieu*,' she exclaimed, lifting her hem a fraction to kneel on the seat. The back was now at the exact height for someone to rest their hands in prayer. 'You have amazed me, sir.' He held out his hand to help her rise. His fingers were warm and strong. 'There cannot be any other such magical forms, surely?'

'There is this.' She heard the almost boyish pride in his voice. A genuine joy in these adult toys. Gone was his stiff formality. He led her to a winged and padded armchair in the Louis *Quinze* style. 'Well, ma'am?'

She chuckled, very much aware that he himself had transformed and was now a man of considerable charm. She ran her hand over the carved wooden wings, searching for a clue. 'You will not catch me out,' she said at last. 'I declare it will become a phaeton and pair.'

He laughed. 'No, ma'am.' In a few swift moves the back had come forward to rest on the front curve of its wings; the hinged seat and back had straightened, revealing a second seat and back beneath. The whole was now a chair with a seat quite six feet long.

'There, ma'am,' he said, sweeping out his arm, triumph shining in his eyes. 'A bed.'

Louise felt her breath crash from her. Gentlemen did not speak of beds to unmarried young ladies. She was suddenly very conscious that only a light linen clothed his arms and chest. Her eyes grew hot. Her head felt dizzy. For a moment she feared she might sink onto the bed itself. She did not dare to raise her eyes to his. Ranulph lowered his arm. He cleared his throat. After the second attempt he said huskily. 'I fear I have detained you, ma'am. My mother must have been awaiting us these twenty minutes past.'

She could not trust her own voice. All she could manage was a shaky inclination of her head. She passed from the room, sure that every inch of her skin was on fire.

Chapter Seventeen

After the meeting in the library which had so affected her composure, Louise kept to her apartment in the East wing as much as she possibly could. Her excuse – that she had no wish to intrude on family meals now that Cressida Henshaw was present to provide company for Lady Trent – was swept aside. Nor could she continue to decline once Mrs Henshaw had departed for her own home. To do so could only offend a lady who had been kindness itself to her.

Therefore whenever she must descend from her rooms, she made sure to take the narrow, twisting stair opposite her door. As Sir Ranulph always used the elegant flight rising from the entrance hall she was confident of avoiding him. The only drawback, of course, was that the route led her past the library. If its door stood open she would linger in the passage, trying to hear if there was any movement in the room. She hurried past only if none emerged.

Two days later her ears betrayed her and she saw him again. He emerged from the library holding two leather volumes as she reached the foot of the stairs. He halted abruptly and regarded her with raised brows. She stammered, much to her chagrin, some sort of excuse she could not afterwards remember. He bowed, his greeting cold but perfectly correct. Her head averted, she hurried past him, painfully conscious that no hint remained of the laughter and approachability she had seen during their exploration of the metamorphic furniture.

It took some hours for her strength of character to revive. The moment of stunning emotion by the chair-bed reared up in her memory. Only by the most rigid exercise of self-control could she conduct herself at dinner as if it had never occurred.

After a sleepless night, she rose with heavy eyes. The small hours had been fraught with lectures on the idiocy of permitting her mind to dwell on whether he, a man of the world, had considered she, a woman of sensible years, to have been ridiculously missish at finding herself beside a bed with a man. All to no effect. She had grown quite hot at the mere thought that he might have done so. At least, that, she told herself, was the cause. Nothing more. Certainly not anything more intimate, more ... no, such thoughts were impossible. Imprudent. Imperilling.

The morning light made it easier to believe it was a nonsensical way to behave. Easier to think she would not succumb to such idiocy, nor let him see she was at all affected by him.

Strong though her resolution was, she could not bring herself to risk another encounter by the library. She took to traversing the corridors leading past the bedchambers to descend by the main stairs once she was certain Sir Ranulph would have long before deserted his apartment. The same did not apply to his valet. Late one morning he emerged into the corridor as she was making her way to her ladyship's bright sitting room at the southern corner of the house. The man flattened himself against the wall, drawing in the tailcoat he was carrying and regarding her with such amazement that she coloured. The scarcely-hidden wave of disapproval that replaced that expression could only mean he thought her about to enter the master's bedchamber. Hurrying past him with only the barest acknowledgement, she vowed she would never again attempt that route. Not even if it obliged her to spend every waking hour in her own apartment.

For the remainder of the day she blushed every time she remembered the incident. Gossip in the servants' hall must be rife. She could not bear to think what they might have concluded.

Self-recrimination dogged her. She swung from embarrassment to anger and back again. He should not affect her mood the way he did. His mother was content to have her living there so he should not demur. The frigidity of a mere man must not... *did not* unsettle her. Try as she might she could not stop castigating herself for behaving like a Bath miss, not a woman of mature years. As often as she could without seeming to be overly anxious to move, she enquired of Lady Trent how the repairs to the Dower House roof were progressing. But she miscalculated.

'My dear,' Lady Trent laughed. 'One might almost think you find Crestings unpleasant.'

'Oh, no, ma'am. It's a delightful house. It's only that... that I fear I am imposing on Sir Ranulph.'

'Do not concern yourself, my dear. I am sure he is perfectly happy to have you here now he has seen how much Christopher has taken to you.'

Delighted, Louise lodged the compliment into her memory. 'He has, hasn't he? I would not have him forget Amelia but it is a relief that he has stopped searching for her every day.' A note of sadness entered her words. 'In fact he only asks for her now if he takes a tumble or hurts himself some other way.'

Stephanie Trent reached forward a hand. 'Do not distress yourself, my dear. Her memory is bound to fade – he is only three, after all. I am sure when he is older he will want to know all about her. It will be a comfort to him to have you there to answer him.' Her gaze rested on Louise's averted face, noticing the flush that had brushed her cheeks and the moisture gathering in her eyes. 'Do you, perhaps, have a portrait of her? Something you could show him?'

The moisture overflowed. 'Papa commissioned one of us both for Mama – to commemorate their silver wedding anniversary.' A finger wiped a tear from under her lashes. 'He took it down when Amelia ran away. I don't know if... if it still exists.'

'I'm sure he would not have damaged a gift to your Mama. It would be too unkind.'

Unspoken words hung between them. Stephanie Trent's next comment showed she had quite understood. 'Perhaps your Mama had it safe before he could think of it.'

A brave smile rewarded her effort. 'I think you may be right. Mama was very attached to it.' She paused, searching her memory. 'There... there may be one of Amelia at Stapley Hall. Now I think of it, I'm almost certain I saw one in Mr Aveley's study when the housekeeper was showing me round.'

'Then you should go over and collect it. It can hang in the nursery if you think it would not distress the child.'

'Would not Sir Ranulph object to hanging a portrait of a complete stranger in his house?'

'My dear, he is not such a monster!' There was concern on her features. 'You cannot hold him in much regard to think so.'

'Oh no, ma'am. It is only that...' Her words faded.

Stephanie Trent pleated the frill at her cuff. 'Ranulph can appear to be a trifle... standoff-ish. I know he holds *you* in the highest regard.'

Louise wished she could believe it. If she had heard it after the day in the library, she might have, but since then he had been as stiff and unyielding as at their first meeting when he had brought her the dreadful news. Nor had he shown any affection to Christopher. Quite the reverse. His orders had been specific and severe. The child was to be kept to the house and the immediate gardens. He was not to be taken into the farther grounds and certainly not to the village. Had it not been such a preposterous notion she could have almost believed he wanted him hidden from sight.

Lady Trent was speaking. 'If tomorrow is as mild as today, we shall drive over to Stapley and collect the portrait. I'm sure Kirkby can be spared from the roofing to hang it for us.'

So it was that the Trents' landau drew through the gates of Stapley Hall shortly after noon the following day. The wheels had barely ceased turning before the housekeeper hurried out of the house with Jedburgh hobbling behind her.

'Oh, miss, we're right glad to see you. Is there any more news of the house?'

Louise had been so wrapped up in her own feelings, her own careering emotions, that she had quite failed to consider Stapley's future. 'I am so sorry, Mrs Nairn, but I have none. Sir Ranulph has not mentioned it to me.'

The housekeeper's eyes lifted to Lady Trent. 'Perhaps, ma'am ...' Her hands clasped together against her bodice.

'I must disappoint you too, I'm afraid. Be assured, though, that I shall ask my son what his plans are before he returns to London tomorrow.'

In the midst of the staff's distress, Louise's heart thumped. Was she glad he was leaving, or was she not? The answer eluded her. She forced her attention back to the anxious housekeeper. 'Mrs Nairn, if I recall correctly, there is a portrait of Mrs Aveley in the house. We thought Master Christopher might like it for the nursery.'

'Yes, ma'am, there is. Mr Aveley is in there at present.'

'Mr Philip Aveley?' Lady Trent said.

'Yes, ma'am. Oh, but where are my manners – will you not step inside? Jedburgh will bring some refreshment to the parlour, I'm sure.'

She opened the carriage door herself and let down the step. Lady Trent rose and alighted, leaning on the housekeeper's shoulder. With Louise following, she entered the house, looking about her.

'I've not had occasion to come here before. What a very pleasant residence it is, to be sure.'

'It is that, ma'am. That's why we're hoping Sir Ranulph will keep it in the family. Master Kit would be sure to love it just like his dear departed Pa did.'

Louise left Lady Trent doing her best to reassure the house-keeper and made her way to the library. Philip Aveley was standing by the wide bank of bookshelves, running his finger along the leather spines.

'Miss Devreaux.' He turned, flushing slightly. 'I didn't hear you arrive.' He bowed and lifted the two books in his right hand. 'I remember some of these. Mama used to read them to us. Gerard was a fine one for reading too.' He replaced them on the shelf. 'Have you brought Kit with you?'

'I'm afraid not. Sir Ranulph —' She broke off to choose her words with care. 'Is anxious to keep him at Crestings.'

'I'm sure he is.' Philip took a turn about the room, his face troubled. After several moments while Louise studied his agitation in some surprise, he turned to her. 'Miss Devreaux, may I speak frankly?'

'Of course, but I cannot imagine what you might wish to say.'

'No. I would hope not. The thought is not one any decent woman would foster.' He bit his lip. 'Miss Devreaux, I am afraid for Christopher.'

'Afraid? Whatever for? He is well. Apart from a slight recurrence of the fever.'

'It's Trent who concerns me. If he is keeping him close … hidden from sight … there may be — I'm sure there is, a reason. A reason one would not care to own.'

'A reason? What ever can you mean?' She steadied herself with a hand on the door frame.

Philip walked to her and drew her into the room, closing the door after peering into the hall outside. 'I fear he has designs on his life. I believe he has already attempted it.'

'Oh, what nonsense. He has hardly seen him.'

'But consider... where was Kit taken ill? And when? As soon as he was in his custody at Crestings. There had been no such problem here. And you saw how he improved when you brought him back.'

'You are wrong. That was the sugar plums. The ones – I must say – that you gave him. He had gobbled them all.'

'Something he's done before. And to no ill effect.' Deep lines of concern marked his face. 'And now you say the fever has returned.'

His accusation perturbed her. Her brows drew together. 'Whyever would Sir Ranulph do what you suggest?'

'Because if Christopher dies, he will inherit Stapley.'

She gasped. 'Surely not. You are the late Mr Aveley's nearest relative. It would come to you.'

'That is what one would think but it is not so.' He took another turn about the room, rubbing his hands. 'You must know that Gerard and I quarrelled. A trifling matter only, but –' He stopped walking. 'Did it not strike you as strange that Trent was chosen as guardian instead of me?'

'I must admit it did surprise me. You are closer to Christopher than he. I would have thought –'

'It did not surprise me.' His hasty words broke in. 'Trent made it his business to enlarge a sibling's spat into a major crime. He leant on Gerry to change his Will into his favour, not mine.'

Louise felt as if the floor had heaved under her feet. 'You must be mistaken,' she said. 'I know Sir Ranulph is... is autocratic but he cannot have such a... such an evil intent as you suggest.' She walked slowly to the desk and sank on the chair pulled out before it.

'You do not know him, ma'am. Not well. Have you not found him a cold, decisive individual? One who does not suffer to have his will opposed?'

His words struck a chord in her but she still protested. 'Yes, but I cannot believe you. No-one with such an amiable mother could contemplate so dishonourable behaviour.'

'You did not know his father. He was such a man − although he kept his dealings from his wife. She will believe them both paragons until her last breath.'

Two strides brought him to her. He grasped her hands. 'Miss Devreaux,' he pleaded, staring deep into her eyes, 'we must save him. Our brother and sister would expect no less.'

She pulled her hands away, rising and brushing past him to stare blindly at the ranks of books. 'No, no you must be mistaken. I cannot believe you.'

'Can't you? Did he try to stop you coming to here today? Or was he pleased?'

She cast over the few words Sir Ranulph had spoken about the visit. He had been in favour of it. Had said it was an excellent idea for Christopher to have a reminder of his Mama. He had even suggested she take time to see if there was a portrait of his father too. The memory sent a chill coursing through her. It was as if he wanted her away from the child for the day.

'I must return. Now! Immediately!' Hurried steps took her to the door. She stopped. 'Please take down the portrait and carry it to the landau.'

Without thanking him she walked as calmly as she could to the drawing room. Lady Trent was sipping a cup of tea.

'I've found the portrait, ma'am. Mr Aveley is lifting it to the carriage for me. Shall we go?'

Lady Trent lowered her cup. 'But Mrs Nairn has brought us some delicious almond tarts. Do try one. I'm sure she will be most disappointed if you do not.'

In the face of this, she could not refuse. Louise forced herself
to enter the charming room and pass anxious minutes eating a
single cake that tasted like ash in her mouth and sipping at tea
that failed to refresh her. When Philip Aveley entered to say the
portrait was safely stowed she had an excellent opportunity to
suggest again that they leave. This time Lady Trent offered no
resistance. The leave-taking of Mrs Nairn and Jedburgh further
delayed the departure until Louise felt she would scream at any
moment such was the fear Philip Aveley's words had sown in her
mind.

The carriage pulled away and she realised that Lady Trent was
watching her closely. The older woman leant forward. 'Forgive
me my dear,' she said, her voice low. 'I should have realised how
trying it must be for you to come here. I should not have delayed
our leaving. I do beg your pardon.'

Louise's uneasy conscience made her squirm on the seat.
'Please don't concern yourself, ma'am. I think I must have the
headache starting.'

'Of course.' Stephanie Trent looked unconvinced. 'We shall
soon be home then you may rest.'

Rest was far from Louise's mind. No sooner was she across
Crestings' threshold than she picked up her skirts and flew up to
the nursery without removing her coat and hat. Fear of what she
might find almost overpowered her mind. She flung the door
open. Christopher sat on the floor of the day nursery permitting
Letty to assist him in building a tower of his brightly-painted
blocks. His face was no longer flushed and the eyes he turned to
her were bright and clear. Hands on the floor, he clambered inel-
egantly to his feet and rushed to clasp his arms round her knees.

'Master Christopher looks to have recovered from his fever,'
she said, lifting him up to cuddle.

Mabson bustled in from the night nursery, folding a small
nightgown in half and quarters against her wide bosom. 'He has

that,' she growled. 'No thanks to Sir Ranulph. He should have stayed where he was. Not be dragged from gate to post the way he has been. We'll be lucky if he settles again.'

Succumbing to Christopher's urgent entreaties to build his blocks into a tower, she removed her coat and hat and applied herself to obliging him while soothing the ruffled feathers of his nurse with a calmness she did not feel.

When at long last she regained the privacy of her bedchamber, scarcely knowing what to believe, she ate hardly a mouthful of the dinner Lady Trent had sent up to her. The lamb cutlets cooled in a piquant sauce that solidified around them. The ham and veal patties and the apple and barberry pie would have been better left in the kitchen. She paced the floor turning Philip Aveley's words over and over in her mind and comparing them with what she had seen and learned of Ranulph Trent. Her mind was no easier by the time she undressed and climbed into bed. Too stunned to toss on her pillows, she lay there, motionless, her lower lip caught between her teeth. Questions tumbled through her mind and drove sleep from her. Not until the cold, small hours of the morning did her fears dissolve and she could drift into sleep.

Chapter Eighteen

The next few days before the rafters and tiles on the Dower House roof were repaired passed in constraint, formality and a marked reluctance for both Sir Ranulph and Louise to exchange more than the absolute minimum of speech. Stephanie Trent, who had permitted the smallest germ of hope to flourish in her bosom regarded the pair with puzzled eyes.

'I don't know what's preventing the boy,' Marius declared to her one evening when his nephew had ridden over to see friends and Louise has absented herself from the drawing room. 'There's nothing to complain about in her. Her breeding's fine. She behaves like a sensible woman. Quite up to snuff. And it's not as if she's an antidote.'

'Marius – what a thing to say! She is far from being an antidote. I think she's very attractive.'

'I dare say, but a pretty face ain't the only thing, y'know.' He drew a snuff box from his pocket and spent more time taking a pinch than was entirely necessary. 'I was never one for the parson's shackle m'self.' He raised his eyes to his sister-in-law. 'You don't suppose Ranulph's the same, do you? He's had his pick of the field for over ten years now and never chosen a one.'

Stephanie Trent plaited her fingers. 'I hope not. I'd thought...' Her words faded. She recalled her conversation with her son,

'You must remember Lawrence did not offer for me until he was over forty.'

'Well,' Marius rumbled, 'he'd better apply himself to setting up his nursery. After me it'll be that fellow up in the Midlands who'll inherit if he don't.' The conscious expression on the face opposite spurred him to comment further. 'Not that you and Lawrence didn't do your best, m'dear.'

The memory of a tiny girl who had not lived out the day and a second son who died before his third birthday hung between them.

'Sorry,' he said. 'Didn't think, m'dear. Not the thing to have mentioned. Not at all.' He cleared his throat gruffly. 'Shall I have a word with him? You know the sort of thing – what Larry would be sure to have said by now.'

'Please don't. If there is any sort of . . . attraction it would only set his back up. We must leave it to him. And to fortune.'

'Huh. Never did any good in my opinion, leaving things to fortune. But if you say not, then mumchance it is for me.'

Kirkby's arrival two days later to announce – with a mixture of pride and anxiety while he inched his hat-brim round between his fingers as was his habit when nervous – that the roof was repaired if his master would care to inspect it, was greeted with relief by two of the household and regret by those of the staff who had been indulging in a considerable amount of gossip on the likelihood of the master taking up with the young master's aunt.

On the first fine morning, the lady herself accompanied Stephanie Trent to the Dower House to choose, at her invitation, which of the bedchambers she would prefer. Sir Ranulph rode beside the open landau, carefully surveying Crestings' grounds and nodding to those of the workers he saw hedging and ditching along the way, rather than speaking to either of the carriage's occupants. He reined in at the pretty mansion's door.

It swung open and Dora Lanthwaite appeared, explaining she had seen them turn in through the pillars marking the start of a short carriage-drive. Her husband hurried to Sir Ranulph's side.

'It all be done, sir. And the missus had two girls up from the village to give the house a good go over. Like a dose of salts they've been – if you'll pardon the expression. I think her ladyship will be pleased.'

Sir Ranulph dismounted and handed him the reins. He walked to the landau, too late to beat Jupp to assist his mother to alight. He was obliged, therefore, to extend his hand to Louise. She descended, her eyes averted and her words of thanks barely audible. Two swift paces took her away from him. She paused, surveying the house before her and wondering if she ought to comment on it.

If she could have chosen the style of residence in which to set up home on her own, Crestings' Dower House would have been it. It was an elegant establishment, in the Queen Anne style, with a pleasing symmetry to its tall paned windows and central door. To the right was a small wing and to the left a covered walkway to a low building.

'Charming, isn't it?' Lady Trent said. 'We have Mr Wren's original plans, you know. Ranulph keeps them in the library at Crestings for safety.'

Louise, who had never seen any plans by anyone, let alone by Sir Christopher Wren, was moved to agree. 'It most certainly is. I cannot thank you enough for allowing me to stay here.'

'Nonsense,' Stephanie Trent moved past her son who had moved to the shallow steps, 'we are delighted to see how swiftly Christopher has taken to you. Aren't we, dearest?'

Sir Ranulph bowed. 'Indeed, ma'am, we are.'

Refusing to discover whether his expression supported his words or not, Louise inclined her head briefly and quickly followed her hostess into the entrance hall. A wide tiled, passage divided the house, running straight to a rear door with glass panes that permitted a brief view of trees in the garden beyond. Mrs Lanthwaite ushered Lady Trent past the doors standing open to the two rooms at the front of the house and into one that overlooked the garden.

'Here you be, ma'am. It's all in readiness for you. Me and Bertha Oakham's two eldest spent all yesterday in here dusting and polishing'

The comment had Lady Trent murmuring about the kindness of the wife of Mr Marius Trent's coachman. Following behind, Louise could see that considerable energy had been expended. The room positively glowed in the mid-day sun that shone through bright windows. The newly-painted walls were devoid of any paintings but the wood furniture standing against them gleamed. The satin and damask on the upholstered sofas and chairs looked fresh and bright.

Lady Trent ran a hand along the back of the nearest chair. 'I am so glad we set the Holland covers about, Mrs Lanthwaite.'

'And me too, ma'am. And you look here,' the housekeeper said, surging past Louise towards one of the rooms at the front.

Louise followed the two women into the hall. Sir Ranulph had not entered the drawing room. Rather he had wandered through the door opposite into what Louise could see was a library. He emerged, bowing briefly.

'You are pleased, ma'am?'

'Very, thank you, sir. It is a delightful house.' Not daring to linger, she hurried after his mother.

Mrs Lanthwaite would not be diverted until she had displayed every room on the ground floor and every apartment on the upper one. By the time Louise had chosen one with a view of the garden as her bedchamber, her nerves were at screaming point. She could only be thankful they had been spared a tour of the attics and the kitchen wing. Sir Ranulph's features had not softened once. Try as she might, she could only ascribe this to his disapproval of her. She still shied from attributing to him the sinister object Philip Aveley had described. The evidence he had quoted was too little. Too flimsy. It was impossible to reach a judgement on it.

She was relieved when the inspection ended and she could climb into the landau to return to Crestings to pack her belongings. 'If you are agreeable, ma'am, I shall remove to the Dower House tomorrow with Christopher.'

'Of course you may, my dear, but there is no rush.'

Sir Ranulph, riding closer to the carriage than before, said, 'I shall ask Wadden to bring down your trunk.'

'Who is Wadden?' his mother asked before she could respond.

'I've employed him to work at the Dower House. Lanthwaite is too advanced in years for any heavy work.'

'There cannot be much heavy work to be done, dear. We are only two women and the nursery.'

'If there isn't, he can turn his attention to the garden. From what I saw of it, it stands in need of work.'

Lady Trent considered. 'You are right, of course. Your Grandmama had a delightful rose garden there but there is no sign of it now.'

'Then he can attend to restoring it.'

Jasper Wadden, when he appeared, did not much resemble a gardener. In Louise's opinion – unversed as she was in matters of staff employment – his eyes betrayed a watchfulness that was unsettling and bore none of the openness she had seen in her father's gardeners. Nor was he much in evidence when there was any lifting to be done. He had a tendency to spend his time walking the boundaries of the Dower House's small park. He made it his business to be first to take hold of the bridles of the few visitors who rode to the house, something that, from their expressions, clearly irritated Lanthwaite and Jupp.

Philip Aveley was not any more comfortable with him. He arrived two days after Louise had moved in. Dismounting he handed over his reins with reluctance.

'Who's that fellow?' he asked her when Lanthwaite had shown him onto the small terrace at the rear of the house where Letty was playing with a muffled-up Christopher.

'Someone Sir Ranulph has employed to help with the heavy lifting. And work in the garden.'

'Lifting? Garden?' His eyes on Letty and Christopher, he lowered his voice. 'He's no gardener. I doubt he could tell a rose from a weed. What is his name?'

'Wadden. Er…Jasper Wadden.' She looked down to twist her cuff. 'I am concerned that you find his appearance here strange.' She raised troubled eyes to his. 'I must admit I have had doubts about his abilities. He arrived so quickly and has done little but walk the grounds.'

'My dear Miss Devreaux, leave it to me. I shall make it my business to discover all about him. He cannot be unknown in the area if he was recruited here.' He stayed only a few moments longer and, after remarking how pale Christopher looked, departed.

It was another five days before he rode up to the house again. Contriving to walk alone with Louise along the overgrown garden paths, his words were laced with anxiety.

'My dear ma'am, it is as I feared.' He cast an anxious glance around them. 'Wadden is known to the Magistrate in Gloucester. I have a connection in the town and he discovered it for me.' He took her hand. 'I fear he has been branded for violence.'

The words struck a chill through Louise's body. 'I cannot believe it. Sir Ranulph would never employ someone like that.'

'Would he not? Could he not have a purpose too dreadful to contemplate?'

'You must be mistaken. You must.' She walked away from him, twisting her hands.

'How has the child been since his return? Can you tell me that he has been in health?'

'He has – of course he has.' She paused.

'What? Ma'am, I beg of you, tell me.' He grasped her hands and forced her to face him.

'He has been a trifle unwell these past two days.'

'What sort of unwell?'

'Sickly. He clasps his stomach and cries.'

'Poison. It must be.'

'No. No.' She pulled her hands free. 'I will *not* believe it. The notion is quite ridiculous.' She could not stand still. She paced the narrow path, unmoved by the rose trails catching at the hem of her gown.

'Miss Devreaux, I beseech you.' Philip hurried after her. 'You do not know Trent as I do. Believe what I say. Please. Help me save Kit. Help me. Do it for the memory of your sister.'

Accusations and denials tumbled in Louise's head. She could not... would not countenance his indictment. But then... but then...

'What can I do?' she begged at last. 'Where can I go with him? My father has banned him from my home and Sir Ranulph would discover us at Stapley within the hour.'

'Have you no other family? Think, ma'am. Kit's life might depend on it.'

She raised a hand to her forehead. 'I have... oh, I have a grandmother. My mother's mother.'

'Where is she?'

'She lives in... in Chippenham.'

'Chippenham? That's on the way to Bath. It can't be more than thirty or so miles. We can easily be there in a day.' He possessed her hands again. 'Let me take you to safety. To your grandmother. He will never find you there.' Her hesitation spurred him on. 'For all we know he might have some dread deed planned for tonight. Or tomorrow. Who's to say? Who's to know what orders he has given that fellow Wadden?' His fingers squeezed hers. 'Madam, say you'll let me carry Kit to safety before it's too late. Imagine how you will feel if – when – the inevitable happens.'

The thought was too dreadful to bear. 'Oh, if you are sure. Can you be sure?'

'As sure as I am that I breathe.' He raised her hands and kissed them. 'Thank you ma'am. Thank you from the bottom of my heart.' He looked into her eyes. 'I shall come for you tomorrow morning. Can you be awake and ready by five?'

'Five? Only if I don't go to sleep.'

'Then promise me, ma'am, you will keep watch. Keep a vigil. Together we can save him. I shall not fail. Shall you?'

Amelia's face swam in her mind. 'No. I shall not fail.'

Chapter Nineteen

The waiting was awful. Alone in her bedchamber Louise sat by the fire forcing herself to read. The words of Mr Coleridge's poem rippled before her aching eyes. She could summon no interest at all in the fate of the mariner or of his albatross. She laid down the book. The handles of her portmanteau poked out from under the quilt on her bed. It was packed and ready, holding the most important items of her belongings and the few of Christopher's she had managed to collect without attracting Mabson's notice.

That subterfuge had sickened her. Only the threat to Christopher had forced her on. Many a time she had faltered, questioning how real it was. At the bottom of her mind she could not bring herself to believe it. No man, no man *worthy* of the name would be capable of such an atrocity, would he? Were there such people in the world? Her experience was limited. A fiercely restrictive father had ensured that. Should she, even now, hold back and flee to him instead, risking that he would not close his door upon her and the child? Her head and the book drooped. No, she could not chance it.

She could not sit. The book was cast aside. She rose and paced the floor, wincing whenever her foot caused a board to squeak. Questions, none of which she could answer, fought in her head. How she wished Lizzie was there to soothe her headache.

Lizzie! She sat up quickly. In all her anxiety about Christopher she had forgotten to take care that her maid attracted no blame. She hurried to the dressing table to write to Lady Trent to explain that Lizzie knew nothing of her flight. She dragged a page from the centre drawer and opened the standish holding the ink and quill in front of the looking glass. The pen hovered over the paper ready to tell the reasons for her decision to leave. It stayed motionless. A drop of ink blotted the clean surface. How did one tell a lady as charming and gentle as Lady Trent that one suspected her son of dire plans against a child? There was no possible way. She could not repay her many kindnesses in such a fashion.

She laid down the quill to hide her face in her trembling hands. There were too many and too few words. For several moments she could not think, then drawing on what surely must be her final strength, she wrote only that Lizzie was not involved and begging Lady Trent to permit her to stay at Crestings until she, Louise, returned. The note was folded, sealed and addressed. It looked so innocuous propped against the looking glass. Nothing gave away its dreadful content.

Louise resumed her seat by the fire, far too anxious to read.

The hours dragged by in mental agony until the hands on the small ormolu clock she had borrowed from the Blue Parlour showed her the moment had come. A chill of apprehension gripped her. Her hat and pelisse lay on the bed. The plume on the hat looked suddenly frivolous, rather than enchanting. She put it on and tied the ribbons in a plain bow. The sleeves of her coat struck cold on her arms. She pulled it up and buttoned it to the throat. Her fingers trembled in her gloves. A fresh candle stood on the nightstand. She wished she had been able to obtain a lantern but that would have meant braving the kitchens or the stables and she could have no acceptable excuse for being discovered in either place. How she would manage to carry the child, her bag and a candle to light her way down the back stairs, she did not know. She must find a way. She must.

The candle, held to the fire, soon caught alight, its tiny flame flickering. She cast a final glance round the pretty room, knowing she could have been happy there with – her breath caught. She would not think of him. Nor of the light in his eyes when he had unfolded the steps from the library table. Cherishing such memories of someone who threatened her darling Christopher was impossible. She opened the bedchamber door.

It squealed on its hinges. She froze. Her heart thumped in her throat. Had anyone heard? Her breathing shallow, she waited.

Silence. No sound reached her straining ears. She hefted the portmanteau and trod along the passage. Not a single lamp brightened the stairs to the nursery floor. With one foot on the bottom step, she paused. Even if she left the bag here, it must be impossible to carry it and the child and the candle. The answer was so obvious a flash of irritation shot through her. The bag must be taken to the outside door. She would collect it once she had Christopher. Then she could abandon the candle and continue her way by the moon and starlight. It took her several fearsome minutes to find her way through the servants' area to the rear door. She deposited the bag by at its foot and stared at it. What if someone should wake and chance upon it? Should she open the door and hide it outside? The stout wood bore iron strapping and a massive lock. Opening it would surely create a noise. She slid the bag into the shadows as best she could and ascended four flights to the nursery, shielding the guttering candle with her hand.

The landing was wrapped in stygian darkness. She paused, straining her ears for any sounds. A slow rhythmic wheeze convinced her that Mabson was wrapped in a deep sleep. Trusting Letty was lost in dreams of princes and castles, or possibly, the second under-footman, she crept towards the door of

Christopher's room. It opened silently. A slight draft fluttered the candle flame. She shielded it with her hand, praying it would not go out. In the dim firelight, the screen Mabson had insisted be placed to shelter the cot from treacherous currents of fresh air barred her way. She crept round it.

Christopher lay fast asleep, his fair curls rumpled on the pillow and his thumb in his mouth. A sweep of dark lashes curved onto his cheeks. Her heart constricted. How could she fail to protect him?

She stood the candle on the chest of drawers by the wall. Murmuring soft platitudes, she lifted him from his cot, wrapping his blankets around his warm little body. He stirred, opened his eyes, smiled sweetly and resumed his slumber. She collected the candle and, treading carefully to avoid catching her shoes in her hem, trod back down the stairs.

He was not heavy but holding him with only one arm soon had it aching like fire. Her steps faltered once or twice but they brought her eventually to the door. Panic rose in her throat. Where was the key? Why had she not looked for it before? Her eyes darted around the wall by the frame. There. There it was, on a hook level with the latch. The candle must be set down. Her knees ached with the effort of keeping her balance while she lowered it to the floor. Christopher's weight burnt more fire into her arm. She straightened, supporting herself with a hand against the wall. Her arm must be relieved. Upright again, she shifted him across her body to the other side. The relief was palpable. She twisted her arm, trying to banish the ache, and collected the key from its hook.

Christopher stirred and moaned. It was all Louise could do not to cry out. He wriggled in his blanket nest, muttering baby nonsense until his thumb found its way into his mouth. In a few moments he settled and she breathed again.

She leant backwards to balance him against her need to bend forward to unlock the door. The key turned smoothly but the drawn bolts shrieked in their brackets. She thought she might faint. That must not be. Christopher depended on her. Her heart thumped. Her breath laboured with effort and trepidation. She wished, most forcefully, that Sir Ranulph had not proven to be such a threat.

Recovering her portmanteau, she stepped outside, her knees aching from her struggles. A long strip of cloud hid the moon, casting deep shadows round the house. A shape emerged from the shelter of a window embrasure. Only the most rigid control stopped her from shrieking.

'You've come,' Philip Aveley whispered. 'I knew you would not fail. Here,' he reached out his arms, 'let me take the child. We must be away from here as swiftly as we can.'

'No, he might wake and cry. You take my portmanteau.'

He grasped it and strode off, soon covering the ground. Louise clutched Christopher in both arms and followed him.

The walk over the dark grass was not long. The clouds streaking the moon passed over and she could see her way quite clearly. Relieved not to face the risk stumbling over an unseen tussock, she tried to ignore the heavy dew that was soaking into her half boots. She took careful note of where she trod, trying to keep her shoes clear of the longest, dampest leaves.

'Here,' Philip called softly through the night. 'Over here.'

She looked up. A gig stood concealed in a copse of young trees, its horse tethered to a branch. She hurried towards it as fast as she could with Christopher heavy in her arms.

'Give him to me and get up,' he commanded. 'I'll pass him to you. Be quick. We cannot be certain Wadden is not prowling the grounds.'

The urgency in his voice, and the thought of discovery, had her passing the child over. He whimpered and she collected her skirts and climbed onto the seat as quickly as she could. Christopher was deposited onto her lap with more vigour than consideration. He stirred again. A muffled wail emerged from around his sucked thumb.

'Shh. Shh, my love.' She rocked him in his blankets. 'Hush now.'

Philip hurried round the gig.

'My bag. Don't forget my bag,' she whispered.

He drew a sharp breath was drawn in through his teeth. Striding back, he collected the portmanteau and dumped it beside her toes, squashing them. In seconds he had released the horse, jumped up beside her and had the gig moving smartly away from the house along one of the lanes through the park.

The motion brought Christopher fully awake. A little hand struggled from the enveloping blanket to rub at his eyes. 'Mabbie,' he wailed.

'Shh, my love,' Louise repeated. 'We're going on an adventure.' She held him closer, alarmed by the gig's increasing pace. 'Can you not go more slowly?' she breathed. 'We shall be shaken to pieces.'

'When we are free of the estate I shall.' Philip's voice was clipped. Almost harsh.

'We aren't going all the way in this are we? Christopher will be frozen before we are a mile down the road.'

'No, of course not.' He reached an arm over the backrest and dragged a blanket forward. 'Use that,' he said. 'We'll stop at Stapley and change into a carriage. He'll be warm enough 'til then.'

'Stapley! It's ten miles. He *will* be frozen. And it will be the first place Sir Ranulph will look for us.'

'Don't fret,' he said tersely, guiding the horse through a low gate standing open at the bottom of the lane. 'We shall not be there long.'

'But the people – Mrs Nairn, Jedburgh – they will see us.'

'No they won't. I've greased their palms too well.'

'What? Oh, I cannot credit that. They're too devoted to Christopher.'

'Ha. You would be surprised what a couple of gold boys can do. I told them they could use it to visit their families.'

Louise lapsed into silence. She could not believe the couple could be so easily bought. 'Would it not have been better to admit them to our confidence? That must have been a better way.'

'No,' he countered. 'It would not. The less anyone knows about this, the better.'

'But –'

'Trust me,' he all but snapped. 'I know what is best.'

The force of his words unsettled her. She clasped Christopher tightly, thinking. The night was dark, the lane hard to see. And their flight was dangerous. At any moment Mabson or Letty might enter the night nursery and discover it. Sir Ranulph could at this very moment be swift on their heels. Mr Aveley must be conscious of it. That must be the cause of his terseness. She persuaded herself all would be well when they reached safety.

No pounding hooves sounded behind them and they reached Stapley as dawn was breaking. Driving the gig into the gravelled circle before the main door, Philip dragged on the reins. The horse dug in its hind legs and skidded to a halt. The abruptness flung Louise forwards, her grasp on Christopher slackening.

'Good grief, sir, take care.' She looked around. 'Where's the coach?'

'I don't know. I'll ask Vintry.'

'Who is Vintry?'

'My groom. I told him to have the carriage here.' He jumped down. 'Come – let me help you inside while I find out. This wind is biting and as you said, the boy must be cold.'

Louise handed Christopher down to Philip and scrambled down, whisking the hem of her pelisse from where it caught on the wheel. The front door opened and a man of dour demeanour appeared.

'Vintry,' Philip said, 'where's the carriage?'

The man looked assessingly at Louise then turned to Philip who continued before he could speak, 'I told you to have it here by now. Take the gig round to the stables. I'll be there as soon as I've seen Miss Devreaux settled.' He put a hand under Louise's elbow. 'Come inside, ma'am.' He helped her up the shallow steps past the stationary Vintry. 'Why don't you put the little chap into one of the beds? He's still the best part asleep.'

'The bed will be cold. I'll keep him with me.'

'It ain't cold, ma'am,' Vintry said. 'I had the girl light a fire in the room with the biggest bed.'

'Girl?' Philip barked. 'What girl?'

'I dunno, sir. A skivvy I think.'

Philip drew a deep breath. 'That's good,' he said to Louise. 'She can make you a dish of tea. I'll see to it now.' He opened the door to the drawing room. 'See,' he said, pointing. 'There's a fire in here too. You will be quite comfortable.'

Louise stepped into the room. 'Do make haste,' she called over her shoulder. 'Sir Ranulph could even now be after us.'

'Have no fear, ma'am. I am here to protect you.'

'And Christopher.'

'And him, indeed.'

The child stirred, whimpering in his sleep. 'I'll settle him on the sofa. He will be warm and comfortable there.' She wrapped her fingers about a hand. 'Oh, the poor little man, his fingers are like icicles.' Her voice hardened. 'I hope he has taken no harm.'

Philip drew a quick breath, seeming about to speak but did not. After a moment, he smiled and said, 'You are so thoughtful, ma'am. Christopher is fortunate to have you to care for him. Take him closer to the fire, he will soon recover. If you will excuse me now, there are things I must attend to.' He bowed and made for Vintry hovering by the door.

As his master passed him, the man muttered, 'No-one said nothing about sending off the skivvy.'

The door closed and Louise heard no more. In the silence, disturbed only by Christopher's little moans, she became aware that her arms were aching. She carried him to the sofa by the hearth and gently lowered him onto it. His breathing was regular. His small face showed no distress, the dark lashes still lay closed on his soft cheeks. How could he have slept through all the travails of the night when her own heart was pounding so loud he must have heard it?

The armchair opposite him invited her to sit. She yawned, fatigue suddenly overcoming her. Not one second of sleep had she had that night. She untied her bonnet and placed it on the arm. Her eyelids fluttered lower. Her pulse slowed. In moments she was as deeply asleep as Christopher.

Philip Aveley entering with a small tray bearing a cup and saucer, a teapot and a small jug stopped on the threshold. He frowned. Louise lay asleep in her chair. That was no part of his plan. He carried the tray to the table in the centre of the room and poured out some tea.

'Miss Devreaux. Miss Devreaux.' He shook her shoulder. 'You cannot sleep now. Here, I have brought you some tea.'

Louise struggled up. 'I am so sorry. Has the coach arrived? Is it time to go?'

He shook his head. 'No, not yet but Vintry assures me it is on its way. Meanwhile drink this. It will revive you.'

He poured her a cup, not bothering to strain it. Dark fragments of tealeaves floated on the surface of the brown liquid. She took the cup from him and sipped. Holding it away, she examined the contents, grimacing.

'What a strange taste. Quite unusual.'

'I found the tea-caddy in a cupboard,' he said, quickly. 'At the back. I assume it has been there for some time. Would you prefer me to find you some wine? I'm sure I can. Gerard liked his wine.'

'No. No, this will suffice. Thank you.' She took another sip. 'I will be much better when the coach arrives.'

'I'm sure it will be soon.'

He stood beside her until she had finished the drink. 'Some more, Miss Devreaux?'

'No, thank you.' A yawn stretched her mouth. 'Oh, I beg your pardon. How rude of me.'

'Pray do not concern yourself. It has been a long night. Nor is it yet over. Be easy, ma'am. Be sure I will tell you the second the coach arrives.'

She yawned again and relaxed in the chair. Her head drooped against the cushioned back. He stayed beside her, watching. At last her eyes closed and her breathing turned as steady as the child's. He moved about the room. She did not wake. 'A few more minutes,' he said. 'Just to be safe.'

An hour later hooves pounding across the gravel woke her. She started up, swaying as she rose. For a moment she was sure she would fall to the floor. She steadied herself and hurried to the window. She pulled at the curtains. Astride his horse, the early sun shining on its coat, was Ranulph Trent.

'My God,' she cried. 'He is come. He is come.' She turned, ready to seize Christopher. She stifled a scream. The sofa was empty. The child was gone.

The door flung back on its hinges, banging against a book-case placed too close. 'Where is he?' Ranulph Trent demanded, his face thunderous, his hand gripping his riding crop. 'Where is he? What have you done with him, you stupid woman?'

Chapter Twenty

'Done with him? I've done nothing with him.' Louise pointed at the sofa. 'He was here. He must be here.'

'Must be?' Sir Ranulph snorted. 'Why in God's name did you leave Crestings?'

His furious tone and words were not her first concern. 'Never mind that, he must be found. He cannot have gone far. He's only three for Heaven's sake.' She started for the door.

'If he went on his own.'

His words halted her. 'What do you mean?'

'That the child has a decent fortune, of course.'

'One that will become yours if... oh my God, if he comes to harm.' Her eyes blazed. 'What have you done with him?'

'Mine? What mad idea is this? His fortune wouldn't be mine. It goes to Aveley.'

Louise raised a hand to her head. Thoughts whirled inside it. 'No... no, it's you.'

'Who told you that?' He gave a bark of humourless laughter. 'Aveley, I suppose.' He swiped his crop at a chair. 'He was lying. Could you not see he was lying? It would be his, not mine.' He turned on his heel. 'That is for later discussion. Finding the child is of the utmost urgency.'

Philip Aveley arrived at the door. 'Trent! You!'

'Where's the child, Aveley?'

'What do you mean?'

Louise ran forward. 'Christopher has gone.'

Philip stared at her, then at the sofa. 'What have you done with him, Trent?'

'Don't seek to blame me. I've but this minute ridden up.'

'So you say.'

'Oh stop arguing, do.' Louise directed her anxious eyes at Philip. 'Where is that man Vintry? It must be he. We must find him.'

'You're distracted. ma'am. Surely the child has wandered about the house. Have you searched the nursery? He might well have gone there, to the place he knows.'

'Of course.' She gathered up the skirts of her pelisse and ran up the stairs calling his name.

In the sitting room Trent and Aveley faced each other. 'If you have harmed the child,' Sir Ranulph snarled, 'I will personally whip you to within an inch of your life. I promise you'll take no profit from him.'

'Keep your threats to yourself, Trent. You may fool women but I know you for what you are.'

'Oh? And what am I? Whatever it is, I am no deceiver of women. And no murderer of children.'

'He's not murdered. What sort of monster do you take me for?'

'The sort who stands in hock to the cent-per-centers.'

'What?' Philip's face whitened. 'Have you been spying on me?'

'Not I. There was no need. Your debts are known in town to anyone who cares to ask.'

'Damn you.' Philip glared at him and flung about the room. His breathing quickened with each stride. He stopped by the fire and swung round. 'What do you know of life? You or anyone like you?' His words ripped out. 'No-one born with a silver spoon – no!' He gave a derisive snort. 'A silver *canteen* in their mouth can have the least notion what it's like to exist on a pittance.'

'Spare me your maudlin whines.' Derision dripped from Sir Ranulph's words. 'You could have lived well enough had you the least smattering of sense. But no, you trod – no, raced down the path to gambling and licentiousness. Gerard knew it. Knew what you were. He didn't trust you with the child.'

'You bastard. I –'

Louise burst into the room. 'I can't find him. He's not in the house. That man Vintry must have him.' She pressed her fingers to her mouth. She swayed. Sir Ranulph reached her in a second, his arm steadying her. 'Be calm, ma'am, I shall recover him.'

Philip Aveley was determined to keep to his plan. 'Then what, Trent?' he demanded. 'Don't think I shall let you have him.'

'Stop! *Stop*, both of you,' Louise all but sobbed. 'I don't know who to believe. We must find him. *I* must find him.'

'Who else is in the house?' Sir Ranulph demanded. 'Apart from this Vintry you mentioned?'

'Um...ah.' Louise tried to think. Her hand strayed to her hair again. 'He said there was a skivvy. I haven't seen her. Have you?' She turned anguished eyes to Aveley.

'No, I haven't. I dare say she has run off.'

'Why on earth would she run off?' Sir Ranulph demanded. 'And where is the housekeeper?'

'He said he gave them some money to visit their families.' She bit her lip. 'I think – I believe he thought them to be in your pay.'

'Did he, by God?' The fury on his face alarmed her. 'Let's find this skivvy.' He pointed his whip at Philip. 'You come too, Aveley. You'll stay under my eye.'

He strode out of the room, ignoring Philip's spluttered protest. Swift steps brought him to the door at the rear of the hall that led to the domestic regions.

A distant commotion greeted them. The closer they came to the back stairs, the louder it grew. Tracking the noise upwards brought them to the linen cupboard. Sir Ranulph unlocked it.

A tear-stained, panicking girl of some fourteen or fifteen years fell into his arms. She wiped a sleeve of a drab gown across her eyes and nose.

For several minutes they could get no sense out of her but eventually, from the comfort of Louise's arms, they had her story. Someone – someone strong and big – had ripped her from her Christian bed, flung a blanket over her head, and bundled her into the cupboard. No, she had not seen them. No, they had not spoken. No, she did *not* know who. Floods of tears resurged. She was an honest maid. She must be returned to her father's home on the instant.

'What vehicles and cattle are there here?' Sir Ranulph demanded.

'There's the gig we came in,' Louise answered over the maid's sobbing head. 'I know not what else there might be.'

'Only my horse,' Philip said. 'In the stable.'

'Where else would it be?' Sir Ranulph shot at him. 'We had best discover if it is still there.' He switched his fierce eyes to Louise. 'Do what you can for her, ma'am. I shall return in a moment.'

He descended the stairs two at a time.

Philip Aveley placed his hand on her arm. 'Have no fear, ma'am. I shall not let him go alone to Christopher.'

He followed Sir Ranulph, leaving Louise patting the shoulder of the sobbing maid and wishing she too could indulge in the luxury of tears.

The gig and its drooping mare was in the stable. Philip's horse was not.

'Ha,' Sir Ranulph barked. 'At least we know your man has him.' Fury narrowed his mouth. Turning on his heel he marched from the stables to his own horse tethered to a bare rose trellis by the house's main door.

'Wait for me,' Philip called. 'I must saddle this nag. I'll not have you go without me.'

Sir Ranulph paused. His inclination had been to leave immediately but that would not serve. God knew what mischief he had arranged. Setting himself to travel the devious byways of Philip's mind, he waited. Whichever road he urged him to take would, he was certain, be the wrong one. He must take care, it was a trick that would only work once. Thereafter he would have no guidance to rely upon. He entered the house, meeting Louise in the hall.

'Aveley's horse has gone so we must assume the blackguard has left. Rest easy, ma'am.' His hand reached out to her. 'He cannot be far. We shall recover the child.' He forced confidence into his tone.

With a bow he was gone, leaving Louise prey to the worst imaginings.

He lingered by the gates until Philip joined him. 'Well? Which way?'

'I don't know. How can I know the man's purpose?'

'Don't try to fool me. It won't work. He's your man. You engineered this. You know where he's taken the boy.'

Aveley looked away. 'Oh, take the road to the left. It leads to Eastcombe.'

'Does it? And why would the villain go there?'

'How should I know what's in his mind?'

'Because you put it there,' Sir Ranulph snapped. 'I think we will head for Stroud. A child is easier to hide in a town than a village. Assuming,' he continued his expression threatening, 'he still breathes.'

He galloped off, obliging Philip to spur his mount to as much speed as its worn-out legs could manage.

They raced through the brightening morning, Sir Ranulph well in the lead, past fields of dozy cows being herded to their milking, and into a village, scattering a clutch of chickens stupid enough to have wandered into their path from a small cottage. A dame, hurrying out of her door, raised her stick and shook it.

'Take you care,' she squawked. 'Take you care.'

Sir Ranulph reined in. 'I beg your pardon, ma'am. Can you tell me if you've seen a rider pass by this morning? With a child on his pommel?'

The woman, well into her sixties to judge by her wrinkles, eyed him and sniffed. 'I don't know as to what the lamb was sat on, but yes. One such went through at first light. Where he is now I don't care to hazard. The way he was pushing his animal he may well be in a ditch. And the lamb with him. With both their necks broke,' she added, her mouth tightening with disapproval.

Sir Ranulph thanked her tersely. He reached into his pocket and tossed her a coin. She caught it with surprising agility and sent them on their way with sharp words to stop trampling her chickens.

An hour further on, both men and horses were labouring. They reached a low inn and a smithy at the edge of a small town. A bay mare stood tethered by the forge, its rear hoof trapped between the smith's thighs. He looked up and ceased his hammering as Sir Ranulph reined in.

'Your horse?' he demanded of Philip. At his sulky nod, he spurred forward. 'Good-day, Master Smith. Can you tell me where the rider is?' He pointed his riding crop at the animal.

'He be taking an ale in Ma Purley's.' The smith jerked his sweat-beaded head at the inn.

'My thanks.'

Ma Purley proved to be a woman of substantial proportions, topped by grey hair inadequately covered by a pristine cap. She met them on her doorstep, amply filling the entrance.

'Good day, ma'am. The smith tells me you have a man waiting here. Did he by chance have a child with him?'

'He did that. And a poor little scrap he is too.'

'*Is*? You still have him?' The words came sharply.

'I do that.' She folded her arms decisively. She eyed Sir Ranulph from his curled beaver to his top boots and back again. 'Though what business it is of yours I don't know.'

Sir Ranulph slid from his horse. 'My ward has been stolen from home. I am anxious to recover him.'

'Stolen?' The arms sagged. 'Then come you in. The babe's in the front parlour, the poor mite. The man said as he was his father, carrying him to a doctor for his fever.' A sniff. 'Not that I'd do so – even if he do have a fever, which I say he don't for he's as pale as a posset. Nor was he dressed as well as the babe. I've set my youngest to watch over him, as your worship will see.' She ceased her jumbled words and sailed into a small hall. Two steps in, she halted abruptly, almost causing Sir Ranulph to collide with her. She turned, her hands twisted together. 'I hope as you don't think I had aught to do with his taking.'

Sir Ranulph bowed. 'I am certain you did not, ma'am. Now, if you will tell me where the man is?

'He's not here. He loped off to ask for the loan of Old Barney's gig. He said the child was in too sorry a state to sit up before him again.' Her hand twisting resumed. 'The poor little lamb is that tired and fretful. All shook up he is, like a flummery.'

Sir Ranulph considered. 'Have you a husband, ma'am? Or a son who might help me? I need to detain the man when he returns.'

'Oh, my lordy.' The hands parted to fly to her wide bosom. 'Never say there'll be trouble like that.'

'I regret there will. A husband, ma'am? Or a son?'

'There's my Davie. My first-born. He's a good lad. He'll stand by you.'

'Excellent. Now if I might see my ward?'

'Of course, sur, of course.'

She led them into a small parlour. Seated on the floor beside a wooden settle spread with folded blankets was a young girl. She looked up as her mother entered the room.

'He's still sleeping, Ma. Hasn't so much as stirred.'

Sir Ranulph strode towards the settle and knelt down, oblivious to the girl's widening eyes as she took in his height and bearing. He laid a hand on Christopher's forehead.

'Has he the fever, sir?' the woman asked.

'No, not at all. In fact he looks no worse for his travels.' He rose. 'I must thank you for your care of him. I hope you will permit me to impose further upon your good nature.'

Mrs Purley was a landlady of some experience. She had no difficulty at all in recognising a member of what she termed the Quality. Such folk did not normally grace her modest establishment but when they did they – if they were half way decent folks as this one looked to be – they dropped their blunt with charming ease.

'I'm sure I'm only too happy to oblige you, sir.' She dropped a shallow curtsey. 'Just you be telling me what you want.'

'I shall need the local Magistrate here – and no doubt the strong arms of your son for the miscreant – and then a chaise of some sort to convey the child home.'

Philip, entered the room. 'It seems the man has run off. According to the smith's boy he no sooner returned and set eyes on our horses than he charged off back to the town. We can be sure we've seen the last of him.'

Sir Ranulph eyed him narrowly. 'If you say so, I'm sure we have.'

Chapter Twenty-One

Louise, left on her own, brought her chaotic emotions under control with difficulty. Fearful that Vintry might — for reasons she could not guess — return to Stapley, she locked and barred the front and rear doors. With the skivvy following her, lost in fidgets and moans, and showing a tendency to clutch at Louise's skirts, she checked the latches of every downstairs window.

'Oo, miss,' she wailed, emerging from her gulping sobs to stop looking behind her at every step, 'be that man coming back?'

Louise collected herself. 'No. No, he is not.'

The girl, whose name was Bathsheba but who was known to all and sundry except her mother as Beth, chewed her lip and huddled her arms into the skirt of her drab gown. 'Are you certain sure, miss?'

Knowing that she should comfort, or at least distract, the unfortunate skivvy, Louise settled upon a plan of action that, she hoped, would also alleviate her own increasing concern. 'I have not breakfasted today. Let us see what food is to be found in the kitchen.'

She marched into the hall with far more confidence than she felt. Beth, struggling to quell her shivers, followed. 'I can't rightly say what there is, miss. Cook don't allow me into the pantry.'

'Well, I shall. Come along.'

The air in the kitchen struck cold. The last embers of a fire burned low in the grate. 'Can you kindle a fire, Beth?'

'I can that, ma'am.' The girl's face glowed. 'Cook says I can do it right proper. It's the first thing I do when I get up.'

'Then you see to it and I'll find us some food.' She scanned the room. A brightly painted door was part-way down the far wall. It opened to reveal a series of shelves on which the remains of a season's preserves stood in orderly ranks above three meat safes. Below them earthenware tubs had *Flour, Bread* and such-like words painted into the glaze. Against the outside wall stood crock of milk with a crocheted circle of white cotton over its top weighted down with blue beads, a cheese dish with a china cover, a basket of nine eggs and a dish of butter.

Not being entirely familiar with any method of cooking eggs, Louise lifted the cover off the cheese dish to reveal revealed a mound of soft white cheese and a lump of mousetrap. She carried the cheese and butter dishes to the table in the centre of the room and returned to delve in the bread crock.

'A simple breakfast,' she said to Beth still on her knees at the hearth, 'but it will serve.'

The girl scrambled up, brushing her hands down her skirts. 'Shall I be making a pot, ma'am?'

'Tea? Yes please, but wash your hands first.'

The skivvy examined her palms that showed slightly grey with darker lines marking the folds. 'If you say so, miss.'

She busied herself. Pride in making some tea – a task she had never before been allowed to perform – glowed in her face. Watching her eagerness gave Louise a brief respite from the anxiety that threatened to overpower her. She ate her bread and cheese with an apple from a box in the pantry and tried to keep a firm hold on her composure. The meal did not take long to consume. The trifling activity quickly lapsed into a still silence. The thought of what might – even as she sat – be happening to

Christopher horrified her. She cast around for something, *any-thing*, that might distract her from her fears.

'Ah,' she said at last. 'I shall collect the remainder of Mrs Aveley's belongings. There are only a few –' She stopped speaking. It had been a task she had been too distressed to complete on her previous visit. Even so, the trial of finishing it would be better than just sitting. Wondering. Imagining.

She forced herself to sound calm. 'Do you know where the bandboxes are kept?'

The tousled head shook. 'No, ma'am. Mr Jedburgh would know but he ain't here.'

'Never mind. I shall make a start and he can bring me them when he returns.' She rose from the table.

The girl's face crumpled. 'You ain't going to leave me down here on my own, are you, ma'am?'

Louise's shoulders drooped. Beth was, in her own way, just as anxious as she. It must be her responsibility to support the girl. 'Of course not, I shall need you to help me. Put the dishes in the sink and then come upstairs.' The maid sprang up, Louise crossed the hall to the sound of cups and plates dropping ungently into the china sink.

The wardrobe in Amelia's bedchamber disclosed the few items Louise had not already folded away. In its depths hung an older one of pale jonquil muslin trimmed with a frill of embroidered primroses. A memory stabbed Louise's stability. She knew the gown. Remembered how prettily it had become her sister. Her throat tightened. She could not leave it here. It held too many memories. She folded it gently and placed it on the pillow. The second pillow dislodged and tumbled to the floor. Neatly folded on the sheet was a man's nightshirt. Louise gasped. She should have realised. Should have known. Her hands trembled. Images of Amelia laughing reared in her mind. Had Amelia laughed in this house? Laughed and loved? Of course she had. Her thoughts careered away to Crestings. Did he wear a nightshirt too? To lie on that metamorphic bed? Her face grew hot. Her eyes prickled. Why was he invading her thoughts like this? In this place where he had no right to be?

She sank unsteadily to the bed, shaken by an emotion she barely recognised. Was this how Amelia felt for ... what was his name ... Gerard? Is that what drew her to abandon her home and family? Then her happiness in Gerard's company must have been great. Perhaps ... perhaps there was happiness in marriage, not the relentless suppression she had seen her mother endure. Perhaps ... perhaps she had been wrong to abjure society. Perhaps –

'Are you feeling poorly, ma'am?' Beth's words broke into her thoughts.

'No I ... no, just a little tired I think.' Louise dragged her thoughts from a quagmire of emotion that threatened to engulf her. 'But I am quite well now, thank you.'

The girl uttered a smiling sigh. 'I'll make some more tea, shall I?'

After more cups of the horrible tea than she really wished to drink, and more painful searches for Amelia's things than she wished to perform, Louise heard the sound she had been longing for. Or was it dreading? She reached the front door and unlocked it to Sir Ranulph's hammering. It flung open. Christopher's howls greeted her. His little arms reached out from Sir Ranulph's.

'Oh, thank God.' She lifted him into her embrace.

'He's unharmed. Go into the parlour and reassure yourself of it.'

In moments she was seated by the fire, rocking Christopher on her lap. Uttering soothing murmurs and running her fingers through his curls, she looked over his head at his rescuer. 'The man?'

'Gone. I could have chased him but bringing the child back to you was more important. I doubt we shall see him again. Not if he knows what's good for him.'

'And Mr Aveley?'

'Stabling the horses.' His eyes rested on her. 'We have to decide what to do.'

'I know what to do,' Philip trod into the room. 'Take Miss Devreaux to her grandmother as I had intended.'

'And how do we do that?' Sir Ranulph demanded in scathing tones. 'She cannot ride with the child. He cannot continue to be dragged about like a parcel. And how do you suggest we get them there? There's no carriage in the coach house. Presumably the servants have gone off in it. So does she carry the child in the gig? In case you had not noticed there's a storm coming. They would be soaked in minutes.'

'Then we acquire another.'

'From where?' Sir Ranulph's voice cut in coldly. 'Or do you have one hidden?'

Philip glared at Sir Ranulph. He laughed derisively. 'Don't bite at me. We can see you're mighty soon defeated.' He glanced at Louise, his features changing and his voice softening. 'Have no fear, ma'am. I shall see you safely to your family.'

'Will you?' Sir Ranulph shot at him.

'Most certainly. Don't think I'll permit Miss Devreaux and the child to be pulled into your grasp again.' He turned back to Louise. 'There must be someone nearby, ma'am, who will lend us a carriage.'

'And proclaim our business to the neighbourhood?' Sir Ranulph said. 'I think not.'

'For consideration of your reputation?' Philip's voice rose. 'Some things are more important than that.'

Sir Ranulph's words overpowered his. 'My reputation is —'

'Be quiet,' Louise cried above Christopher's resurgent sobs. She jumped to her feet, almost staggering with the weight of the child she was holding. 'Be *quiet*, both of you!'

The men stared at her. Gently bred young women did not shout at anyone, much less at men older than herself.

'Ma'am –' Philip began.

She waved a distracted hand at them. 'No. No. This is no time for such … *squabbling*.' She clutched at Christopher who was wriggling off her knees. 'I must get him to a place of safety.'

'Safety from whom?' Sir Ranulph's words cut at her. 'From him, or from me?' The tension in his face and voice showed the strong effort he was making to control himself. 'You precipitated this crisis,' he flung at her. 'You had no need to run from Crestings.'

Caught between defending herself and comforting Christopher, she glared at him. 'Had I not? How did I know that? How could I be sure he was safe there?' She struggled up, clutching the whimpering child. 'Get me a carriage one of you. I don't care how you do it, or who does it. Just get me a carriage. I must change his clothes.' She turned from the fire. 'He is exhausted. I must settle him to bed.'

'But how can we find one?' Philip asked, steadying her round the sofa. 'I cannot leave you here. Alone. With him.'

'And don't expect me to leave you alone with him,' Sir Ranulph countered. The men's furious stares clashed.

Her scathing gaze swept the pair. 'Then both go! I shall be pleased to be rid of you. Spend the night in the stables for all I care.'

Protests burst from Philip.

'No.' She cut him off. 'I cannot permit you to remain here.'

'But it would be quite improper for you to remain here alone.'

'Not as improper as an unmarried woman staying under the same roof as two gentlemen to whom she is not related,' Sir

Ranulph said, his eyes locked on Philip's face. 'Especially when her own maid is left sobbing her innocence at Crestings.'

'But —'

'No.' Louise broke into another protest. 'Either you two depart or I shall.'

Sir Ranulph bowed. 'As you wish, ma'am. We shall spend the night at the inn. Together.' Heavy emphasis accompanied his words. 'We shall return at nine tomorrow morning.'

'With a carriage of some sort, if you please.'

The men departed, each as stiffly correct as the other. As soon as they were out of the Hall, Louise locked the door behind them, struggling to keep Christopher close.

He took his face out of her shoulder. 'Bye bye,' he said sleepily.

His little voice was almost her undoing. She lent her head against the solid door. 'Hush, darling,' she said after a moment. 'We must find little Beth and make sure the windows are all still latched. Then we shall sleep. I must be ready in good time tomorrow.'

Christopher's tear-stained face turned up to her. 'And Mama?'

Louise choked back a sob.

After a sleepless night spent in the same bedchamber as a troubled child and an anxious maid, with a chest of drawers dragged across the door, Louise left Stapley Hall the following morning in a coach borrowed from the local squire with Christopher on her lap and Beth, now garbed in Amelia's oldest gown and shawl, squashed on the seat beside her.

Sir Ranulph had been adamant that the girl should come. 'You may not have a care of your reputation, ma'am, but I have.' He had said. 'She will accompany you.' He had cast a scathing glance at the cowering Beth. 'I assume Mrs Aveley had a gown to replace that...' he had scanned Beth's drab garment, 'that one. Put her in it, if you please.'

Once dressed, the girl was too overcome by her new garb to speak, much to Louise's relief. All she could do was run her reddened hands over her skirts and sigh with ecstasy. For himself, Sir Ranulph had managed, by means quite unknown to any of the party, to procure a neckcloth that was startling in its freshness. For reasons she could not satisfactorily explain, Sir Ranulph's neckcloth reassured Louise. Abjuring herself to stop being so nonsensical, she returned her attention to Christopher.

He rode behind the carriage as it pulled away. A crumpled Philip Aveley followed on a plough horse, about which he did not cease to grumble.

That the girl was still lost in a vision of fashionable heaven could not be denied. Her ecstasy increased at the timbered Fleece Hotel in Cirencester. Picking her skirt up as daintily as she could she followed Louise inside to partake of refreshments the landlord was only too happy to provide. Eager to impress her temporary mistress with her nascent talent as a lady's maid and not a scullery skivvy, she managed to upend a dish of buttered eggs onto the table cover. The accident subdued her for quite three minutes. Despite her clumsiness, Louise was grateful for her presence. The girl was only too happy to amuse Christopher, playing pat-a-cake with him for mile after mile, causing him to chuckle with delight.

Philip was not chuckling with delight. He had suffered the bitter pleasure of watching Sir Ranulph disburse the funds to enable Miss Devreaux to transfer to a post-chaise and for the squire's coach to be returned to its owner. He stood in the hotel's galleried courtyard, fully aware that the deference paid to Sir Ranulph did not extend to him. Fury bubbled in his head. Being forced to depend on those same funds to send the plough horse home and hire a replacement was degrading. His resentment burst into unwise words.

'I'm amazed your valet hasn't been awaiting your pleasure here,' he barked, mounting the hired nag that replaced his slug. 'No doubt the landlord would have only been too happy to run off and fetch him.'

Sir Ranulph regarded him from under lowered lids. 'Had you paid attention to Mrs Purley's apologies this morning, you would know her husband had departed on the only available horse at the inn in order to attend his father's sickbed. Thus he was not available to render me any service at all.'

A derisive snort greeted this remark. Philip turned his horse's head and urged it under arch and into the street.

After speedy change of cattle at Malmesbury, they soon reached the small town of Chippenham nestling in a bend of the River Avon. Louise had been a mere ten years old on her only visit to her grandmother's house which made her efforts to direct them into its park somewhat hazy. A terse conversation between Sir Ranulph and two men wrestling to lay a hawthorn hedge on the slope down to the town resulted in a turn down a side lane which led them through the fields to Frannington Court.

The Melthorpe's ancestral residence, situated in a sweeping park above the town, had begun life as a modest Elizabethan manor. Its modesty had not recommended it to its subsequent owners, none of whom were particularly modest, and each of whom had added to the original in ways that had now rendered the whole an inconvenient tangle of incompatible styles. Wings rambled, stairs rose and descended in peculiar places, corridors and passages wound and enclosed courtyards met confused guests at regular intervals.

Lady Albina's eldest son, who much preferred to lodge in his London town house, was rarely seen there unless he was minded to hunt or shoot. His wife, however, occasionally resided with her mother-in-law as did those of her daughters whom she had not yet married off. Now the Season had started she had removed with them to town to pester her spouse into funding new gowns for the various balls, breakfasts and other amusements to which she would shepherd them.

The butler who opened the double doors was far too well-versed in his role to permit his eyebrows to rise at the sight of Louise bearing an indignant infant. Her lack of visiting cards surprised him but as her name was stored in his exhaustive memory he did not hesitate to stand aside for her to enter. He spared no glance for Beth but did incline his person fractionally to Sir Ranulph and Philip Aveley.

'If you would condescend to wait in the Green drawing room, ma'am, I will appraise her ladyship of your arrival.'

Some moments later, he informed Louise that her ladyship would receive her in her apartment. Depositing Christopher into Beth's lap, Louise followed the butler up a flight of wide stairs to scratch on the door he indicated.

After several moments it was opened by her ladyship's dresser. She regarded Louise's crumpled gown with superior eyes for several seconds.

'Don't fiddle-faddle in the doorway, Twitton,' her ladyship called. 'Let her in. '

Seated at her dressing-table, Lady Albina eased a particularly becoming cap onto her thinning grey hair. 'Think yourself fortunate to be here, my girl. I don't allow anyone to see me before my cap is on so think yourself honoured, girl.' Turning her head side-to-side in front of her mirror, she patted a frill into a better line. 'I'm not one of the desperate females who messes about with wigs, trying to convince the world she hasn't as many years in her dish as she has.' She took a pair of lace mittens held out to her by her dresser. 'You can always tell them by their hands anyway.' She eased the mittens over her knotted fingers. The lacy tips were so long, her little fingers almost disappeared.

Satisfied with her appearance, she swivelled round on her chair. 'Now, girl, tell me what you are doing here with a child and two men I doubt I've heard of.' Her gimlet eyes bored into Louise. 'Not another scandal, I hope.'

Louise coloured furiously. 'No, ma'am. Certainly not!' Her quick glance at the dresser told her grandmother all she wanted to know about the style of confidence she would hear.

'Off you go, Twittor. I've finished with you now.'

No more was said until the door snapped shut behind the disapproving dresser.

'Now then, miss. What have you been up to?'

To her exquisite embarrassment, Louise felt tears well in her eyes. 'Oh, Grandmama, I am in such a fix.'

Chapter Twenty-Two

Informed, amazed, intrigued and determined, Lady Melthorpe thanked Sir Ranulph and Mr Aveley for delivering her granddaughter and great-grandson to her care and dismissed them. The gentlemen found themselves directed to Chippenham town, which, they were assured, boasted some excellent hotels. Riding past the Buttercross in the Market Place where several country women were selling chickens and anonymous portions of meat, Sir Ranulph announced they would stay at the Angel, a fact that raised Philip's hackles again. He set his horse skittering.

'Mighty high-handed of you, Trent. Why choose the Angel over the Bear?'

'Because I wish to.'

'You mean because you wish to keep me under your eye. Let me tell you –'

'Tell me nothing, Aveley. I've known your game these past weeks and if you think I'll permit you to succeed, you are several leagues off the mark.'

'I have no idea what maggot you've taken into your head,' Philip blustered.

'Yes you have. You know precisely what I mean. Don't think you can dupe me, even if you have succeeded in bamboozling Miss Devreaux.'

Guiding his horse to the hotel's entrance, he slid out of the saddle and tossed the reins to the brown-jacketed ostler who hurried out of the door. The man lingered by Philip.

'You be staying too, sir?' he asked in a burred accent.

Caught between flouncing off in a show of independence and succumbing to Sir Ranulph's autocratic decision, the straightened contents of his rapidly diminishing purse forced Philip into acquiescence. 'As you wish,' he grunted.

His temper was in no way improved to hear the landlord reporting that, yes, Sir Ranulph's valet had arrived and yes, his groom was presently securing his curricle in the stables. The man's bowing and scraping set Philip's teeth together. Left in the private parlour he eyed his temporary benefactor scathingly.

'I see your valet and all your traps are here. What magic was that? That landlord returned?'

'No, I sent for him from Malmesbury if you must know.'

Philip snorted. 'Can't manage without them, I dare say.'

'Say what you wish.' Sir Ranulph stripped of his gloves. 'Your opinion of me in no way interests me. My opinion of you should bear some weight. You have plunged too deeply at Faro. That is no surprise. It's the reason Gerard appointed me as guardian, not you. He had no wish to see his son beggared by your profligacy.'

'How dare you? You know nothing of me nor of –'

'Spare me your splutterings. I know what you are about and you will not succeed. The child will be safe from you.'

'And from you?' A snort accompanied Philip's snarl.

'He will always be safe from me – with me.' Sir Ranulph's contemptuous eyes swept over the younger man. 'What will it take to buy you off?'

'Buy me off? Don't be ridiculous. You couldn't.'

'Oh, I could. Let me see now. Stapley produces slightly over a thousand a year. Your debts – as far as we've been able to discover – amount to some four and a half. Even if you gained control of Stapley, it follows that you cannot expect to retrieve yourself from the Greeks unless you sell it. If you do that, you will have no income worth the mention.' He paused, judging his adversary. 'I will give you six thousand to take yourself away and leave Christopher alone. Neither you, nor any agent you care to employ will go near him. I want no more Vintrys.'

'You're ridiculous,' Philip snapped. 'Your sort think money will buy everything. Well, you're wrong. And your ridiculous accusations are wrong. I have no designs on Christopher. Other than to keep him safe from you.'

'As you wish. It's not an offer I shall make again.'

Before Philip could do more than open his mouth to reply, the landlord entered the room followed by a manservant bearing a tray laden with wine and glasses. Philip flung away to the window and stared furiously at the scene below.

'I've sent my eldest off post as you wished, sir,' the landlord announced. 'And the head ostler's away to Frannington Court for the coach.'

Dragging his attention from a woman lumbering across the market square after an escaped chicken, Philip wondered just who Trent was sending the landlord's boy to. He hoped it was not the local magistrate. Or worse, the Runners.

Albina Melthorpe penned two invitations at the escritoire in her drawing room. 'There, my dear,' she said, affixing wafers to them with a flourish. 'We shall have the pair to dine and I shall see what I make of them.'

'Do you think that is wise, Grandmama?'

'Of course. How else am I to judge them?' She picked up the silver bell on the elegant desk and rang it with vigour. 'I know of Ranulph Trent. His mother is the daughter of a dear friend. Helena, the Earl of Windlesham's third daughter. You won't know them of course. He had six of them. They were mighty pleased when she caught Trent's eye, I can tell you.'

Louise, relieved for the time by Christopher falling asleep in Beth's lap in a hastily revived nursery, endeavoured to follow her grandmother's charge through the *ton's* upper five thousand.

'Philip Aveley is unknown to me. He gave every appearance of being of gentle birth.' She sniffed. 'Have to say I found his spaniel eyes enough to turn my stomach.'

'Spaniel eyes, ma'am? I found him most sympathetic.'

'I dare say you did. His sort know that it always turns a girl's head.'

'He has not turned my head. Nothing of the sort. It'd only that...that he seems to enter into my feelings for Christopher which Sir Ranulph seems not to.'

Lady Melthorpe would have been surprised to discover that the thoughts now churning in her venerable head bore a remarkable similarity to those that had caused hope to spring in Stephanie Trent's breast. She was not surprised when Sir Ranulph presented himself correctly attired for dinner in knee breeches and coat. Philip Aveley she regarded with faint displeasure, eyeing his riding dress with disfavour but allowing herself to be consoled by his elegant apology and the information that only the urgency of Christopher's rescue had prevented him from packing his evening dress.

'I dare say it was. Never having been obliged to rescue anyone from anything I cannot say how it must have been.' Well aware that Sir Ranulph met her every idea of a suitable *parti*, she obliged Philip to sit at the far end of the settee on which she was arranged in a gown of midnight blue silk. 'I don't know your family. Who was your mother?'

Across the room, Sir Ranulph's lips twitched. 'I see your grandmother takes an interest in connections, ma'am.' he said to Louise.

'As do many elderly ladies, sir.'

'Indeed.' He indicated a pair of armchairs slightly removed from the inquisition. 'If we leave them to their exploration, you will have chance to tell me how Christopher fares.'

Louise allowed him to hand her to the nearest and sat. The newly-ironed folds of the evening gown she had crammed into her portmanteau prior to her flight from Crestings draped around her feet. 'He does very well. Beth has quite taken to him. And he to her.'

'That must be a welcome rest for you.'

'How so, sir?' A pair of fine eyes rested on him. 'Do you think I find my sister's child a burden?'

He bent his elbow on the arm of the chair and regarded her with amusement above the long fingers half-hiding his mouth. 'No, I do not. I merely observe your determination to take sole possession of him. It must, to a young woman unused to infants and devoid of a nurse, be a continued effort.'

'It is, but it's one I'm delighted to make.'

'I am pleased to hear it.'

'You were far from pleased when I first suggested it. You forbade me to see him.'

'That, ma'am, was my mistake and one I happily confess to. Being – like yourself – unused to infants it had truly not occurred to me that he would grow to trust you so swiftly'

'To trust me?'

'Indeed. There is a family resemblance that must comfort and reassure him.'

'But I look nothing like my sister. She had fair hair.'

'You are mistaken, ma'am. Her hair might have been differently coloured but there is a great similarity in the eyes. And the mouth and chin.'

'How can you say that? You did not know her.'

'Mistaken again, ma'am. I did meet her. Not above twice, it is true, but the portrait you had carried to Crestings was an exact likeness.'

Louise floundered. 'You'd met her, sir? I had not expected that.' Her lips trembled. 'Tell me, was she happy? Did she strike you as such? I did not... I had not –'

'Calm yourself, ma'am. Mrs Aveley – once she had overcome her shyness with me – gave every appearance of being ecstatically content. Gerard was the same. I was pleased to see him so fortunate in his wife.'

That he should speak of Amelia with such generosity was something she had not thought him capable of. His words caused tears to prickle her eyes and tie her throat. For a moment she turned her head away. His interest in her sister's happiness confused her. It cast an entirely different light on what she had made of his character. As had the memory of his own delight in his library. Her cheeks coloured. She pleated a fold of her gown, still pondering, unaware that speaking of Amelia's joy had set him thinking that one sister's happy marriage might presuppose marriage to the other might well be equally successful.

Watching the play of expressions across her face, Ranulph began to dwell on what he knew of her. She was maddeningly independent. Wilful. She was most certainly courageous. Few gently-bred women could defy two men as she had yesterday. And also her domineering father. Her duty, her *imagined* duty, had brought her from the protection of her home to the uncertainty of his, where – he must admit – he had not welcomed her. Although his mother had. That gave him cause for reflection. His mother was not one to be taken in by merely a pretty face and good manners.

Lady Melthorpe's summons drew the pair from their silent deliberations. She permitted Sir Ranulph to lead her into the lofty dining room, a chamber clearly designed to impress, if not cower, visitors. Behind them. Philip possessed himself of Louise's hand.

'My dear ma'am,' he whispered, 'pray do not hesitate to tell me if Trent gives the least sign of pressuring you into an unwise decision.'

Almost of a height, she stared him in the eyes. Spaniel eyes. Her grandmother's description wiped the charm from his expression. Had she set too much store by his sympathetic demeanour? No. She was five-and-twenty and had learned enough in her two Seasons to discriminate between the genuine and the false.

'I have no concerns of that nature, sir. He has made no such attempt and even if he had, Christopher and I are safe with Lady Melthorpe. Sir Ranulph has shown no desire to prevent our staying here.'

The last was certainly true. That he had also shown no inclination to permit such a stay was also true, but she did not mention that.

It would be unfair to say the meal passed in an atmosphere of distrust and dissention. Sir Ranulph was perfectly at ease, regaling his hostess with all the latest *on dits* from London but without removing his lazy gaze from Louise and Philip for more than the moments necessary to avoid ruffling the Melthorpe feathers. For her part, Louise was relieved to be under the protection of a woman who, she was sure, would prevent any attempt at coercion. Philip was the least happy of the guests. Incorrectly attired, irritated by Trent's superiority of manner, and conscious that her ladyship's gaze was uncomfortably direct, he addressed himself whenever his attention went unclaimed by his hostess to assuring Louise of his continued concern for her safety. And that of Christopher.

When the ladies rose, he rejected the offered port and suggested accompanying them to the drawing room instead.

'You think I am unable to find my own drawing room, sir?'

'No, my lady, but I do think Miss Devreaux has had a trying few days and might be glad to retire early. I would not oblige her to sit for another half hour until we joined you.'

Albina Melthorpe sniffed. 'Very considerate of you. Very well.' She turned a blank face to her butler hovering by the open door. 'Have the tea tray brought in immediately.'

The man bowed wordlessly, casting his gaze over an under-dressed gentleman, the like of whom he had never yet been called to wait upon in Frannington's dining room, not in all his long service with the family.

Sir Ranulph and Philip departed a bare twenty minutes later. About to climb into Sir Ranulph's curricle, Philip paused. 'I thought your tiger came with us. Where is he?'

'Not that it's any concern of yours, but I sent him back to the hotel.'

'On foot?' A derisive snort. 'Typical of you.'

'I doubt on foot. He's well able to take care of himself. And Frannington is a sufficiently well-ordered household to oblige him even if he were not.'

'Do you intend to leave Miss Devreaux and the child here?'

'For the time being.' He caught the speculative glance Philip directed at him, despite the darkness surrounding them.

'Oh, do not bother to accuse me of any scheming.' Sir Ranulph said, favouring him with a look that had been known to make presumptuous sprigs of fashion shrivel in their boots. 'I leave any such machinations to you.'

Unable to think of any response that would prevent a scathing riposte, Philip sat silently throughout the short journey to Chippenham. Alone in his bedchamber he turned the events of the past few days over in his mind. That Louise Devreaux now seemed less inclined to believe his account was clear. Her manner had changed. Not by much, but by enough to permit him to conclude that her trust in him had faded. He hoped that he had sown sufficient doubts of Trent's purpose in her mind. Sufficient to let him to recover his position. He stripped off his coat and paced the small room. What if he could not? He had left London knowing it would not be long before a certain hefty individual hammered on the door of his lodgings there, dunning him for payment. If the narrow-eyed gentleman was not immediately reimbursed, word would be spread in London and more dunning fiends would arrive. If he was forced into recourse to the usurers again, the four and a half thousand pounds Trent rightly knew he owed would expand to proportions he had even less chance of meeting.

Chapter Twenty-Three

'I shall be returning to Crestings tomorrow,' Sir Ranulph said the following afternoon, lowering his teacup in Frannington Court's vaulted drawing room. His eyes were fixed on Louise's face. He failed to interpret the expression which crossed it.

'As you wish, sir.' Her words displayed no emotion. 'I must thank you – and Mr Aveley – for bringing me to Lady Melthorpe. I much appreciate it.' Suddenly conscious she looked down and up. 'I take it you are permitting us to stay here?'

'I am, ma'am. I am sure you will be quite safe in her ladyship's company.'

'Then…' She laced her fingers in her lap.

'Then what?'

'Then would you be good enough to have my trunk packed and sent over, please? I…it was not possible for me to bring much with me. If Lizzie…' She hesitated, fully conscious of his eyes upon her. Her chin lifted. 'If you could arrange for Lizzie to accompany it, I shall be most grateful, sir.'

'You surprise me, ma'am. You are so resourceful, I had assumed you had contrived to have all your worldly possessions and your maid concealed and waiting for you somewhere.'

Only the knowledge that she was begging him for a favour kept her from uttering a hasty rejoinder. He knew Lizzie was not with her because he had mentioned her at Stapley. And Lizzie would have been questioned about her belongings. She could barely keep herself from directing a malevolent glare at him.

Her grandmother looked across at them. She regarded Sir Ranulph over her half-moon spectacles. 'I fail to see why you should leave. The Season has barely started and town will be rather flat. If you stay here, you're welcome to cast a line in our river.'

'Thank you, ma'am, most generous of you. I cannot speak for Aveley but I have business to conduct at home. And Lady Trent will be anxious to have word of the child.'

Her ladyship shrugged. 'As you wish. If you must go rather than write to her, say all that is proper to her for me. I don't expect we shall ever meet again in this life.'

Sir Ranulph bowed as much as he could without rising.

Philip, acutely conscious of his inability to pay for his transport to Stapley Hall, let alone for his shot in Chippenham if he remained there as he wished, uttered similar regrets. 'Would that I too could stay, ma'am, but I regret I must also take my leave. I hope, though, that I may have permission to call upon your ladyship to see Miss Devreaux and my nephew.'

Lady Melthorpe inclined her head without noticeable enthusiasm.

Thus it was after a bare three days in northwest Wiltshire that Sir Ranulph, driving his curricle with Philip up beside him, and his travelling chaise bearing his valet, Lizzie Sutton and several corded trunks behind him, turned for the Cotswolds' rolling hills. They had barely reached the Malmesbury road before Philip, screwing his neck round to stare at the chaise demanded,

'Where's your tiger? He ain't in the carriage.'

'I sent him to London.'

'Not like you to be without all the trappings of your state.'

'You have not the least idea of what is or is not like me.'

'Have I not? Don't fool yourself Trent. Your family are all the same – haughty and above your station.'

Sir Ranulph pulled on the ribbons causing his pair to sink onto their hindquarters and halt. The coachman on the box of the following chaise heaved on his team and muttered direfully under his breath.

'Do not hesitate to inform me if you would prefer to walk.'

Philip's face flushed. 'Don't be ridiculous.' He folded his arms. Thereafter, he spoke as few words as possible during the swift journey to Stapley Hall that soon left the chaise behind. Only when he had been deposited at its gates did he mutter his brief thanks.

'Stay away from Frannington, Aveley. It would not be good for you to call there again. And collect your traps from here and leave.'

Sir Ranulph flicked his whip and the curricle moved off.

Philip glared at his retreating back. 'Don't tell me what to do,' he muttered. 'I'm not one of your lackeys.'

He hammered on the main door but no one came to open it. He cursed and marched round to the stables, hoping to find some signs of life there. He found them. Mesdames Nairn and Farrow were comforting a sobbing woman in an old-fashioned bonnet and shawl while Jedburgh was begging a red-faced man to cease shouting and listen. The entire group turned on Philip.

'Oh, Mr Aveley,' Jedburgh uttered with every sign of relief. 'Here's the master's brother.' This to the red-faced man. 'He'll know what's become of your girl.'

Bemused, Philip looked from one to the other. 'What girl?'

Mrs Nairn ceased patting the distraught woman's should and hurried forward. 'Beth,' she said. 'Her as was kitchen skivvy.'

'Bathsheba,' sobbed the woman.

'Oh, her. She's gone to Chippenham.'

'Chippenham?' the woman shrieked, falling against the butler's thin chest with redoubled sobs.

The unknown man, his face noticeably redder, advanced. 'Why be my lass a-going there?'

'She's acting as maid to Miss Devreaux. Miss Devreaux is sister to the late Mrs Aveley.'

'A lady's maid?' The mother's sobs ceased on a breath. 'That's a good step up for her.' She wiped her damp cheeks with her slipping shawl. 'Her wages will be going up too I don't doubt.'

'I don't know about that,' Philip said. 'I do know I've been wearing the same linen for almost a week. Is my bag still inside, Mrs Nairn?'

'It is, sir. In the bedchamber you like to use. Shall I fetch it for you?'

'Not at all. I'll go up and change. Make me some dinner while I do. And bring up a bottle of burgundy, Jedburgh. I'm parched as we'll as hungry.'

Tempted as he was to stay, and disappointed not to have Vintry crawl back to see him, the next morning Philip packed one or two small items of silver into his portmanteau and set off for the single room that composed his lodgings in London. The silver, when hocked, allowed him to place some coins into his suspicious landlady's outstretched hand while she muttered about outstanding rent, and left him sufficient to meet his needs for a couple of weeks. Always assuming he stayed away from the card tables and Tattersalls.

It took him three days to find Vintry, and that at his third visit to a gin house in an area he loathed. It was too close for comfort to the kennel where he owed considerably more than the price of the hocked silver.

'I don't know,' Vintry muttered into his tankard, casting suspicious eyes at his neighbour slumped across the top of the table they shared. Satisfied the man was beyond consciousness, he continued, 'Don't know as I want 'owt to do with that Trent's business. He looks to be a mite too handy with his fists if you ask me. And I wouldn't put it past him to shoot a man for no more than a little filching.'

'If you're such a coward,' Philip hissed, 'find me someone who isn't. You know where to send them.'

Vintry was not the only one who knew where to find Philip. As he was weaving his way home through a narrow, dark street of poor houses, so jug-bitten that the ground seemed to undulate before him, a bulky figure emerged from the shadows.

'Well, well,' it uttered. 'If it ain't Mr Aveley.'

Philip staggered, reaching a hand to the nearest wall. 'Burndock? Is that you?'

'It is. Now,' he pulled Philip upright, 'you tell me where the money is else London'll be too hot for you. You'll have no more chance to go about fleecing decent shopkeepers.' His face leered closer. 'I'll have you know my brother's in the Marshalsea a'cos of you. Folks like you have driven his business to the wall for not paying your shot. I want what you owe him and I want it damn quick.'

'I haven't got it.'

'Then you'll find yerself as uncomfortable as my brother. Only less in the eye of the Beadles, if you take my meaning.'

The threat and the fumes on the man's breath convinced Philip his danger was grave. 'What if I say I can get it?'

The man' snarled. 'You've been saying that for months.'

'But I've almost managed it. It's my brother's place. It'll soon be mine, there's only his kid in the way.'

'I don't hold with them as forgets their family and does away with their brother.'

'He's already dead. He died last month. He –'

Philip found himself raised on his toes by two hands grasping his coat lapels. 'Seen to him already, have you?'

'No! No, I haven't. Though there's some who think I have.'

'What of this babe then? You'll not be doing away with him, will you?'

'No. No. I'll ... I'll find a way to get his fortune without that.'

'There's no time for lawyers. My brother's sickening with nothing to grease the warder's palms neither.'

'No lawyers. I can just move into his house. There's the rents to come.' He did not explain that Stapley had only two tenant farmers, both of whom paid the smallest of amounts. 'And I can sell the carriage and such.'

The grip on his coat slackened. His feet flattened against the cobbles. For a second he had to steady himself against his inquisitor.

'Well then, you be about that and I'll be back here in four days to collect.'

'Four days? That's impossible.'

'No it ain't. And don't think of disappearing. I'd know where to find you and if I didn't, I'd know who to ask. Someone who can read of the deaths in the journals. Your brother'll have been mentioned there, I don't doubt.'

Standing Philip steady, Burndock dusted his coat, rearranged the crumpled lapels and disappeared into the night. Weak with relief, Philip unlocked the house door, not without difficulty, for which he blamed the flickering light from the dying flambeau rammed in a sconce several houses away, rather than the effects of gin and the discouraging effect of Burndock's conversation.

The screech of the key turning in the iron lock caused his ears to wince. It also caused his landlady to emerge from her room on the ground floor. A guttering candle showed her to be gowned in her usual sombre black.

'Ah, Mr Aveley at last,' she announced, her face dour and hands clasped at her waist. 'This is a fine hour to be entering a decent house.' A scathing glance swept him from hat to boots and back again. She sniffed, scenting the spirit on his breath.

'And a fine state to do it in, to be sure. Mr Fairford as has the room by yours has a decent position in a counting house to keep up. He doesn't need to be woken at all hours of the night by someone who can spend his time in ways no decent body would approve.'

It was borne in on Philip that decency exerted a major pressure on his landlady's mind. 'Ah,' he replied, swaying gently and grasping at the newel post for support.

'So, I'll thank you to have your traps packed and be gone. You can stay 'til the end of the week seeing as how you've paid your rent 'til then. I'm a decent woman. I won't rook you for that.'

'Ah,' Philip repeated to her departing back as she re-entered her lair and shut the door with a snap.

He ascended unsteadily to his room and sank onto the narrow bed, fully clothed, including his boots. The swirling head he laid on the pillow produced feelings of nausea and convinced him the room was heaving about him. He sat up. The swirling increased; he lay down again and closed his eyes. Much inclined to resent his eviction, he cursed for several minutes until reason triumphed through the haze of gin. Leaving would ensure Burndock would be unable to dun him again. A smirk moved his features. That would teach the blackguard. The smirk wilted. If Burndock could not find him, he might pursue his stated intention of announcing to the world that he was the cause of his brother's fate. That would not do. No, he would pen a note to the creature assuring him of the imminent arrival of funds. In fact he would attribute his departure to the necessity of leaving town to collect them. He doubted for a moment that the man knew his letters but decided he had enough wit to find someone who did. That would secure him a few more days, but it brought him no closer to easing his predicament.

The smirk faded into the dark. Burndock's words, such of them as he could recall, turned over in his mind. He was right. There was no time for lawyers. They pounced on every possibility to prolong their activities in the name of profit. Wills meant lawyers. Disputes over property meant lawyers. Lawyers meant a protracted wait for a decision and therefore funds, always assuming a challenge to Gerard's Will was successful. If it wasn't, then his debt would increase. Through the swirling effects of the gin he applied as much of his mind to the problem as he could.

After several sweating minutes he concluded that disposing of Christopher was not the answer. His mere disappearance would give Trent the chance to drag the matter out. It might even mean the Runners. And danger to himself. There had to be a better way. After an hour he was no nearer discovering what was. He shifted uncomfortably on the thin mattress. He shivered. There was no fire in the room and the small hours of the night struck cold. He sat up, heaved off his boots, levered off his coat and dived under the two worn blankets. Sleep crept closer. His eyelids drooped. The swirls lessened. The day's troubles receded. In a second, the clarity of thought that can cut through the most inebriated mind brought him upright. That was it. No smirk now, only a wide grin. The solution was so obvious he was amazed he had not discovered it before.

He lay down, pulled the blankets up round his ears and slept.

Chapter Twenty-Four

Frannington Court's nursery floor had been designed to accommodate some dozen or so children with ease. It had lain unused since Lord Melthorpe, ascending to his father's dignities, had declared that the new Lady Melthorpe preferred to occupy the second of his mansions on an elevated site in the South Downs. It placed her near her Mama, a lady much given to bemoaning her widowed state. The decision placed no restriction upon his lordship's proclivities. Whenever his mother-in-law descended on one of her frequent, unannounced visits, he invariably found estate business that required his urgent attention elsewhere, although he did occasionally wonder which house the lady considered herself to inhabit – his or her own.

The echoing nursery corridors did not recommend themselves to Louise. Planning her words carefully to avoid offending her grandmother, a woman who was, to all intents and purposes, a stranger to her, she ventured to suggest a better arrangement.

'Do you think, ma'am, I might move Christopher and his nurses to the rooms alongside mine? Nurse tells me he is finding it hard to settle as I suppose he must. In the past few weeks he has been moved from –

Lady Melthorpe's raised hand halted her. 'You must do as you deem best, my dear. This rambling old place is quite large enough for you to set up an apartment for yourself that permits you to have the child close enough.' Her head tilted and her appraising gaze dwelt on Louise's face. 'But not too close. It's a shame you've none of your own.' She paused. 'I'm surprised you weren't contracted to marry in your first Season before Amelia cast that shadow. It's not as if your birth is debatable and I must own you have grown into an exceedingly pretty girl.'

'Hardly a girl, ma'am. I'm five-and-twenty.'

'Pooh, a mere infant. There's too much nonsense talked these days about any girl who isn't snapped up as soon as she pokes her nose round the schoolroom door. I know several men who would have sooner jumped into the Avon than marry some chit of that age with no thought in her head but of gowns and balls.' She tapped her fingers. 'There's Conniston for a start. He fixed on the elder Harcourt-Spence girl. Eventually, of course.' More tapping. 'And there's Ellonby's heir too. His wife was no mere girl.' She shook her head. 'Sad that was. He was a fine young man until he took himself off to Portugal and the heathen French. There's too many been done for out there.'

Desperate to change her line of thought before it turned, as she suspected it would, to Ranulph Trent, Louise said, 'I think I saw mention of the new canal in yesterday's journal, ma'am.'

'Canal? Ha! I'll eat the plumes of my new bonnet if that ever comes to aught. You should have heard the furore about the last one. What possessed the idiots to stop it short of the town, I shall never know.'

'Did they, ma'am?' Louise leapt upon the comment.

'Of course they did. Bah! What do they want with their tunnels and locks? Who wants coal around here? There are plenty of trees for the fires and if those people in the Midlands – wherever that is – want coal, they should use their own instead of making people cut up the countryside.'

Louise, possessed of only the haziest knowledge of life in the Midlands or why they should need so much coal, listened to the continued diatribe, relieved that she had hit upon a means of diverting her grandmother's mind from Sir Ranulph. Her own mind, she discovered, much to her chagrin, was apt to dwell on him whenever there was no immediate crisis to distract it. The man was positively haunting her. She thought of him on waking and it took considerable strength of mind not to wonder, as she fell asleep, what he might have been doing that day.

'Now Ranulph Trent,' declared Lady Melthorpe, causing Louise to jump, 'he's the sort of man who wants a wife of some sense.' Encouraged by the colour that rose in her granddaughter's cheeks, she moved swiftly on to avoid being too obvious. 'And there's Hubert Nevis, rather older but still in his prime. I never thought his first wife suited him. Far too giddy a girl. He's older and wiser now, I dare say. Three children already. Two boys and a girl, I think. Or Major Cardross? Do you know him? Probably not, he spent quite some time in the Guards. Only sold out when the Earl turned up his toes. I daresay he's had every handkerchief thrown at him this past year.'

'No, ma'am, I have not the pleasure of Cardross's acquaintance. If he is only lately returned I would not. It is some time since I went about in society. Apart from visits to my cousins.'

'Not still being coy after Amelia's bolting, are you?' Lady Melthorpe dismissed every concern. 'That must be forgotten by now. No one will be interested in it. A five day's wonder as it was. You should go up to town more. Get Marston's new wife to take you about. Assuming she's not yet in an interesting condition. Is she? Do you know?'

'I ... er ... er no, ma'am. But surely not. They were only married in February.'

'Well then, it's ideal timing for you. I'm sure Lady Marston would appreciate your company. As I recall she's not yet turned twenty. She'll need some guidance from a slightly older head.' She lapsed into thought. 'I shall write and suggest it to your Mama.'

'No, really, ma'am, I could not go even if I wished to. There is Christopher to consider. He has lost so much I cannot desert him too.'

'Nonsense. He barely knows you. Children know their nurses better than their families. It cannot harm him to be without you.' Louise received another examination from the elderly eyes. 'How certain are you that you are not with him for your own relief, not his? As I recall you were exceeding close to Amelia.'

Her words caused Louise to catch her breath. A sob knotted her throat. It was several moments before she could reply. 'We were close, ma'am. I loved her dearly. I … I …'

'You think you would fail her if you left the child?'

Her bowed head whipped up. 'That's it, ma'am. That's it exactly. And I must admit he is … he is all I have of her.' Her head lowered again. She could not continue.

'There, there, child. You have had a difficult furrow to hoe but you must be able to see your way by now.' Leaning on her cane, she heaved herself to her feet to cross to her granddaughter. She patted her bowed curls. 'Do not cut yourself off from life, child. Amelia would not want it and the child does not need it.' A gnarled finger poked through a single tress to lift and drop it. 'If there is someone who's taken your fancy, for whom you think you might form a lasting passion, follow it. Life soon goes by. Faster than people of your age think. Regrets and sorrows are cold comfort in your old age.' She hobbled towards the door. 'Think on what I have said, my dear. Now, I must take these old bones for a rest.'

She passed from the drawing room, leaving Louise to stare at the prospect beyond the tall windows and contemplate her advice. Deep in thought, it was some time before she noticed Letty running, albeit very slowly, across the sweep of lawn with Christopher. The child legs lurched in an unstable fashion. When he turned his head to see if she was catching him, his feet tangled and he fell laughing onto the grass.

The sight brought a smile to Louise's face and pleasure to her heart. Rising, she hurried up to her bedchamber for her coat, hoping she would be in time to join them. The quickest route downstairs took her past the servants' hall. Magdale, emerging in his authoritative manner, drew back. Louise cast a quick wave at him with a gloved hand.

'Master Christopher is playing outside.'

'Yes, ma'am. Charming lad, if I may be so bold.' Re-entering his domain he descended from his lofty height and divulged to a favoured few that Miss was mighty taken with the young master.

Louise rounded the corner of the house in time to see a small man toss a ball to Christopher. She halted. Something about him touched a memory. The precise one eluded her. Christopher ran forward, hands ridiculously too far apart to catch the ball. She reached a laughing Letty as the child's arms closed on thin air.

'Who is that?'

'Oh, ma'am, you gave me a start. It's Sir Ranulph's tiger, ma'am. Lester.'

'I see.' Louise was very much afraid she did. The man came forward knuckling his forehead.

'Afternoon, ma'am. I was playing with the boy. He likes to catch a ball – in a manner of speaking, that is. He's not caught it yet.'

'You're Lester, I hear. Sir Ranulph's tiger.'

'That be right, ma'am. He's left me here to look out for his horse. He couldn't – or to speak more rightly – wouldn't take it back a-tied to the curricle. Wouldn't ever take the notion into his noddle. Cares a lot for his cattle, he does.'

'I see. Not a heavy task for you, I assume.'

'Feed it. Curry it. Ride it out to shake the fidgets off its legs.'

'He trusts you to do that? To ride it?'

'He does that, ma'am.' He nodded confidingly. 'Don't you fret. I may be a small ru – a small person, but you'd never guess how quick and strong I am.'

'Probably not.' She was uncertain as to whether his presence was an advantage or a danger. 'Don't let me keep you from your duties. I am here to play with Master Christopher now.'

The man bowed, tapped his forehead and strolled back round the corner of the house with his hands thrust into his pockets. If the master required him to watch after an infant, then watch after him he would. It was no skin off his beak. Nor would he go against orders and reveal to the lady that the gent whom he was delighted to serve was now shacked up in the Bear Hotel in Chippenham waiting for him to report any alarm.

'He does like Master Kit,' Letty said. Her face crumpled. 'I hope as I didn't do wrong, miss, to let him play with us.'

'No, of course not.' Louise bent down to take the ball Christopher was thrusting against her knees.

'Frow, frow,' he demanded.

Obliging him, he trotted after it and she continued. 'We must take great care of him. Don't leave him with anyone else but Nurse, will you?'

'Oh, no, miss. Mr Trent – Sir Ranulph, I should say – was most firm about that. *Letty, my girl*, he said to me, *you have a good care of Master Kit. We don't want any accidents, like the one with the pony.*'

'Did he? It was most kind of him.' She gnawed her bottom lip. 'I didn't see the accident myself. Only Sir Ranulph riding to the rescue.'

Christopher wobbled towards her with the ball. 'Frow. Frow.'

'It were a mighty near thing, miss. It seemed...' Her face closed.

'Seemed?'

'Well, miss...I don't know as I should say.'

'You most certainly should, Letty. If it concerns Master Christopher's safety.'

'Frow. Frow,' came the demand.

Louise took the ball and threw it absently. 'Well?'

'It's only that it looked to me as if Master Philip smacked the horse and then started limping. He was alright afore that.'

Fear and delight tangled in Louise. 'Before the pony bolted?'

'As near as I could say. I wasn't paying much mind to him afore that for Betty — her with the red hair — had come out of the still room and called to me so I'd only just turned back.' She took her turn with the ball and Christopher lurched off after it again. 'I must say, though, as she thought the same.' A frown pleated her juvenile forehead. 'I dare say we're mistaken, miss. It's a puzzlement to me why he should do anything as daft as smack it with the young master on its back.'

It was not at all a puzzle to Louise. It was, in fact, a relief. All the suspicions she had held about Ranulph Trent dissolved in an instant. He was not the danger. He was the saviour. He and his ridiculous delight in silly furniture. She bent to take the ball from her clamorous nephew. 'I'm sure there is nothing to it,' she assured Letty, her heart light.

Chapter Twenty-Five

Ranulph Trent occupied himself in the Bear's private parlour reading an account by James Perry in *The Morning Chronicle* that must surely be libellous of the King. If it did not result in Mr Perry's prosecution he would be surprised. He laid the newspaper down. The room was, for someone accustomed to only the best, surprisingly comfortable and well-appointed, as was his bedchamber. Its two arched windows did not, happily, overlook the market place so he remained undisturbed on those days when the clatter, cries and general hubbub would otherwise have wakened him early. Unfortunately the eight bells in the tower of St Andrews church so kindly cast by Mr Rudhall were not as easily ignored. Consequently he did rise early and occupied himself in trotting a hired horse down the High Street and over the bridge to hack around the country lanes and fields. He would much have preferred his own, but Apollo was the reason for his tiger remaining at Frannington Court. Being unknown in the area, he had no fear of being recognised. The only person who might do so was Philip Aveley and he caused Sir Ranulph no concern at all. His anxiety for Christopher would mount if the man was hovering in the neighbourhood but that eventuality was well in hand. Lester was a resourceful fellow, and reliable. He could rely on him to follow his orders to the word.

Returning from a canter along the lanes between the sprouting fields he found Lester lingering opposite the archway into the hotel's courtyard. Seeing his master arrive, he scurried across the cobbles towards him.

'Problem?' Sir Ranulph asked.

'Not as such, your honour, but I saw that fellow you've suspicioned when I was in the Fox's taproom yesterday night.'

'What were you doing there? I told you to stay at the Court.' He dismounted and looped the reins over his arm.

'Ah, well.' The tiger took hold of the bridle and stroked the horse's soft nose. It whinnied warm breath into his ear. 'I thought I saw him when Miss took the lad out in the gig to see the deer in the park. Thought it'd be a smart idea to make certain.'

'First of all, how does it come you were with Miss Devreaux, and second, why did you think he was in the Fox?'

The tiger presumed to look offended. 'Sir, you know how I wouldn't fail you. I've made myself right useful in the stables and took the gig round to her. Not that it's difficult to be useful, there's only Gawber as can tell one end of a horse from t'other.'

'Who might Gawber be?'

'Lady Melthorpe's coachman. He's from Devon too.'

Well aware that his tiger was exceptionally proud of his Devonian heritage, Sir Ranulph suppressed a smile. 'Go on.'

'After Miss had seen the lad into his cot for the night and Letty were in his room – she's a sweet girl that Letty, very obliging with the left-over cake.'

'Never mind about your adventures with maids, get to it.'

'So knowing the lad was safe – as I said – I asked Gawber where to go for a heavy wet and some company and he said the Fox was the best place. So I toddled down there and what do you think?'

'I'm living in hope that you will eventually tell me.'

'Yes, well, there was the Aveley chap with someone I wouldn't say was of a Christian turn of mind. Far from it, if you ask me.'

Sir Ranulph's interest sharpened in his grey eyes. 'Describe him.'

'Short fellow. Grey in the face – too much time in Newgate with nowt to garnish the warder's palm if you ask me. Up to no good in company with your Aveley, I'll be bound.'

'He's not my Aveley,' Sir Ranulph said, somewhat absently. After several moments he continued, 'I'll send for Wadden. When you see him, describe this fellow and direct him to the Fox. He's to fall in with him, if he can. He should know what Aveley looks like for he saw him at Crestings. If he meets this man you've seen, I want to know about it. And quickly. Now get off back to the Court.' The tiger released the bridle and turned away. 'And Lester...' The man turned back. 'Thank you.'

The tiger chuckled. 'Don't you fret yourself about Miss and the lad, sir. We'll keep them safe. You'll see.'

Sir Ranulph drew breath to shatter any notion his tiger might have that he was given to fretting about anything, not even the stubborn and recalcitrant Miss Devreaux, but the man was strolling off towards the market, whistling and with his hands in his pockets. Passing under the arch into the hubbub of the hotel's courtyard he permitted a groom to relieve him of his mount. He would admit to a decent concern for the safety of his charges. Charges? Did he now number Miss Devreaux as a charge? Certainly not. His pace quickened. She was a grown woman. Well able to take care of herself. A maddening woman. Absolutely relied upon to flout his every wish. Obstinate. Opinionated. Wilful. She was enough to irk any man.

His steps took him up to his bedchamber. Divesting himself of his hat and whip, he stopped halfway across the room. Did she irk him? Most certainly she did. But she was ... what? His mind travelled the path it had carved before. Resolute? Steadfast? Loyal? Loyal Louise? Louise Eleanor Devreaux. He could picture her clearly, laughing at him with her foot on the library steps. Far too clearly! He pushed the image away and rang the bell for breakfast. He ate it energetically, determined to stop debating with himself whether her eyes really did show violet when she was angry or were simply a very deep blue. He failed.

Vintry sat in the corner as near to the Fox's inglenook fireplace as he could manage without attracting curious stares from the regular inhabitants occupying the prime, and warmest, benches. A pock-marked table of inadequate proportions protected him from unwelcome approaches by the natives. Not even the buxom maid who delivered his fourth tankard could elicit a pleasant word from him. He sat there his eyes fixed on the ale's dying foam, casting only the occasional sulky stare at the rest of the crowded and fuggy room. Not even Wadden's entrance occasioned more than a sniff.

Wadden acquired a tankard from the tapster and ambled towards Vintry's corner without once meeting his eye. Seating himself with a nod and a grunt, he gulped a deep draught. Staring at the remaining contents he permitted a more satisfied grunt to escape.

'Humph.' He reached inside his shabby coat and extracted a clay pipe from its pocket. For several minutes his entire attention focussed on wedging shreds of tobacco into the bowl. Satisfied, he lifted a taper from a battered tankard lodged on the mantle above the fire and kindled them into a decent glow. Puffing, he unfolded a crumpled copy of The Journal and applied himself to reading, apparently with some difficulty, to the report of a lurid crime on the front page.

'Bah,' he said, after a few minutes. 'Any fool who goes forking on his own deserves what he gets. Bulk and file's the way. Or a bungnipper.' He grunted again and laid down the newspaper to take another pull at his tankard.

Vintry eyed him, apparently unwilling to discuss the relative merits of picking pockets in company with one or two assistants or on one's own.

'Is this a decent lay-up?' Wadden asked. 'No rum-dubbers as gets at yer belongings?'

A shrug. 'Can't say as I know. I ain't no thief.'

'Nah. Not my line o'work, neither.'

Interest sparked in Vintry's breast. 'Oh? And what might be your line of work?'

He observed Vintry from narrowed eyes. 'I don't know as I go around telling that to the curious.' The caution sounded strangely at odds with his previous spurt of thieves' cant.

He was subjected to a searching examination of his features, hands and apparel. 'If you're looking for work, mebbies I knows of summat.'

'Oh, yeah?'

'Yeah. There's this flash cove I know. Has a little task in mind.'

'Oh? And how come the likes of you know a flash cove?'

'That ain't none of your business.' Vintry hunched forwards. 'Are you interested?'

'What might it be? Tell me first. I ain't looking to dance at Tyburn.' He rubbed his neck. 'Or if'n I was to risk it, I'd be wanting a sight more than hangman's wages.'

'Well,' said Vintry after a quick cast at the nearest imbibers, 'it might be like this.'

Sir Ranulph, appraised by his tiger of a possible offer of nefarious worth to Wadden, leant over the parapet on Chippenham's bridge and propped his mouth against his laced fingers, heedless of the dust the stonework was adding to his elbows. Below him, three urchins waded into the water with make-shift nets. Bare footed, they swept unsuccessfully for fish.

'What will you be wanting me to do, sir?' Lester asked.

Several moments passed before he received an answer.

'For the present nothing, but keep a close watch on Miss Devreaux and, particularly, on the boy.'

Lester had passed several years in Sir Ranulph's service; he presumed upon them. 'Do you think that's wise, sir? Wouldn't it be better to take them back to Crestings?'

'It would be.' His master straightened. 'But it would only make for a delay in whatever Aveley has planned. The threat would remain.'

'Perhaps then you should warn the miss.'

'I can't do that. She's a woman. Females can't be expected to bear that sort of thing.'

'I bet as she could. She looks pluck to the backbone to me. It's not every girl of her kind that charges about the country with no abigail.'

'First,' the reply came with less terseness than he expected but in a voice charged with concern, 'she does have an abigail – and had one of sorts at Stapley, though I can't recall her name. And second, if you want to continue in my employ, you'll speak of her with respect.'

'I still say she'd bear up well.'

'I'll not have her troubled.' Fierce eyes swept over him. 'Keep that in mind.'

'If'n you won't tell her, you could have the man taken up instead. That'd keep the boy safe.'

'No I could not. He's done nothing wrong. As yet.' He straightened up. 'Now, take yourself back to Frannington Court and watch over her – them,' he corrected. 'If anything occurs, borrow a horse and ride to me immediately.'

'And if I'm not free, like? If someone's cracked my napper?'

'Don't get yourself where you could be knocked about. Keep your distance. Wadden's the one for that work. You're there to listen and learn and tell me when it happens.'

'You're certain it will then?'

'As certain as I am that you'd best be off. Now.'

Lester tapped his cap and hurried away up the hill, leaving his master to return to his contemplation of the River Avon. He was mighty relieved that he only had to do what he was told and not be the one who must decide what action to take. Or not take.

The walk from Chippenham to Frannington Court was a good five miles by road, most of it uphill. Lester took to the fields, much to the alarm of the cattle and sheep therein. In the final field outlying Frannington's park his progress was arrested by the sight of a lady he knew well in a blue riding habit racing a familiar mount towards the gates. A man – Gawber the coachman, unless he mistook – laboured a considerable distance behind her on a brown cob.

'My gawd,' he gasped. 'She's on Apollo. She'll be off him afore she's gone a half mile.'

He forced his way between a pair of badly-laid hawthorns and ran non-stop to the stables.

Arriving breathless he was confronted by Lady Melthorpe, her butler, her dresser, three anxious grooms and a maid who was supporting a sobbing Letty who had a stained handkerchief tied round her head. 'In gawd's name, what's up?' he shouted. 'Why's the Miss gone on Apollo?'

Lady Melthorpe turned, pointing her cane at him. 'You're Sir Ranulph's tiger, aren't you?'

'Yes'm.'

'His ward has been kidnapped. You'd best get yourself mounted and go to Crestings to tell him.'

'There's no need, ma'am. He's in Chippenham.'

'What? What's he doing there?'

'I can't rightly say, ma'am. But he'll be wanting to know about this. And why Miss is on his horse?'

'She's chasing them, of course. Ewan,' the stick swung to the youngest stable-lad, 'give him a horse. Sir Ranulph must know immediately.'

Fidgeting while the horse saddled and brought out, he leapt into the saddle and galloped back to Chippenham.

In a short space of time Ranulph Trent and his tiger bore down upon the odorous establishment known as The Fox. Its denizens were few, there being gainful labour of various lowly sorts to be had elsewhere. The landlord, a thin-faced man of uncertain years was taking his ease by a small fire and quenching his thirst before the evening's effort.

'You,' Sir Ranulph said. 'Have you seen a man by the name Wadden?'

'Me, your honour?' The landlord lurched to his feet, spilling half of the tankard's contents down his cord breeches. 'Why, no, your honour. Not as I could rightly say.'

Sir Ranulph advanced, his whip clenched in his hand.

The landlord eyed it and backed to the safety of his bar. 'O'course if he be the one with the broke nose, I might of seen him.'

'Here?' The word was barked.

'Only to wet his whistle. He don't stay here. Said it was too mal...mal...mulderous for a man of his standing.' He spat. 'The swine.'

'Where is he then?'

'He's at the old cot down by the stream a mile off. That should be more to his liking, being as it's green damp up the walls.'

Sir Ranulph turned on his heel. Lester, outside with the horses, held out the second reins to him.

'Not there?'

'No, but he's managed to tell them where he'll be.'

Sir Ranulph leapt into the saddle. He dug his heels into the horse's flanks. 'He's a bare mile away. Or so the landlord says.'

'Do think he has it right? You know what these folks are with their country miles.'

Sir Ranulph flicked a glance at him as the horses raced along the lane. 'I hope it's true.' He stopped by a broken down gate. 'In here. The river's the other side.' He spurred through. 'Pray God we're in time.'

Chapter Twenty-Six

Louise was by no means a poor horsewoman but Apollo's exuberance at being galloped anywhere, let alone through delightful countryside on a bright afternoon tried her skill to the utmost. The shabby carriage she was chasing had vanished from view. She only knew from the lodge keeper that it had turned away from the road to Chippenham. Where the road led, she knew not. Nor had she ever passed along it for even the shortest distance. Her rides, such as they had been, had amounted to no more than a sedate canter around the park on a mare whose staid gait would not have tried even the most inexperienced of riders.

The gently rolling land formed itself into a steeper hill. She urged Apollo forward. 'They cannot be far ahead,' she panted, leaning forward, the reins tight in her hand. The carriage disappeared from view between stands of trees round the fields. She urged Apollo forward until she glimpsed it again. It looked to be passing through the fields far down the hill. There must be another lane somewhere ahead. By a venerable elm, half-clothed in spring green leaves, she found it. The lane turned sharply off and slid downhill under the touching branches of more elms. A bend in the lane's descent hid the vehicle from view, and its worn surface became increasingly uneven. Stones littered it, weeds grew on it. Apollo stumbled. She barely held him up.

'Pray God it's not much farther,' she whispered.

She pressed on through the dim green light of the natural tunnel until she could make out a vehicle a fair distance ahead where the trees were sparsely separate. It was rumbling towards a cottage standing at the lane's lowest reach where the silver Avon wound through flat water-meadows. 'Please God,' she whispered, 'let it be them.'

She slowed Apollo to a walk, afraid that another twist in the lane might bring her suddenly upon her quarry before she had time to prepare. Prepare for what? She drew to a halt by a wide oak rising from a scrappy hedgerow. Keeping the horse as concealed as possible by the wide trunk, she bent to peer under a low branch. Ahead, the lane curved out of sight. A group of three trees stood by the entrance to a neglected field, half concealing the cottage's roof. As she watched the top of the vehicle came into view. It stopped by the front wall. Two men jumped down. Even so far away she thought she had seen them both before. Yes, the thin man had been at Stapley. He was the one who had stolen Christopher. Her heart, scarcely steadied from her tumultuous ride, quickened again. And the other? A large, lumbering man. She knew him. The gardener. So-called. The man Ranulph Trent had sent. The one who had spied on her at the Dower House.

Her thoughts were chaotic. Was Sir Ranulph the threat after all? Had he sent the man after the thin man's attempt had failed? Did it mean the two had been in league all the time? Finding a way for one to win her confidence by making the other appear the villain?

Panic gripped her. She drew back into the shadows cast by the tree. It must be impossible to seize Christopher while they were near. Perhaps, when it was dark ... Perhaps they would go out somewhere. She tried to remember how bright the moon had been last night. Clouds had filled the sky, blotting out the moon for some of it. If they were here again tonight, the way to the cottage would be pitch black and treacherous.

Kicking her foot free of the stirrup iron, she slid her leg over the saddle's top pommel and slid to the ground. For a moment the hem of her habit's trailing skirt caught on the saddle. She tugged it and it slithered down around her. Her throat dried. She tried to swallow but could not. She must calm her thoughts. Plan what to do. First, Apollo must be hidden. If either man left the cottage and saw him, they would know someone was near. If it were the man from the Dower House he must recognise the horse. He must know he was about to face him. Unless ... unless ... No, she could not truly believe it of Sir Ranulph. If they thought he was about to come upon them, they might leave Christopher and flee. Or they might ... they might ... She could not bring herself to think of his possible fate.

With considerable strength of will she set her mind to forming a plan. Nothing could be done until it was fully dark. The answer would be to creep up then and rescue him. The field between the trees and the cottage was enclosed by ragged hedges. She could go part of the way in their shelter now, while there was some remaining light in the sky. How she wished she was not clothed in bright blue velvet. She must take great care not to be seen.

Apollo took exception to being tied to a tree but a hand over his nose and soothing words settled him.

'You stay here,' she whispered. 'I shall soon be back.'

With the skirt of her habit swept over her arm, she stepped into the lane, taking careful note of which field he was in. Readying herself to dive into a ditch at any unexpected approach, she made her way forward. A few hundred yards further on, she smelt smoke. The cottage could not be far. She pushed through the thinned hedge into a field and, crouching, inched forward.

There it was. It was filthy. No place for a child. The thatch was green with moss and mildew. The walls that had once been bright were mired at the base and as green as the roof above. One window had a rag of a curtain at it but the others were bare. The door, which bore few traces of paint, was shut.

She huddled by the hedge until the light drained from the sky and the moon rose to glow palely through inky clouds. Her heart pounded as she left the protection of the hedge. She stumbled on her hem and tripped headlong, only just preventing herself from gasping out loud. The ground was rough. It grazed her cheek. Tears sprang to her eyes. She blinked them away and crept further on until she could cower behind the remains of a stone wall. To judge from the gnarled and broken trees beyond it, it must have once enclosed a small orchard. Her ears strained to catch any sound of Christopher. She could hear nothing. No voices. No child crying. Even the nag tethered to a broken fence post was silent.

The clouds thickened. Shadows deepened under the largest apple tree. What warmth had been in the early April sun was gone. Some of her courage had drained with it. She wished she had not been so impetuous and had waited for Gawber to stay beside her. She shivered and wrapped her hands together to stop them shaking. Her nerve was shaking too. Summoning up stern words she did her best to rally her forces. Christopher must be saved. There was no-one else here to do it. She gathered her habit skirt closer and waited for a shaft of moonlight to show her the way to the cottage door.

Sir Ranulph and his tiger rode up from Chippenham, disregarding the rights of anyone else on the road to a gentle passage.

'It must be close to the river,' he said, 'I could wish the landlord's directions had been clearer.'

'I don't think he knew of its whereabouts. Just hoping to see us gone, sir.'

'It can't be too difficult to find. He said a mile. And by the river. If we have to trace down every lane and byway we'll find it.'

Lester forbore to comment. He did not need to, his face declared his thoughts quite adequately. Nor did the first four lanes they galloped down improve his outlook. 'We could be doing this all night,' he grumbled as the regained the wider road from the fifth lane.

'If that is all you can say, be silent.' Sir Ranulph road on, then drew rein. 'We'll go down the next and if that is not it, we'll take to the river bank.'

Lester cast his eyes heavenwards and followed his master down the sixth track they had discovered since leaving the inn.

The gloom had deepened into night by the time they reached the river. Turning his horse's head upstream, Sir Ranulph guided the animal through the water-meadow. It sank up to its fetlocks.

'You want to be up a mite,' Lester called, 'or it'll be in up to its hocks.'

His mouth grim, Sir Ranulph heeded the advice and moved up from the water's edge. A cluster of willows impeded his progress. He rode round it to see a cottage inside a skeletal beech hedge. He raised a hand. 'Dismount,' he whispered. He slid to the ground and handed his reins to Lester.

'Wait here. I'll see who, if anyone, is there.'

He disappeared into the gathering gloom. Lester swung his leg over the pommel and landed on his feet. He looped both reins round a weeping trail of willow and looked about him for a stout stick. His master might have his pistol in his saddle but Lester had never fired one and doubted he could hit a house side if he did. Shooting his master by mistake was not in his plan.

The ground proved too damp for him to stand for long. With a care for his shoe-leather as well as his cold toes, he re-mounted and continued to wait. Minutes passed. On the brink of inching the horses forward to see what had become of Sir Ranulph, a figure emerged from the darkness.

'It's not the one. There's only an elderly mother there, and her son. He said the place we want in another mile or so upstream.'

Lester grunted. 'Said as the landlord didn't know a mile from an inch.'

'You didn't, but he wasn't correct as to the distance.'

'What did the old biddy's son say about the place?'

'That it's stood empty for a couple of years since someone who rejoiced in the name of Fodderty and his daughter disappeared off to Bristol with her sailor husband.'

'Heard the life story did you? I thought you were gone a while.'

The feeble joke lessened the tension of his master's face. 'I think she has few visitors.' He nudged his horse forward.

Louise waited in the shadows, shivering, until the clouds cleared the moon's face and its gleam struck cold on the land. Her hands trembled. She tried to put her shaking knees down to the chill night air but she knew it was untrue. Never had she been in a situation such as this. What fate might befall her if the men captured her she barely knew but she was certain it would not be benign. Several of her mother's veiled warnings haunted her. If she emerged unscathed she would never dare tell anyone.

Trying her best to summon courage from her shaking nerves she pulled up her hem and picked her way over the broken wall. At the far side of the derelict orchard the second wall gave way to some sort of garden between it and the cottage. Nothing remained of it now save weeds and a few stakes. She stopped by one of them. It was iron. Rusted, but stout enough to deliver a helpful blow. Grasping it in her gloved hands she wiggled it backwards and forwards until it pulled free of the ground. Holding it before her, and carrying her hem, she trod closer to the cottage wall.

A child's wail broke the silence.

Christopher.

He was there.

The sound gave her courage. Surely she could reach him. Halting by the window nearest the front door, her ears strained to catch another sound. Men's voices were raised. An argument? Were they debating his fate? Creeping on her toes, she inched to the rear. Another door, in a worse state than the first, hung on worn hinges. She let her encumbering habit drop to the ground. With one hand she grasped the latch, the other tightened on the iron stake. Her breath stopped. Slow-moving fingers lifted the latch. A faint squeal of old metal caused her to halt. Her heart pounded. Had they heard? She waited. The men's voices continued. She raised the latch further.

The door swung open on hinges that creaked. She felt as if her heart would burst out of her pounding ears. Her eyes strained to see into the room. A narrow shaft of moonlight showed it contained a few broken sticks of furniture and quantities of rubbish. Christopher lay huddled on a decrepit bed by the wall, whimpering softly.

Her breath escaped in a single burst. She crept to him and placed a hand over his mouth. His eyes flew open.

'Hush, hush, my love,' she whispered. 'I have come to take you home. You're safe now but you must be quiet. Can you be quiet for me?'

The small head with its terrified eyes showing above her hand nodded.

She laid the stake on the bed and lifted him into her arms. The skirt of her riding habit dragged across the grimy floor. She kicked it out of her way. Christopher clung his arms round her neck. They dragged the ribbons of her hat, tipping it sideways. She tried to nudge it back into place before it slid over her eyes. The attempt had to be abandoned. The more she tried the more he clung to her neck. She staggered, fearful of dropping him.

'Hold tight, my love,' she whispered. 'We shall soon be out of here and riding home to Letty.'

She reached the door with her trembling burden. Her trailing woollen hem caught in what had once been a chair but was now a seat with three legs. It toppled onto the floor. The noise sounded like thunder to her. She ran.

Behind her the door to the first room was flung open. Two men dashed through.

'What the deuce ..?' Vintry raced across the floor and into the night.

Hampered by the child and her habit, there was no escape. Vintry's hand grabbed her arm. Christopher screamed.

'Let me go!' she shrieked.

Christopher's arms were wrenched apart. Wadden caught him before he hit the floor and carried him into the cottage. Vintry dragged Louise after him in an ungentle grasp. She screamed and screamed and kicked and struggled until he flung her onto the bed, cursing as she sank her teeth into his grubby hand.

'The bitch has bitten me, damn her. I'll soon see to her.' He bent towards her.

Feeling frantically over the noisome blanket, Louise's fingers found the iron stake. She grabbed it and swung it at Vintry. It caught him above the ear, causing him to stagger.

'The bitch,' he yelled again. His hand swiped at her, knocking her head against the wall.

The last thing she saw before darkness enveloped her was Wadden comforting a sobbing Christopher.

Chapter Twenty-Seven

Someone was banging her head. No...no, the throbbing was inside it. It was her hand that was throbbing. No, someone was patting it. Her eyes flew open. The scene that met them appalled her. Three men were wrestling in the moonlight filtering through the filthy window. A tall, bulky individual had his arm crooked round the throat of a shorter, wiry man who was doing his utmost to kick at the third. She started up only to find her head reeled with the movement. A strong arm slid round her shoulders, supporting her from falling back onto the vile bed.

'Be still, ma'am, there's nothing to fear.' The voice struck her as familiar. She turned her head which was resting against a strong shoulder. His face outlined by the cold light, Ranulph Trent cradled her against the capes of his greatcoat.

'Oh, it's you,' she told him, unnecessarily. A swift motion brought her upright, though her head swirled. 'Christopher?' She scanned the dark room, trying to see. 'Where is he?'

'Aunt Looz, Aunt Looz,' came a small voice. A small figure clambered over Sir Ranulph's lap.

'Oh, my darling,' she cried on a sob. 'You're safe.'

'You are both safe.' Sir Ranulph lifted Christopher into her open arms. 'We shall have you back to Lady Melthorpe's in no time.'

The scuffling that occupied most of the small room and threatened to collapse onto the bed, ceased. 'What do you want done with this one?' Wadden asked.

'We'll take him back with us and hand him to the magistrate in the morning.'

'You don't want to be doing that.' Vintry wrestled to break an arm free of Wadden's rigid hold. 'I'm not the one as wanted the brat held.'

'No?' Sir Ranulph's voice cut coldly through the dark.

'No. It were Aveley,' Vintry said. 'He wanted a ransom for him.'

'Oh, it cannot be.' Louise broke free of the restraining arm. 'He would not be so cruel to one of his own family.'

'Yes he would. The devil's been dancing in his pocket for months.'

Vintry's words confused her. 'What?'

'He's cleaned out. Been drawing the bustle as if he were swimming in lard.'

'He means he's in debt,' Sir Ranulph explained. 'I have known it for some time.'

'But he can't be. He always looks so presentable.'

'He'll be off on French leave now this hasn't fallen into his lap.' Vintry snarled. 'Leaving me to carry this.'

'Oh, good God,' Louise said, her hand to her forehead. 'I have no idea what he means.'

Sir Ranulph's arm tightened about her. 'That Aveley will leave the country to escape his creditors,' he explained.

Wadden shoved Vintry at Lester. 'Here, miss, you look.' He pulled the fold of newspaper from his pocket. 'It says in here that one of his creditors is fit to die in Marshalsea.'

'Put it away,' Sir Ranulph told him. 'Miss Devreaux may read it later, there is not enough light in here.'

'Yes indeed. I just want to go home.'

A few minutes saw her seated in the shabby coach, Christopher on her lap with Sir Ranulph's greatcoat wrapped about them. Wadden had command of the reins. Sir Ranulph, reunited with Apollo, led Vintry who was tied to the pommel of his hired mount. Lester brought up the rear, grumbling loudly at the side-saddle he was obliged to use now Sir Ranulph had commandeered his previous saddle for Apollo.

Albina Melthorpe sat rigidly upright in her lofty drawing room, spurning her dresser's offers of hartshorn, a vinaigrette or a snifter of brandy.

'You're nothing but a doomsayer,' she told her, quelling her own fears with difficulty. 'You would greet the Second Coming with complaint and reproach. If you cannot find anything useful to say, keep silent.'

'But your ladyship —' began Twitton, clutching the spurned vinaigrette and three spare lace handkerchiefs.

'But nothing.'

Further recriminations were cut short by the door opening. Magdale, his face austere, ushered the coachman into the room.

'Have you found her, Gawber?'

'No, ma'am.' He shuffled, supremely conscious he was shod only in thick woollen socks, his muddy boots having been forcibly removed from him in the kitchen by an unimpressed footman under the severe direction of the housekeeper. 'Lost sight of her down by the lambing shed and couldn't find her again. I tried every lane there was but she'd disappeared like a ghost.'

The dresser wailed, unstopped the vinaigrette and inhaled deeply and unwisely. She covered her splutters with all three handkerchiefs.

'Very well, Gawber. Take yourself down to the kitchens for a mug of ale.'

The coachman backed himself out of the room, bowing over the hat clutched in his hands.

'Magdale, see to it that all the menservants are dressed and out at first light. We must search for my granddaughter.'

The butler bowed. 'Yes, my lady. And would you wish me to summon the doctor now or later?'

'Not at all. Not yet. I declare I'm surrounded by worrywarts of the first order. There'll be time to summon him if Miss Devreaux is in need of his services and not before.'

He withdrew, leaving his mistress in the company of her dresser who was muttering under her breath of people brought home on hurdles with their necks broke.

Her ladyship's rigid control was rewarded some two hours later when her granddaughter carried an exhausted and sleeping Christopher into the room.

'My dear girl, you have him.' She rose from her seat, leaning heavily on her dresser's arm. 'Is he hurt? Are you?' She pulled her gaze from them to the figure behind. 'Sir Ranulph, my thanks to you. I dread to think of the consequences had you not come to the rescue.'

He advanced and bowed over the raised hand. 'The merest bagatelle, ma'am. Restoring Miss Devreaux to safety has been a privilege. Might I suggest she takes some rest? She has suffered a blow to the head.'

'Has she? Have you? What happened?'

'Perhaps I might tell you, ma'am,' he replied, 'while the child at least is settled.'

'If you have quite finished organising me, I shall take him to bed and change out of my habit.' She peered over Christopher's head at the hem. 'I doubt it will ever recover.'

'I'm sure it will. Twitton, accompany Miss Devreaux. When she has changed, do what you can to restore her habit.'

Her head down and her mouth pinched, the dresser followed Louise out of the room, still clutching three lace handkerchiefs and the vinaigrette.

'Now, Sir Ranulph, tell me all.' Lady Melthorpe settled herself in her chair. 'What happened to my great-grandson? And who was responsible?'

He told the history concisely, starting with the bolting pony and including mention of Marius Trent's discoveries in London.

'I see.' Lady Melthorpe leant back, surveying him closely. 'An unedifying tale. You are sure of it?'

'Regrettably, yes, ma'am.'

'This uncle? – Aveley, wasn't it? He wanted to ransom the child, not...'

'I doubt he would have killed him, ma'am. He needed money too urgently for that. A disappearance would mean time taken to search. And then there'd be due legal process to complete. Far too long for his needs.'

'What do you think he'll do next?'

'I am hopeful that he will leave the country of his own volition. If not he must be encouraged to do so.'

Watching him closely, she said, 'And my granddaughter?'

His face stilled in the light of the guttering candles. 'She is unlikely to be ... welcomed at her father's home. It had been – as I understand it – her intention to set up home on her own with the child.'

'I do not approve of young girls setting up home on their own. Especially with a child even if it is not hers. Tongues will wag. They always do. There are far too many noddlecocks with no intellect to do otherwise.' She glared at nothing in particular. 'And too many vicious cats.'

'Miss Devreaux is welcome to continue residing with my mother if she so chooses.'

He grew hot under her silent scrutiny.

'I can think of a better solution.'

'Ma'am?' The word was a croak.

'I'm no fool, Trent. I've had plenty of years to recognise when a man has developed a lasting passion. They give themselves away. They look up when a door opens only to show a fit of the glooms when it is not the one they wish to see.'

Sir Ranulph cleared a throat suddenly dry. 'I fear you are mistaken, ma'am. I have no such interest in Miss Devreaux.'

'Haven't you?'

'No. She is not what I look for in a wife – charming as she is,' he added quickly.

'What do you look for in a wife?'

'Breeding, of course. A certain elegance of mind. Someone presentable.' He shifted uneasily in his seat. 'Not the sort of noddlecock you described earlier.' The disquiet that had kept him unwed for so many Seasons spilled out. 'There could be nothing worse than being greeted with mindless chatter over the table for years to come.'

'I would not call Louise a noddlecock. Would you?'

'No, ma'am.' He swallowed, feeling like a callow youth under her gaze.

'And she certainly possesses all the other qualities you mention.'

'But, madam ...' he sprang from his chair to pace to the fireplace, 'she is ... wilful.' He faced his interlocutor. 'Stubborn.' His hands flew up frustratedly. 'God knows she never takes advice. It's like taking to the doorpost.' The hands drooped. 'Say what you will, she will have her way.'

'Rather like your good self, I believe.'

The protests drained from him. He sank back onto the chair. 'She sees me as her enemy, ma'am. Ever since we first met when I had such a painful duty to discharge. I believe she has held it against me ever since.'

'If that is what you think, she must be dissuaded from it. I shall set about it. She may remain here for the present and I expect you to do your part. If you don't, you're not the man I think you. In the meantime, you will rack up here for a day or two. You've been careering about the countryside and cannot have slept any more than the rest of us. I will have an apartment made ready. Shall I summon the magistrate to take charge of this Vie – Vet –?'

'Vintry. I think not, ma'am. Not for the moment. I need to consider all the ramifications of making this public before we take that course.'

'I agree. We will lock him in one of the cellars for tonight. You may talk it over with Miss Devreaux when the child is settled. It will give you another excuse to be in her company.'

'Another, ma'am?'

'But of course. You are joint guardians. The child's future must be gone into. In a spirit of conciliation. If you cannot display enough address to bring her to accept you after that, then I wash my hands of you.'

Sir Ranulph stiffened. 'You suggest, ma'am, that I take advantage of a lady in a distressed state of mind for my own benefit?'

'Try for a little consistency, man, do. A bare moment ago you had her as wilful and stubborn and ignoring your advice. You can't now have her a die-away miss fainting after a torn frill. Pooh!' A be-mittened, dismissive hand flapped at him. 'Take yourself off and find your own mind.'

More or less ordered to his room like a recalcitrant juvenile, Sir Ranulph bowed with as much civility as he could muster. Wearing an expression that caused the footman lingering in the expansive hall to maintain a vacant stare into the middle distance, he followed him to a bedchamber of no mean proportion. Divesting himself of his coat, he loosened his cuff bands and heaved the shirt over his head in a single movement. He availed himself of the warm water and towels on the wash-stand. He lifted his shirt. A critical examination showed every hallmark of The Bear's inexpert laundrymaid. Lady Melthorpe had clearly invited – no, commanded him to stay for several days more, making Dursham's attendance vital. Not least because he had not carried a second evening shirt to Chippenham with him. He sat at a table, standing on its gracefully carved legs between the pair of windows, and penned a brief note to his valet. A footman answered his bell in less than a minute.

'Give this to my man Wadden, please. Ask him to take it to The Bear as soon as he is sufficiently rested to depart. And have him ensure the man Vintry will still be guarded when he has gone.'

The man bowed and withdrew. Sir Ranulph looked longingly at the high bed. Two bulbous columns of dark oak supported one end of a heavily-carved tester and an equally intricate headboard supported the other.

'Elizabethan,' he said. 'I hope the mattress is not.' He hesitated, but not for long. He had endured the less-than-charming facilities of the Bear for longer than he liked. Not bothering to remove his boots or turn back the covers, he tested it.

A deep feathery comfort embraced him. He stretched out. With his hands laced behind his head, he stared up at the ruby-dark tapestry lining the wooden canopy overhead. So, the autocratic woman thought he should offer for her granddaughter, did she? The slight irritation the thought produced gave way to amusement. The *Grandes Dames* of her generation were disappearing fast. It was a shame. The generation that had replaced them was, he decided, basing his conclusion on various mamas who had tried to spark his interest in their daughters, far less entertaining and far more likely to dissolve into a fit of the vapours. And most of their girls were either giddy idiots without a serious thought in their heads, simpering schoolgirls or watering-pots. None of them were the equal of Miss Louise Eleanor Devreaux.

Louise Eleanor Devreaux ... he pictured her easily. Too easily. She was everything he had described. Wilful. Stubborn. Far too sure of herself and much-given to argument. He would never know a moment's peace. Or would he? There was a restful air about her – when she was not arguing. She was undeniably courageous. Taking to the heather on a strong and untried mount, in solitary pursuit of villains who might offer her God-knew-what offence was undeniably foolhardy but it was certainly brave. And when she laughed her face changed from solemn into one with traces of mischief. What a beautiful *debutante* she must have been. And beautiful she still was. He tried to remember if he had seen her on her come-out. The vaguest image of a graceful girl hovered at the edges of his mind. He had seen her then. Why had he not noticed her the more? Because she was younger? Too young? Then there had been all the talk of her sister and he had not seen her again although she had, very occasionally, braved the cats and returned to town with her cousin ... cousin ... Marston, that was it.

Now there was a man whose opinion he respected. No court card he. He had run across him several times at the Discourses at the Royal Institution. George Winchilsea, the President spoke well of him too, when the Earl could be persuaded to dampen his enthusiasm for cricket. If Marston enjoyed her company, then he, Ranulph, had not mistaken her worth.

Worth? Good God. He sat up. He was reviewing her as he would a horse. What had Albina Melthorpe said? That he looked up to see if it were she entering the room? He most certainly did not. Did he? He searched back through his memory. The evenings when his mother had persuaded her to join them for dinner had been enjoyable. And the scene in the library when she had laughed in his face with sheer delight almost haunted him. But after that, all he had seen was a cold expression and a turned shoulder. Which was her true character? The laughing, beautiful woman, or the frosty termagant? All his experience could not help him now.

Chapter Twenty-Eight

Louise entered the nursery with Christopher in her arms. Mabson's prostrated, lachrymose figure launched itself from the chair like a soul departing the grave for the joys of Heaven.

'My lambkin.' She lurched forward as swiftly as her bulk permitted. 'My lambkin. Come to your Mabbie,' she warbled, reaching out.

The nurse's overweening fuss irritated Louise. Her words came sharply. 'Have a care, he's asleep.'

'Oh, how can he sleep after all his terrors?' The voice whispered in sufficient volume to disturb the occupants of the floor below.

'Very easily, it seems.'

Mabson's eager arms dragged the child into a fierce embrace. 'Oh my poor little lambykin,' she moaned. Tears dripped onto his face. He stirred and his eyelids fluttered.

'For goodness sake, control yourself. He has been disturbed enough tonight.'

The nurse pulled him closer, glaring at Louise over his tousled head. 'He'll sleep sound enough.'

'Then I have not the least idea how he does it. It amazes me he can be so full of interest one second, then deep asleep the next.'

'It's the way with them,' she pronounced, her words dripping with superiority. 'When you've your own you'll see it often enough.'

The comment brought a knot to Louise's throat. She sank into the chair the nurse had vacated. Her fingers plucked at Sir Ranulph's coat that still hung on her shoulders. Realising, she stilled them and pulled it closer until its collar rubbed her cheek. The material's strength comforted her. She shook away the memory of his care for her and rose.

'I must change and return to her ladyship.' She looked around but Twitton had disappeared. Clutching the coat and looping the muddied skirt of her habit over one arm, she hurried to the seclusion of her own bedchamber.

The door snapped shut as she leant against the wood, her eyes closed, her breath coming unevenly. The coat slid from her, and her control dissolved with it. Tremors shook her legs. She wrapped her arms about her, gripping at her sleeves. Her mouth trembled. Folding her lips she held her breath, hoping to steady it, until her head felt it would explode. Breath burst from her. 'Don't be ridiculous,' she cried out loud. 'There is nothing more to fear. You are safe. With Christopher.' The words did not banish the shakes. She knew a moment of fierce longing to be held again in a pair of strong arms.

Her hands came up to cover her face. 'No. No.' She would not think that. Her eyes fell on the tapestry bell pull by the fireplace. Suddenly impatient to be downstairs to hear what punishment would be meted out to Vintry and Aveley, she reached it with quick steps and tugged it fiercely for a maid. The coat still lay by the door. She picked it up. It was still warm. Her warmth, not his. She laid it on the bed and started to remove her habit. Trembling fingers tugged at the row of buttons down its front. They refused to co-operate. She stamped her foot, well aware she was still trembling.

'Everything is fine,' she told the bed curtains. 'For goodness sake don't be such a wetgoose.' Even so, she had to steady herself against the bedpost. Her head drooped.

The door opened. Lizzie Sutton's troubled face peered round it. 'Miss, are you well? You ain't faint, are you?' The maid hurried across the floor. 'You're looking right pale.'

'Don't fuss. I have a slight headache. Nothing more.' She submitted to having her jacket unbuttoned.

Lizzie's nimble fingers met no trouble. 'They're saying downstairs as the young master was almost dead.'

The chatter steadied Louise. 'Nonsense. He was cold. And tired. That is all.'

'If you say so, miss.' The jacket was off. In moments, the habit skirt fell to the floor. 'You step out of it and I'll brush it.'

'Her ladyship has told Miss Twitton to see to it. Take it along to her when we're finished.'

Lizzie's face indicated quite clearly how much she enjoyed that commission. 'Yes, miss,' she said in resounding tones. She would send little Beth to make her wish known; that would pay off the slights my lady's snooty dresser had cast in their direction. 'Will you be wearing your pink muslin?' she asked, contented.

While Louise changed, the conversation between Lady Melthorpe and Sir Ranulph filled the drawing room with lively comment. It ranged from her ladyship's *bête noire* of canals, to what he knew of the scandalous Old Price riots at the Covent Garden theatre, and on to the King's failing health. The latter topic was set fair to descend into a fiery exchange on the likelihood of a Regency until the twin doors opened.

'Ah, here she is,' Louise's grandmother announced, forgetting all about the King. 'Has the child settled?'

'I think he will, ma'am. As soon as his nurse lets him.'

'Clucking like a hen with one chick, is she?'

'She is. But at least she had stopped sobbing by the time I left.' Her hands gripped together. 'Sir Ranulph, I cannot thank you enough for rescuing us. If you had not arrived with your man when you did, I shudder to think –'

'Don't,' her grandmother commanded. 'No good ever came from fretting over might-have-beens.'

Sir Ranulph arrested in his bow said, 'Lady Melthorpe is correct. Pray do not concern yourself, ma'am. All that matters is that you and Christopher are safe.'

'But is he?' Louise cast an anxious look at him. Her fingers kneaded together. 'How can we be sure? We have captured that dreadful man who took him but Mr Aveley is at large. He may try again.'

He held out his hand. 'Permit me to lead you to a chair.' His action wrapped her nervous fingers in his. 'You will be safe here, you know. Or indeed at Crestings, too.'

'That may well be true, sir, but I cannot spend my life as a prisoner.' She sank onto the chair, her eyes raised to his. 'Mr Aveley must be found and brought to justice.'

'Found certainly, ma'am, but not handed over.' There was reassurance in his gaze.

'But –'

'Child,' Lady Melthorpe broke in, causing Sir Ranulph to straighten and turn, still holding her hand. 'Do you want this scandal aired in public? I do not. Nor will your father.'

'But if he is not taken up, how may I be certain he will not try again?'

'I have every belief that he may be persuaded to leave the country,' Sir Ranulph said.

Suddenly conscious of the warmth of his touch, she snatched her fingers away. 'Leave?' She looked from him to her grandmother. 'But how?' She rose from her chair, her eyes switching from one to the other. 'You surely don't mean to pay him?'

Sir Ranulph regarded her steadily. 'I fear it will be the only way.'

'Oh, no! No!' She could not stay still. 'That is to reward him. It's unthinkable. Unthinkable.' Her skirts whipped round her ankles as she paced the carpet.

'Calm yourself, child. It will be for the best. It's the quietest way to dispose of him.'

She turned about the room. 'It must not be. And what of that man of his?' she demanded, stopping in front of her grandmother. 'I must believe he was to ... to *dispose* of us. He must be punished.'

'There is no difference between handing Aveley over and doing the same with him.'

'No, no I cannot agree. He is a vile character. I insist he is punished.' Her voice crept higher with each word.

Sir Ranulph stepped forward. His hands grasped hers. 'He will be, ma'am, I assure you.'

Louise pulled away. Her anger and distress pierced him.

'I shall set Wadden to deliver him to a friend of mine tomorrow. He is a serving captain on one of his Majesty's frigates. Have no fear. The man will not be made ... comfortable.'

She looked from him to her grandmother.

'Leave it to Sir Ranulph, my dear. I am certain you may repose complete confidence in him.'

Louise plunged from anger and amazement to disappointment. Unexpected and unwanted tears gathered on her lashes. 'It seems I have no choice.'

She sank onto the chair beside her. A globe of figured walnut stood waist-high on curved legs beside it. Conscious that her control was growing increasingly fragile, she tried to hide her agitation by tracing fingers over the highly-polished surface.

Lady Melthorpe's gaze became unusually abstract. She said, 'If you will bear Miss Devreaux company for a few moments, Sir Ranulph, I will have Magdale provide for your man.' She allowed him to open the door for her. On the threshold she turned. 'Louise, my dear, I believe you said once Sir Ranulph took an interest in unusual items of furniture.' She pointed at the globe. 'That is a Biedermeier piece. My son gave it to me for my ... well, it need not bother you for which birthday, but he did. Pray open it for our guest and see if you can find the secret drawer.'

Sir Ranulph bowed her out of the room. He shut the door, his mind occupied by the news that Louise must have spoken of him with, presumably, interest.

'I am intrigued,' he said, approaching the globe as if there had been no disagreement, no distress.

Its gleaming surface was banded round its equator with an inlaid brass scroll. He placed his hands gently of either side. The front of the top half slid up revealing a quadrant with a level quarter-floor and a vertical back which held a small drawer on either side of a central mirror. He lifted out the floor to reveal two more drawers and a curve of wood.

'I cannot see a secret drawer, Miss Devreaux,' he said, knowing that the curve was certain to conceal it. 'Would you care to try your luck?'

Louise rose listlessly. 'If you cannot, sir, I doubt I can.' She examined the interior and pushed a disinterested finger at the wooden curve. Nothing moved. She opened and shut one of the little drawers.

'Perhaps it conceals a switch,' he said, bending closer.

Her expression displayed no interest. Nevertheless she slid her fingers into the cavity. After a sharp click the curve rotated revealing a secret compartment. 'Oh! There it is.'

'Well done, ma'am.'

'It is hardly world-shattering.' She made to push the curve back into place but it would not move. She pushed again. Still no movement. 'Oh, the wretched thing. How stupid of it.' A final push, harder than the others still failed to close the compartment.

Her fingers trembled. She tried to shut down the top quarter sphere. It jammed on the drawer she had removed. 'Oh, no.' Her hands shook. Tears rushed to her eyes. 'Why won't it shut?' A sob. 'Why won't the stupid thing shut?' The tremors reached her shoulders. She hid her face in her hands.

Sir Ranulph's arms ached to enfold her. His fingers gripped into fists. 'Please, ma'am, I beg you, do not distress yourself.'

A shaken head was his only answer. He knew beyond doubt that the terrifying events of the last few days – the last evening – were finally exacting their price.

'Miss Devreaux, ma'am, please do not.' Chancing everything in one fateful move he gathered her into his arms. 'You are safe now, I promise you. I shan't let anything harm you ever again.'

Her shaking increased. For a moment he thought he had played and lost, then her fingers crept from her face to grasp the lapels of his coat. She gave herself into the emotional release of tears.

Rocking her gently he whispered her name into her curls. Murmuring soothing nonsense until the sobs that wracked her body subsided.

Behind him the door opened. 'So?' said Lady Melthorpe from the threshold. 'I assume I am to wish you both happy.'

Louise twisted away from Sir Ranulph's arms and lifted her cuff to mop her tears.

'You are a little premature, ma'am,' Sir Ranulph said thickly.

'Then I suggest you get to it. I shall return in a few minutes.' She whisked herself out of the room as quickly as her years allowed.

Sir Ranulph regarded the back of Miss Devreaux's head. 'Ma'am, please say you will marry me. Louise ... Louise, please. I want so much to marry you.'

Her head with its disordered curls shook. 'You cannot possibly want to. You don't like me.'

He turned her gently towards him. Tears had streaked her face and reddened her eyes. 'Oh, I do. Even when you ignore my requests.'

'Requests?' she croaked. 'You mean orders. You only ever give me orders.'

'But I can give you so much more. Oh,' he waved a dismissive hand. 'Not wealth and position. They would not sway you, I know. You have proved that beyond doubt. But deep love. And protection. You deserve so much more than you have ever been given. Please, I beg you, let me cherish you as you were never cherished before.'

He held her reddened gaze, hoping that he had said enough. 'Your eyes really are violet,' he said, irrelevantly.

Despite herself, she gurgled with rueful laughter. 'Violet and crimson by now, I think.'

He pulled her close, his hands on either side of her face and kissed her closing lids. Her hands slid between his arms and crept round his neck.

'Yes?' he said. 'Is that yes?'

'Only if you promise never to give me orders ever again.'

'I promise.'

She laughed, disbelieving and let him kiss her.

Chapter Twenty-Nine

A discreet but thorough search by Lester and Wadden proved Philip Aveley was nowhere to be found in the environs of Frannington Court. Sir Ranulph ordered them to Chippenham to acquaint themselves with various of the staff at the several hotels and lodging houses.

'If he is still loitering hereabouts, I want him found.'

Lester and Wadden put considerable effort into avoiding each other's eye. Neither held any hope of finding the man, not least because they had already expended considerable thought and energy in trying to do so.

'Right, sir,' Lester said as he and Wadden absented themselves from their master's stern gaze.

'We won't get him,' Wadden pronounced when they reached the safety of the Court's stableyard. 'No matter how many maids and flunkies we charge with it.'

Lester mounted into the gig her ladyship's head groom permitted them to borrow. 'We'll give The Angel one more try. You never know, the swine might have slunk back.'

Sir Ranulph stood by the library window, watching the gig leave. If Aveley was in Chippenham, he was confident his pair of scallywags would soon be hauling him back to Frannington Court. In the meantime, he had a letter to write to Captain, the Honourable Justen Fairburne. He seated himself at the substantial desk that occupied the centre of the impressive room only to discover inspiration flagged. He had no doubts of Justen's accepting his request; what concerned him was how much he might reasonably expect to hear of his reasons. In the end he settled on the briefest of outlines, but one which would ensure Vintry paid for his crimes.

> *My dear Justen,* he wrote.
>
> *May I prevail upon you to assist me in ensuring that someone who has caused distress to a lady of my acquaintance has the opportunity to regret his action? His name is Vintry and I feel sure some time in the fresh sea air will suit him admirably.*
>
> *I believe you are at present refitting in Plymouth. My man, Joseph Wadden will bring Vintry to join you.*
>
> *Yours as ever,*
> *Trent*

Among the items arranged on the desk was a polished wooden tray that held a small tinder box, a twisted wick on a stand and two sticks of red wax, one with a rounded end that showed it to be already in use. Sir Ranulph kindled the wick and dripped melted wax onto the folded letter. Before it had cooled and set he removed his signet ring and pressed it into the red pool. Returning his ring to his finger, he slipped several bank-notes from his pocketbook and laid them with the letter. After a moment he added two more notes. The last thing he wanted was for Wadden to be unable to deal with any unforeseen event during the journey. He would be exercised enough in preventing Vintry from escaping. A smile lifted one corner of his mouth. If he had Wadden's measure, Vintry would be no more comfortable on the journey than he would be once at sea.

His thoughts moved from Vintry's fate to the problem of Philip Aveley. He had decided – always assuming they found the man – that the most satisfactory option was to despatch him out of the country. To one of the colonies, perhaps. India was a land of opportunity, but did he wish to give the man an opportunity? Canada was not as distant as that. Or there were the Americas, a country that welcomed peoples of various classes and talents. Sir Ranulph knew he would, of course, have to meet the man's debts first else a stain would be set against the Aveley name. Marius had set them at four thousand, a not inconsiderable sum but not one that would cause him any problems, merely annoyance.

He was still pondering when the door opened and the love of his life entered. He rose, holding out both hands. 'My darling.'

Louise slipped hers into his grasp and he kissed her fingertips. 'Have you any word of Phil – of Mr Aveley?'

'Lester and Wadden have gone to Chippenham to watch the hotel he has used.' He saw the change in her face from hope to anxiety. 'Do not fear, my love. We shall have him.'

'And when you have? What then?'

He slipped his arms around her waist and pulled her close. 'I am minded to let him choose between India and the Americas.'

'Let him choose?' She placed both hands on his chest to lean away, staring up at him. 'Has he any right to choose?'

'No, but if we let him do so he is more likely to depart without a fuss.' He lifted a hand and kissed her fingers again. 'Trust me, my love. I will ensure he never troubles us again. Now,' he drew her to the padded seat at the farther window, 'tell me what you have done to prepare for our wedding.'

'I have written to Mama and Papa of course. Also to my cousin Hugo and his new wife. I thought perhaps Lady Marston might stand as Matron of Honour for me. My other female cousins are so very much older than I. And anyway –' she made an attempt at a smile, 'Grandmama says they are a pack of woebegones fit only for funerals.'

'Then we shall most definitely *not* invite them.'

'Are you quite happy that we shall marry here? Perhaps Lady Trent...' Her expression held a degree of anxiety.

He squeezed her hand to reassure her. 'My mother will be happy for me to marry anywhere. Apart from Gretna, of course. In fact I suspect she and Lady Melthorpe have had their heads together over us already.'

'Their heads together? But they don't know each other.'

'Oh, I think they do.' He pulled her closer. 'And even if they do not, do you think either would hesitate to correspond with the other? Matchmaking is surely the most entertaining of occupations for venerable ladies.'

She rested her head against his shoulder. 'Perhaps you are right.'

'I know I am. Now, will you be going to London for your bride-clothes?'

She rose abruptly, snatching her hand from his grasp. 'Oh, how can I think of bride-clothes when that man is still at large?'

He stood to wrap his arms around her again. 'I beg your pardon, my love. I did not mean to annoy you with trivia. Only to give your thoughts a happier direction.' His hand under her chin tilted her head. 'Do you doubt me? Doubt that once my mind is set I shall be diverted?'

'No. No, of course not.' She ran a finger along his lapel. 'It's only that I know I shall never be truly at peace until he has been set on a ship and sailed.'

'I know, my love. I can only repeat, trust me.'

She sighed. 'I do. I *do*.' He felt the superhuman effort she made to put her worries from her. 'Tell me how...how, oh, what was the name of your mare? The white one?'

'Luna.'

'Luna, of course. Has she foaled yet?'

'No.' Her question brought a light to his eyes. 'She has four more months to go.'

'Oh, dear. I don't know much about horses.'

'That, my love, is obvious.'

She allowed him to tease her and they passed a considerable time discussing nothing very much at all until Sir Ranulph caught sight of the gig returning. Three people were squashed onto the seat.

'Ah. I think, my love, you had best return to Lady Melthorpe. Unless I mistake, Aveley has been taken.'

Louise looked up sharply. 'Oh. Oh, yes. I don't want to see him. When I think how he cozened me, played upon my grief for Amelia...' She swallowed.

'I know. Come now, off to your grandmother.'

She permitted him to open the door for her to pass from the room. Aveley was shown into it a short time later. Or, to be exact, he was escorted into the library with Wadden on one side and Lester on the other.

'For God's sake, Trent, send these pests of yours away.' Aveley shrugged a shoulder at Wadden's bulky presence.

A slight nod of Sir Ranulph's head dismissed the pair.

'We'll be outside, sir,' Wadden said with heavy emphasis, his eyes on Aveley.

A smile twitched Sir Ranulph's mouth briefly at the thought that Aveley stood a chance of overcoming him. The man might affect the appearance of an athlete but Sir Ranulph knew he lacked the ability to defeat anyone like himself. His mouth settled back into a harsh line. There was no amusement in what he had to accomplish.

The door closed behind the two men leaving silence behind them. Sir Ranulph stood calmly by the desk. Aveley drifted round the room, inspecting this item or that, this bookshelf or that. Eventually he stopped and faced Sir Ranulph.

'Well?'

'Not especially. You have brought trouble upon yourself. Worse, you have brought it upon a lady I hold in high regard.'

'She's caught you then, has she? The words were a sneer.

'I advise you not to render your position even more uncertain by speaking of her in such terms.'

A shrug. 'So what have you to say that has caused me to be dragged here?'

'Don't play me for a fool. You know very well what it is. You tried to harm Christopher and when that failed you tried to abduct him. To put the best face on what you did, you meant to hold him to ransom. At worst, to kill him and inherit Stapley.'

'Don't be a fool. What had I to gain from killing him? You're the one who would inherit Stapley.'

'I would not, but that is irrelevant. It was ransom you intended.' Sir Ranulph's expression hardened. 'How much? How much were you intending to sell the child's life for? For selling is what it would be.'

Aveley spurned his scathing gaze and turned a shoulder.

'Come, not so modest. Your debts were approaching five thousand.'

His head spun back. 'How do you know that?'

Sir Ranulph snorted. 'Have you lost your memory? We have had this out once before when I offered you six thousand to absent yourself. If you had found the sense to accept then, you would be debt-free by now. That can no longer apply. With the rates the cent-per-centers charge their claim must have increased.'

Philip Aveley faced him, unable to hide the speculation in his eyes. 'So you are offering more?'

'I told you not to think to play me for a fool. If I were to do that, you would turn and turn and be back for more for ever after.'

Concern replaced the speculation. 'So what is it you have to say? Stop wasting my time and come to it.'

'Heaven forbid I should waste such a valuable commodity. What I will do is buy your ticket to a country of your choice. If you undertake to remain out of England for your life I will pay your debts and give you two thousand pounds.'

'Country? Which country?'

'The Americas or India would be my suggestion.'

'The Americas? No. Not at all. It's full of mutineers and revolutionaries. Not the least part civilised. India, now ...'

'America sounds exactly the place for your ... talents,' Sir Ranulph scoffed, eyeing him with contempt.

Aveley took a turn about the room. His wandering stopped. His head came up. 'Make it America then, and four thousand. Enough to set myself up.'

'Are you of the opinion that this is a barter? India and two.'

His offer received a scowl. For several moments silence hung between them then Aveley shrugged.

'Very well. Give me the money and I'll go.'

His comment raised Sir Ranulph's eyebrows but did not produce a bark of laughter. 'For the last time, disabuse yourself of the notion that I am a fool. My lawyer is due here to tomorrow to draw up the Settlement between my fiancée and me. Before he does that, you will travel to Bristol with him and Lester. When they have seen you to the gangway shortly before the ship casts off, Mr Ellstone will hand you the money – discreetly of course, we have no desire for you to be tipped over the side by an avaricious captain. Lester will remain until the ship has sailed out of sight. And you with it.'

For several moments Aveley remained silent.

'The alternative,' Sir Ranulph said, 'is for us to endure the inevitable gossip and hand you over to the magistrate.'

There was nothing in his expression to give Aveley the least hope his persecutor was bluffing. 'Very well,' he said, his voice filled with loathing. 'Have it your way. I'll return tomorrow to –'

'You will spend the night here, in company with Wadden. I know her ladyship will agree when I tell her you have accepted my offer.'

'Accepted?' Aveley spent several minutes venting his opinion of the offer and its instigator.

Entirely unmoved, Sir Ranulph moved to the door. Wadden and Lester were standing outside. 'Lady Melthorpe's butler will direct you to the room set aside for our ... guest,' he told them. 'See that he spends his time there and nowhere else.'

He stood back and watched Aveley submit himself to the waiting company.

Chapter Thirty

Barely had Aveley and his wardens left Frannington Court's elegant park than a rather elderly coach bearing Mr and Mrs Devreaux bowled up the carriage sweep to the main door. Mrs Devreaux had been employing her handkerchief for much of the journey. Mr Devreaux viewed it with dislike.

'For goodness sake, woman, stop this incessant snivelling. Anyone would think there was reason to be sad.' He twitched a coat-tail across a knee. 'To think that after all these years the girl has caught herself a husband.' The coat-tail was brushed away. 'Not that it would have been so bad if she hadn't. We're bound to need someone to take care of us when we can no longer do so.'

His wife sobbed. 'How can you be so ungenerous, sir? After all her trials?' The snivels expanded into sobs.

Mr Devreaux raised his eyes to the roof of the carriage and clenched his teeth.

Magdale had been notified of the carriage's approach by one of the pair of powdered footmen waiting by the double doors. He moved across the lofty entrance hall at a stately pace. A majestic nod to the other man had them both leaping to open the doors. Their action afforded the butler a view of a lady of advanced years alighting from the carriage without waiting for anyone's aid. He affected not to notice how much she had aged since her last visit, or the state of her eyes so she looked to be attending a funeral.

'Where is she, Magdale?' she demanded, handkerchief fluttering damply. 'Where is my daughter?'

'Miss Devreaux is with her ladyship in the Blue salon, ma'am.'

The anxious mother took three steps past him across the marble tiled floor. Her progress halted abruptly; her husband was laggardly in his entrance.

Magdale permitted an eyebrow to rise fractionally. 'If you and Mr Devreaux will follow me, ma'am, I will conduct you to her ladyship.'

Mrs Devreaux entered the salon. She saw nothing of the elegance of its furnishings, the excellence of the Aubusson carpets or the charm of the various ornamental pieces that she had known in her youth. All she saw was Louise rising from a sofa beside her grandmother. The anxious mother brushed past Magdale. She reached Louise before she had taken three steps and clasped her to her bosom.

A gale of sobs broke from her. 'Oh, my love. My love. I thought never to see you again.'

'Mama, please. Please.' Louise struggled to part her mother's grasp that was pinning her own arms to her sides. 'There is no need for such unhappiness. I would always have found a way to see you.'

'Oh, but I am not unhappy,' she sobbed. 'It is so wonderful. Where is the child? Do show me the child. He is all I shall ever have of Amelia.'

'For goodness sake, Eleanor, try for some control.' Lady Melthorpe regarded her daughter with disapproval. 'You have yet to greet your future son-in-law.'

Mrs Devreaux's head spun round. Her reddened eyes encompassed her mother and then Sir Ranulph. He had risen from a chair by the sofa and now bowed.

'Good day, ma'am. It is a pleasure to meet you again. And on such a happy occasion this time.' He nodded at Louise's father. 'And you, sir.'

Mr Devreaux was not to be won over by the elegance of his bow or his words. His words showed his resentment at his skirted authority. 'In my day, sir, it was customary to speak to a girl's father before paying one's addresses to his daughter.'

'Papa, no. I am five-and-twenty. There was no need for him to do so.'

Sir Ranulph took her hand. 'Hush, my love. It would have been polite for me to have at least told your father of my intentions but, if you remember, matters progressed so quickly.'

Matters thereafter proceeded at a considerable pace. Mrs Devreaux ascending to the nursery floor spent hours every day playing with Christopher, and could rarely be persuaded to leave, much to Mabson's discontent. Sir Ranulph, after discussing legal matters in the library with his future father-in-law, took tender leave of his fiancée and departed to prepare Crestings for its new mistress. After a suitable interval during which his bride acquired such bride-clothes in London as she felt necessary — of a quantity her grandmother several times declared quite insufficient — he returned to Frannington Court with his mother and Cressida Henshaw. Louise, driven to the brink of distraction between her mother's frequent requests that she visit the nursery to see Christopher's latest triumph, and the demands of Lady Melthorpe's favoured *modiste* summoned up from Bath to prepare more bride-clothes at speed, greeted Sir Ranulph with relief.

'Oh, I am so happy to see you,' she said, slipping her hands into his and permitting him to lead her into the small morning parlour she preferred to use.

He wrapped his arms round her. 'Has it been dreadful?'

'Not dreadful but I shall be … be *thankful* to be away.' She ran a finger down is cheek. 'Papa has been … difficult.'

'More difficult than your Mama?'

'Good gracious, no. Mama hardly ever leaves Christopher.' Her voice quavered. 'Papa has seen him only twice. I could wish …'

He brushed a strand of hair from her temple and kissed the delicate skin. 'There's not much longer to wait before I can have you away from here with Christopher.' He studied her. 'Will he be happy at Crestings, do you think? You had so many concerns that it was too large a place after Stapley.'

'He will be fine, I'm sure. I'm amazed at how quickly he has accepted me.' Her lashes lowered over eyes suddenly moist. 'It's as if Amelia is already fading from his memory.'

'Do not fret, my love. He is bound to adapt. Or so Mama tells me. Sad as it is, he is very young and Amelia *will* be forgotten. But you will be able to tell him about her when he is grown enough to understand.'

Her face lifted and she smiled shakily. 'You have been listening to Lady Trent. That is exactly what she said.'

He had the grace to look a trifle guilty. 'Correct as ever, my love.' He pulled her close and kissed her. 'The last of the Banns will be read on Sunday and after that … tell me,' he said, a smile sweeping his face, 'how your trivia is progressing.'

Her eyes sparkled at his teasing. 'By trivia I assume you mean my bride-clothes.' An expression of grave disdain informed her features. 'I have to tell you my choice fell so far beneath what Grandmama considered sufficient that Madame Rannville and her ladies have been working ceaselessly to ensure my appearance will be a credit to her. And Mama has even descended from the nursery to inspect the occasional gown.'

'Great Heavens,' he said, in mock alarm. 'I fear the arrangements I have set in train at Crestings will fall sadly short of your standards.'

'Indeed they might. Not that I expect to see much of them. From what I can tell I shall be spending most of the time in my apartment changing from one gown into another.'

'I can guarantee you will be spending much of the time in your apartment but it will not be for the purpose of changing your gown.'

A deep chuckle bubbled up her throat. Winding her arms round his neck, much to the detriment of his exquisite *Trône d'Amour*, she gave herself to convincing him how much she approved of his plan.

On Sunday the sixth of May, the entire party loaded itself into a medley of carriages and had itself conveyed to St Andrew's church in Chippenham. The vicar, a ponderous man much conscious of the significance of his task, looked down from his pulpit at the faces turned up to him and announced, "I publish the Banns of Marriage between Ranulph Burnett Trent of the parish of Charlton Kings and Louise Eleanor Devreaux of the parish of St Albans. If any of you know cause or just impediment why these two persons should not be joined together in Holy Matrimony, ye are to declare it. This is the third time of asking.'

Seated between her grandmother and mother in the Devreaux family pew Louise held her breath. There was no reason at all for anyone to declare an impediment because there simply was none. Even so, she crossed her fingers inside her new feather muff.

Sir Ranulph seated immediately behind her leant forward. 'All done,' he whispered.

She half turned her head folding her lips together to preserve her countenance in suitably solemn demeanour. His laugh came low and slight, convincing her he knew of her struggle. She heard him sit back and had no need for further control.

'Behave, miss,' her grandmother whispered.

Startled, Louise glanced at her only to discover she too was trying to suppress a smile.

Three days later the party re-entered the church, this time without Louise and her father. Prey to unaccustomed nervousness, Sir Ranulph stood before the chancel steps with his uncle as groomsman at his side. After several anxious minutes his ears caught the sound of a carriage drawing to a halt outside. More anxious moments passed then the church door swung open on its screeching hinges. The Seede organ burst from the dirge it had been emitting into a rousing rendition of Beethoven's 'Ode to Joy'. Louise, clothed in silk and gauze, caught up in ruffles with bands of pearls, and carrying a posy of gardenias brought with great care from Crestings' glass houses, advanced up the aisle on her father's arm.

Sir Ranulph turned. His breath caught. Mrs Devreaux, in the front pew, her mother on one side and Christopher standing on the seat beside her, swivelled round. Louise's ethereal beauty caused her to have immediate recourse to her handkerchief. Her grasp on Christopher's arm slackened. He scented release, pulled free and pattered unsteadily along the pew seat. His triumphant laughter clashed with the organ notes. Heads turned. Louise laughed.

'Oh, catch him do. He'll be away to the horses if you don't.'

Letty shot out of her seat among the Frannington Court servants and headed him off at the south aisle. Order restored, the vicar ceased scowling and intoned, 'Dearly beloved…'

Some twenty minutes later, Sir Ranulph and Louise walked from the church as man and wife, not to be put asunder by any man. He could barely turn his eyes from her glowing face to acknowledge the hails and cheers of the crowd that clustered round them. Assisting his bride to climb into Lady Melthorpe's landau, he raised his hand against the shower of petals being flung over their heads by her enthusiastic servants.

'There cannot be a single flower left whole.' He brushed two pink rose petals from Louise's veil.

'Oh, don't stop them. It makes me so happy.'

He flopped down beside her. 'Only rose petals to make you happy? Then you shall have roses every day.'

She moved her hems aside from his careless feet. 'I fear it will try you somewhat to find roses in the winter so don't talk nonsense.'

'No? Must I not talk nonsense?'

Her eyes danced. 'Yes, do. I like it.'

He proceeded to talk nonsense to her whenever the opportunity to do so arose in the lengthy wedding breakfast and social manoeuvres that followed until he kissed her fingertips in the hall as she prepared to climb the stairs to her apartment with her mother.

Nonsense was not what he talked to her father who had not ceased to scowl for most of the day. They stood isolated by the flower-filled fireplace.

'Let me assure you, sir, that I shall do everything in my power to ensure your daughter's happiness.'

'So I should hope.'

He laboured on. 'And your lawyers were satisfied with the Settlement.'

'They were.'

Sir Ranulph could only wonder that Louise's perseverance in her duty to such a miserable individual had not broken years before.

'My dear boy,' Mrs Devreaux wafted back into the room, still clutching a handkerchief and making him jump. 'I shall bid you goodnight.' He feared for one dreadful moment that she was about to embrace him. She did not but dabbed her eyes instead. 'So happy,' she sighed. 'So very happy.'

He bowed. 'I thank you, ma'am. Please excuse me. I must bid my mother and Lady Melthorpe good evening.'

This accomplished he betook himself from the room and past an unconscionable number of servants, all doing not very much in the hall and landings, to gain his wife's suite.

'Ah,' he said, opening her sitting room door and finding her standing beside a large, draped item tied with a silk ribbon in the centre of the carpet. 'It is here.'

'It? What is *it*?'

He closed the door. 'A surprise.'

The bow loosened under his hand and the cloth slid onto the floor revealing an armchair in the Louise *Quinze* style.

'A chair? Why have you brought a chair? I don't —' Louise stopped speaking. Her eyes sparkled. Her mouth spread into a smile. 'Not a chair then,' she said.

His eyes met hers. 'I think perhaps not.' His hand lifted the back. It tipped forward. In seconds the chair she had first seen in Crestings' library had become a bed.

She peered at him over the fingertips covering her smile. 'A bed, sir? You've brought a bed when there is a perfectly adequate one in the next room?'

His smile answered hers. 'I thought so unconventional a lady as yourself might care to try it.'

She laughed and walked into his arms.

THE END

22345134R00160

Printed in Great Britain
by Amazon